THE
Roman

SYLVAIN REYNARD

everafter ROMANCE

EverAfter Romance, New York

❧ Praise for *The Raven* ❧

"A fabulous Gothic treat of a book filled with ancient vampires, dark vendettas, and star-crossed love."

&ₒ*Deborah Harkness,*
#1 New York Times bestselling author
Discovery of Witches trilogy

"This book knocks over genre and swirls it into an addicting mix of mystery, romance and fantasy. With nearly lyrical prose and magical characters that step right off the pages, *The Raven* is going to make SR diehards and newcomers alike nurse an epic book hangover."

&ₒ*Christina Lauren,*
New York Times bestselling author
Beautiful Bastard series

"Reynard never disappoints, especially when it comes to creating well-developed characters and granting readers an invitation to use their imaginations. This dark, sexy tale is nestled in the mysterious city of Florence and will amaze and enchant readers throughout. The author tries the paranormal genre on for size and, not surprisingly, it's a perfect fit."

&ₒ*RT Book Reviews*

"I'm loving this series…Sylvain Reynard's writing is exquisitely beautiful and it evokes such emotion and vivid imagery…Compulsive reading as the reader is swept away in an intriguing sensual romance set in the heart of Florence. Raven and William's story is addictive and mesmerizing as new meets old with humour, passion, danger and mystery."

&ₒ*Totally Booked Blog*

"Sylvain Reynard's dark and mysterious world of The Florentine and its vampires is sensual, passionate and deadly."

&ₒ*The Reading Cafe*

❈ Praise for the Gabriel Trilogy ❈

"I found myself enraptured by Sylvain Reynard's flawless writing."
ᚵ *The Autumn Review*

"Emotionally intense and lyrical."
ᚵ *Totally Booked Blog*

"The Professor is sexy and sophisticated…I can't get enough of him!"
ᚵ *Kristen Proby*
USA Today bestselling author

"An unforgettable and riveting love story that will sweep readers off their feet."
ᚵ *Nina's Literary Escape*

"Sylvain Reynard's writing is captivating and intense…It's hard not to be drawn to the darkly passionate and mysterious Gabriel, a character you'll be drooling and pining for!"
ᚵ *Waves of Fiction*

"A must read whether you're a longtime fan of [Sylvain Reynard]'s or have never read a word he's written. The writing as always deserves special mention for its style and beauty."
ᚵ *Bookish Temptations*

"The story was magnificent, the characters and world complex."
ᚵ *Romance at Random*

Books by Sylvain Reynard

Gabriel's Inferno
Gabriel's Rapture
Gabriel's Redemption
The Raven
The Shadow
The Roman

Novella

The Prince

EverAfter Romance
A Division of Diversion Publishing Corp.
443 Park Avenue South, Suite 1008
New York, NY 10016
www.EverAfterRomance.com
For more information, email info@diversionbooks.com

First edition, December 2016

The characters and events in this book are fictitious.
Any similarity to real persons, living or dead,
is coincidental and not intended by the author.

ISBN: 978-1-68230-676-5

10 9 8 7 6 5 4 3 2 1

Cover Design by Heather Carrier Designs
Interior Book Design by Coreen Montagna

Printed in the United States of America

To Florence, Rome, and Prague,
with gratitude

Prologue

May 2013
Florence, Italy

S he was dying.

The Prince heard her heart stutter and slow and her breathing grow even shallower. The young woman with the brave soul and the great green eyes was dying.

The humans had smashed her skull into a wall. No doubt her brain was injured. The skin on her arms was pale, almost translucent. Her face was bruised and smeared with blood.

The Prince had seen goodness die, not once but twice. He'd held it in his hands and seen the life ebb out of it, like sand sifting through his fingers.

He would not let such beauty die.

Out of sight of the other vampyres, he retrieved the illustrations he'd left on the roof. He cradled them along with the woman as he flew across the Ponte Vecchio to the other side of the Arno River. With every step, he focused his ancient hearing on the sound of her heartbeat, worried it would fall silent before he reached the safe haven of his villa.

He would have to give her a great deal of vampyre blood in order to heal her. It was possible she was beyond help. And it wouldn't be his blood he would give to her. Not even to save her life.

The Prince quickened his pace, his figure moving like a jagged flash of lightning up the hill. When he reached the heavy iron gates that surrounded his home he paused, holding the woman more tightly. With a cry, he leapt over the barrier, landing like a cat on the other side. The woman groaned at the movement, and her eyes flickered open.

"*Cassita*," he whispered, his gray eyes meeting hers. "Stay awake."

Her eyes rolled back into her head.

"*Sard*," he cursed, sprinting to the front door of the villa and barrelling inside.

He didn't bother calling for his servants; he had mere minutes, perhaps even seconds before her heart stopped beating. Forever.

To his massive library he flew, pressing one of the volumes on the shelf. A wooden panel on a nearby wall moved, revealing a hidden door.

Without hesitation, the Prince entered the absolute darkness that shrouded the doorway and descended a staircase, stepping nimbly until he reached the lower level. He ran down the hall until he reached a heavy iron door. He pressed a secret code into a number pad and waited impatiently as the door opened.

The woman's heart grew fainter still.

He held her close, pressing her face into his neck, as if his strength could be passed to her. As if, by his touch, he could keep her from death.

He wound his way through row upon row of wine bottles, carefully stacked in tall, wooden racks that reached over six feet in height. He moved to the very back of the wine cellar, where his oldest vintages were stored.

Placing the woman on a wooden table, he put his illustrations to one side. He'd attend to them (and his revenge) later.

The Prince chose one of his most precious vintages, the blood of an old one he'd destroyed in the fourteenth century. He uncorked the bottle and swept his finger inside, retrieving a black substance. He placed his finger in the woman's half-open mouth.

It wasn't the best way to feed her. She was unconscious and unable to swallow. He could only hope that the vampyre blood would dissolve into her system, staving off her imminent death.

Within a minute, the woman drew a sharp breath.

He withdrew his finger, noting it was clean. He jammed it into the wine bottle once again, coating it with more life-sustaining darkness.

He placed his finger in her mouth, and this time her tongue moved. A weak half-swallow followed.

He whispered old words in her ear, lapsing into Latin as he exhorted her.

The woman's heart skipped a beat, then increased its movements until it was beating slowly but steadily. Her lungs drew a deeper breath. He could hear her veins begin to hum as the foreign substance mixed with her blood to flow through her body.

But these were reflexes—the body hungering for life while the mind remained unconscious.

He fed her a little more blood by mouth. Although she was breathing, her pulse remained weak. She needed vampyre blood in greater quantities than she could take orally. But he couldn't risk moving her until he was satisfied she'd survive the time it would take to set up a transfusion.

The Prince cursed the animals that had attacked her.

He fed her twice more before choosing several valuable vintages from his collection and jamming them under his arm. He'd leave the illustrations behind, for the present. They were safe enough in his wine cellar. Although the thief had taken them from his home before…

He lifted the wounded lark into his arms and transported her to the hallway. He whispered to her as he climbed the staircase, begging her to hold fast to life.

He was far from certain she'd survive the transfusion. But for the sake of the goodness of her soul, he would try.

Chapter One

August 2013
Florence, Italy

"The human is dead." Gregor's Russian accent was far more pronounced as he spoke nervously to the Prince of Florence.

The Prince had just regained control of his principality and was closeted with his former assistant, out of reach of prying eyes and ears.

"Dead?" The Prince's stoic expression slipped.

"Yes, my lord. Apparently, he was trying to protect your pet and her sister when Maximilian killed him. He came with the sister from America."

"Where's the body?" The Prince abruptly unsheathed and sheathed his sword.

"With the police. There's to be an autopsy." Gregor hesitated.

The Prince speared his assistant with a look. "And?"

"The human intelligence network is concerned about a policeman named Batelli. Although he isn't involved in the murder investigation, he's aware your pet and her sister have disappeared. He's claiming a connection between all of this and the robbery of the Uffizi."

The Prince bared his teeth. "An autopsy will expose us. Instruct the network to claim the body as soon as possible. They are to keep it until I give them further instructions."

The Prince strode toward the door of his study without a backward glance. Raven and her sister would be devastated to learn that Daniel was dead. That is, if they were still alive.

He touched the handle of the door. "Assemble the army and order them to stand guard along the borders. Word of the attempted coup will spread. It's possible even one of our allies will take this opportunity to attack us. We must be prepared."

Gregor bowed. "Yes, my lord."

"Tell the loyal the treasury will be opened in order to reward them. You and Aoibhe are to oversee the distribution, and I task you with keeping her generosity moderate."

The Prince placed his hand on the hilt of his sword. "You and she are the last remaining members of the Consilium. I'm sure you're aware you cannot trust her. It seems she's been colluding with Ibarra, who is still alive and roaming the city. I've dispatched a hunting party to locate him."

"Ibarra?" Gregor's eyes widened. "But you executed him."

"I did." The Prince wore a grim expression. "It seems he was… resurrected."

Gregor blinked. "He's as powerful as Aoibhe, if not more so. A hunting party will have difficulty felling him."

"That is why we must be on our guard and why I'm tasking you with overseeing the security of the city. Keep a close watch on Aoibhe, and see that Ibarra is destroyed. I shall be at my villa, trying to stave off a war with the Curia."

Gregor fidgeted with his hands. "Beg pardon, my lord. I thought the gift of the human females would be enough to placate them."

The Prince's expression tightened. "Only if they arrive unspoiled. The conflict with Machiavelli delayed me in sending couriers to our neighbors. And there are other dangers."

A look passed between the two vampyres.

"I hope they will arrive safely, my lord."

"We may hope, Gregor, but over the centuries I've learnt not to surrender my fate to hope. See to the army and be cautious. Either Ibarra or Aoibhe may try to take your head."

The Prince opened the door and entered the corridor, striding purposefully toward a secret underground passage.

Once he entered the passage and closed the hidden door behind himself, he broke into a run.

He hoped he would not be too late.

Chapter Two

W*illiam is dead.*
The realization repeated like a maddening refrain in Raven's mind.

Machiavelli had seized control of Florence and sent Raven and her sister as a peace offering to the Curia. He'd probably executed William already, making his ascent to the throne complete.

Raven shut her eyes, too distraught to cry.

William's last act had been to break his promise. He'd sworn they'd stay together, but he'd allowed the soldiers to take her away. He hadn't even drawn a sword.

Je t'aim, he'd mouthed, as the soldiers dragged her. A last look, a last meeting of the eyes, and she was torn from him.

Now he was dead.

The vampyre who was carrying her stumbled. Raven hung over his shoulder, her face at his back. She fisted his shirt in order to hang on.

He smacked her bottom. "Let go, you cow. You'll fell us both!"

Anger, quick and hot, overtook her. She made a fist and punched him in the kidney.

Her fist met something hard and unyielding.

"Ow!" she shrieked, cradling her hand. "What was that?"

The soldier laughed. "Kevlar. We're wearing vests."

Raven grabbed his shirt over the vest, pulling it taut against the front of his body. "Touch me again and you'll answer to the Curia."

Her words were enough to halt the vampyre. His chest erupted in a growl. "*What did you say?*"

"You heard me. When we get to Rome, the Curia will want to know how I was treated. And I'll tell them."

"You're just a human," he spat. "You need to learn your place."

"So do you. The Curia has sworn to eliminate you and the others. Do you really want to give them another reason to kill you?"

The soldier didn't move. It was as if the wheels of his mind were turning, measuring her words.

"Be smart," she continued, releasing his shirt. "Keep me and my sister safe, and you'll be rewarded."

"A reward from the Curia is worth nothing," he snarled.

Before Raven could respond, footsteps approached.

"You there," a deep voice barked. "Keep running."

"Yes, commander." The soldier took off at high speed.

Raven noted with satisfaction that he now held her closely but cautiously. Her threat had worked.

She had a piercing headache and was nauseated after bouncing on the soldier's shoulder for hours. The landscape was still bathed in blackness. She was fairly sure sunrise was approaching, but she had no idea of the time. She wasn't wearing a watch, and her cell phone was tucked into a pocket. The soldier hadn't seemed to notice it.

She still wore the gold bracelet William had given her some months ago. It signified their connection. But the soldier hadn't seemed to notice it, either.

She called out to her sister, earning a command of "*Silence.*" She defied the soldier twice, but Cara didn't respond. She must still be unconscious.

Cara's current state was Raven's fault. She'd failed to protect her from their stepfather when they were children. She'd failed to protect Cara when a vampyre attacked them in Florence. Now Cara's fiancé was seriously injured, and they were at the mercy of ten vampyre soldiers and their leader.

The soldiers had been tasked with delivering the women to their old friend Father Kavanaugh at the Vatican. They were a peace offering given by the new Prince of Florence to his enemy, the Curia. William had…

Raven halted her thoughts.

THE ROMAN

She didn't have time to dwell on the past. She didn't have time to grieve his loss or curse him for what he had or hadn't done. Through a great force of will, she ignored the feeling in the pit of her stomach and focused on the present.

She needed to protect her sister. She needed to ensure they reached Rome alive.

A shout sounded to Raven's left, and her captor slowed. They climbed what seemed like a steep, rocky hill and went about twenty paces before he heaved her roughly to the ground.

The soldier took a large step back, staring down at her with undisguised contempt before striding away.

He'd deposited her in a copse of trees, seemingly protected. She searched the darkness, eagerly looking for her sister. Thankfully, Cara had been placed on the ground nearby, sprawled across the roots of a tree. Raven crawled to her side.

"A short rest," announced Stefan, the leader of the group. "We'll take cover for the day in Umbria. Princess Simonetta is an ally, and the Prince's couriers should have informed her of our presence."

Raven only half-listened as she examined her sister. Cara was breathing steadily, eyes closed.

Raven squeezed her hand. "*Cara.*"

She didn't respond.

Raven tried again and again. Cara made no movement.

Raven struggled to her feet, ignoring the searing pain that shot from ankle to hip in her disabled leg. She stumbled toward Stefan, biting the inside of her cheek against the pain.

"I need you to examine my sister."

The French Canadian gave her a scornful look. "I don't treat human beings."

"She's been unconscious for hours. She may be in a coma."

Stefan favored her with his back and began to speak to the largest soldier, who was commanding the detachment that surrounded them.

"I'm talking to you." Raven lifted her voice in Italian, barely keeping hold of her temper.

"I don't engage in conversations with food. Especially food that suffers from hysteria." Stefan spoke over his shoulder before continuing his conversation.

9

"Hysteria?" Raven seethed. "You misogynistic asshole."

A series of growls rose from the soldiers, and she watched as they approached her from all sides.

Stefan glanced pointedly from the soldiers to Raven. "You were saying?"

"That you're an asshole. You all are." She limped sideways, placing herself between the vampyres and her sister. "We belong to the Curia. She may be dying, and you're neglecting her. What do you think the Curia will do when you show up with a corpse?"

Stefan twitched, his gaze moving to Cara.

Raven followed the path of his eyes. "Maximilian attacked her. Aoibhe gave her some of her blood in order to heal her. She's been unconscious ever since."

"Lady Aoibhe?" One of the soldiers laughed. "That wench wouldn't spare a drop of blood to save her own mother."

"She fed her," Raven insisted. "Not much, but enough to heal her."

Raven switched her attention to Stefan. "You need to examine my sister. Now."

Stefan sniffed. "You don't give orders. Your master is dead; you're chattel to be traded for peace. I have the priest's letter in my pocket."

Her green eyes flashed. "We belong to the Curia. If you don't help my sister, they'll kill you."

"Knock it on the head." One of the soldiers swung his sword. "Then we won't have to listen to it prattle."

"Touch me and you're dead." Raven turned in a circle, staring each of them down. "What do you think the Curia will do if we arrive damaged? They'll kill you. All of you. And I'll dance around your corpses."

"Difficult to dance with a crippled leg," a soldier mocked, miming her disability.

"Enough." Someone moved forward.

All grumbling and growling ceased.

He was a head and shoulders taller than the others, placing him at well over six feet. His chest was broad, and his arms and legs were wide and powerful.

He stood toe to toe with Raven, peering down at her with dark, fathomless eyes.

"Sunrise approaches." His Italian was spoken with an Eastern European accent. "Stefan, see to the human. Then we must go."

"You aren't in a position to issue commands, Borek." Stefan crossed his arms over his chest. "Prince Machiavelli placed me in charge."

Borek's grip tightened on the hilt of his sword, his eyes never leaving Raven's. "I'm in command of this detachment. My mission is to deliver the females to the Curia, unharmed. Don't make me kill you."

"You wouldn't dare," Stefan sputtered, uncrossing his arms. "I'm a member of the Consilium."

Borek turned his head a fraction, and his eyes met Stefan's.

"Fine," the physician huffed. He turned on his heel and walked toward Cara.

"Thank you." Raven hazarded an appreciative look at the commander.

He bent toward her, his expression unchanged. "*Curia whore.* If I had my choice, you and your sister would already be dead."

Raven took a step back, surprised by his sudden show of anger. She quickly collected herself. "We want the same thing, commander. We both want to get to Rome as soon as possible."

"You know nothing of what I want." He jerked his chin in Cara's direction. "Attend to the girl and get ready to move."

Raven returned to Cara's side just as Stefan concluded his examination.

He stood and brushed off his hands in distaste. "She's unconscious, but that's likely a side effect of the blood. Aoibhe is a powerful vampyre."

"Will she wake up?"

"Yes." Stefan didn't bother looking in Raven's direction. "Don't ask me when. I don't know how much blood she ingested or what her injuries were. Some humans have this reaction to vampyre blood — their systems shut down, and they sleep for hours. She could awaken at any time."

"Thank you."

Stefan's upper lip curled.

"You'd better hope the Curia actually wants you." He dropped his voice. "I wonder what would happen to you and your sister if they change their mind."

Raven's hands curled into fists.

Her curse was drowned out by the clanging of steel as the soldiers drew their swords, faces set against the perimeter. A few vampyres positioned themselves around the tree under which Cara lay.

"What's happening?" Raven's gaze moved from soldier to soldier, finding their faces uniformly tense.

Something rustled amongst the trees and pounded against the earth. Then, all of a sudden, an animal leapt into the clearing, knocking one of the soldiers to the ground.

The animal roared.

"Ferals!" a soldier cried, lifting his sword. "To arms!"

Out of the corner of her eye, Raven saw something move. Before she could scream, a great hulking beast emerged from the tree behind her sister.

Chapter Three

August 2013
Cambridge, Massachusetts

"How did he know?" Julia whispered to a lightless room, her hand low on her abdomen. She lay in bed with her husband, long past the hour at which they'd retired.

Still sleeping, Gabriel grunted and rolled toward her.

She examined him in the shadows—the curl that clung to his forehead, his beautiful features and stubbled face, his naked chest and shoulders.

"How did he know?" she repeated, pressing her hand to his face.

Gabriel drew a deep breath and leaned into her touch. A moment later, his eyes opened.

He blinked. "Huh?"

"The man from the Uffizi. The one who came to you in Umbria and told you I was sick. How did he know?"

Now Gabriel was awake.

A muscle jumped in his jaw. "I don't know."

"Dr. Rubio says it was a good thing we demanded an ultrasound. One of the fibroids has grown so large." Julia shuddered.

Gabriel lifted her hand from his face and kissed it, lacing their fingers together. "You're going to be fine."

"Dr. Rubio wants more tests, but the fibroids explain so many things—the pain, the low iron, the bleeding."

Gabriel winced. "I should have paid closer attention."

Julia pressed their conjoined hands to her heart. "I thought the symptoms would go away."

"You need to take better care of yourself." His dark brows knitted together. "You have a husband and a daughter who love you. Who need you."

He brushed his lips over hers.

She sighed appreciatively. "I promise I'll do better. But I don't understand how a stranger could know something so personal."

Gabriel pulled back. His blue eyes studied hers. "I don't know who or what he is. I'm glad you and Clare are far away from him."

"I'm grateful he warned us. My symptoms were worsening. I can only imagine what would have happened if things had continued." Julia shuddered once again.

Gabriel's hand slid to her abdomen. "It's all right now. Let's not worry about what might have happened."

He leaned over and kissed her, his tongue tasting the curve of her lip.

Julia responded, looping her arms around his neck and drawing his body atop hers.

The baby monitor on the nightstand crackled, and a low cry was heard.

Gabriel froze, as if he were an animal trying to avoid a predator.

"I'll go." Julia shifted from beneath him.

Gabriel grabbed her wrist. "Wait. Let's see if she goes back to sleep."

Julia laughed. "You always say that, but she never does."

He huffed grumpily, running his fingers through his thick, dark hair.

"I'll go." He kissed her forehead. "Mummy needs her sleep."

Julia smiled and sank under the covers, watching as her husband pulled on a pair of boxer shorts and padded toward the nursery.

She toyed with the cross she wore around her neck, wondering why the man who had threatened her husband had gifted them with important information about her health.

She had no answer to this question.

Chapter Four

Raven moved instinctively, covering her sister with her body. Animalistic snarls and hoarse vampyre cries filled her ears, along with the thundering of footsteps from all directions.

She heard a growl by her elbow and an Italian oath, accompanied by the whistle of something metallic slicing through air. A heavy object thudded to the ground some distance away.

A hairy paw grabbed the ankle of her injured leg and pulled, almost yanking her hip out of its socket. She released her sister and kicked, twisting violently.

"Let go!" she cried. "Help. Help!"

The grip on her foot tightened, and she felt the bones in her ankle groan in protest. She rolled to her stomach and clawed at the ground, trying to catch hold of something. The stench of blood and unwashed flesh filled her nostrils.

She retched.

Something flipped her to her back. She looked up into dark, insect-like eyes.

Raven screamed, lifting her uninjured foot and kicking. The feral howled as she made contact with its face.

It grabbed both of her ankles and squeezed.

She yelped in pain and began to flail, fearful the creature would crush her ankles.

Then, all of a sudden, the feral released her.

Raven scrambled toward her sister. She huddled over her, examining her for injuries.

Borek stood a few feet away, his broadsword dripping black blood onto the body of a headless feral.

Their eyes met.

"Stay here." He kicked the corpse aside and strode into the fray.

It was difficult to see, but Raven discerned a feral grappling with soldiers at the center of the clearing. Stefan stood off to one side, awkwardly clutching a sword.

The feral moved like an animal, hunched on all fours and rearing up only to strike. It appeared to be male and was of average size, but stronger than its vampyre counterparts. Raven counted one injured vampyre, who was kneeling on the ground, clutching his shoulder.

She blocked out the feral's screams, interspersed as they were with incoherent mumblings and profanity. Her attention focused on her sister, hoping Cara wouldn't choose that moment to regain consciousness.

A cry of triumph rang out, and Raven saw Borek standing with his sword held high, a feral's head dangling from his other hand.

"We need to move. Now." Borek tossed the head to one of the soldiers. "Retrieve the heads. Carry them a mile and drop them."

"What about the corpses?" Stefan stepped forward, sheathing his sword.

"Leave them."

"But they could reanimate."

In two steps, Borek was towering over the physician, his sword still dripping feral blood.

Stefan cowered, blinking up at the commander.

Borek pointed his sword at Stefan's chest. "Do you wish to announce our presence to everyone in the region?"

The French Canadian shook his head.

"Leave the corpses." Borek turned in a circle, gesturing to the group. "Move."

While the party lined up and prepared to run, he crossed to the injured soldier. Ignoring his pleas, Borek lifted his weapon and beheaded him with one sure stroke.

Raven staggered to her feet, leaning against the trunk of the tree as she tried to gain her balance.

Without emotion, Borck retrieved the head and sword of his fallen comrade. He directed two soldiers to carry Raven and her sister. The vampyres snapped to attention and walked toward the women.

Raven locked eyes with one of them as he approached. "Why did he kill his own soldier?"

The vampyre shrugged. "Guillaume was bitten by a feral. He would have become one of them."

Raven swallowed, trying to quell her nausea.

Vampyres appeared to be human. Even she, who'd become the lover of one of the most powerful vampyres in Italy, forgot how different they were from human beings. Their cold-blooded actions and lack of empathy were all the more disturbing precisely because they looked human.

Raven resolved to keep the difference between the two species firmly in mind.

She couldn't help but remember her previous encounter with a feral, near her apartment in Santo Spirito. She'd thought she would die until, inexplicably, the feral had stopped some feet away, cursing her for having a relic.

She wished she had one of William's relics now. Borek had seen to it that Cara had medical attention, but he hadn't done so out of compassion. He'd done so because he feared the Curia.

Raven needed to bolster her defenses.

"Commander Borek." She lifted her voice, evading the soldier who was supposed to carry her.

The commanding officer ignored her.

"Commander Borek," she repeated, louder.

He turned his head in her direction, as did the remaining members of their party, with the exception of Cara.

"We need to leave," he growled. "Or you'll end up dead."

"I need a sword." She extended her hand.

He stared at her incredulously. "No."

She took a few limping steps in his direction. "I'm not afraid to fight. What if we encounter more ferals?"

Borek glared.

He walked toward her and held out Guillaume's sword.

As soon as she took the weight of the weapon into her hand, it slipped from her fingers, toppling to the grass.

Laughter rippled across the vampyres.

Stubbornly, she tried to retrieve the sword from the ground. It was so heavy she could barely lift it with both hands.

Borek snatched the sword away from her, thrusting it into his belt. "Much as it pains you, you'll have to rely on us for protection."

He barked an order to the soldier assigned to her, and the vampyre bowed before taking off at a run. In his stead, Borek lifted her over his shoulder. They descended the hill at a high rate of speed.

Raven was surprised the commander would deign to carry her.

After they'd gone some distance, Borek slowed. He passed his hand down her uninjured leg and slid it under the hem of her jeans.

She jerked away from his touch. "What are you doing?"

"Keep your voice down."

She felt something cool slide into her sock. Borek pulled the leg of her jeans down to cover it.

"A dagger." His voice was low. "Conceal it from the others."

Raven placed her hand at the small of his back, indicating that she'd heard.

"Aim for the throat," he rumbled. "A dagger will be of little use against a feral or one of us. But it will buy you time."

"Why are you helping me?"

Borek fell silent.

Raven had given up all hope of receiving an answer when his voice came out of the darkness.

"For now, at least, your fate is tied to mine."

Chapter Five

By the time the first rays of sunlight scattered across the Umbrian landscape, Raven was sitting on the floor of a ramshackle wooden building.

Borek was seated beneath a covered window, staring.

He hadn't carried her long. In fact, he'd passed her off to another soldier shortly after hiding the dagger in her sock.

Raven had examined the weapon after they'd stopped, using the excuse that she had to go to the bathroom in order to gain some privacy. The dagger appeared to date from the Renaissance and would easily take pride of place in a museum. It was also extremely sharp. Even now, she had to be careful to extend her leg in a certain way so the knife's edge didn't breach her skin.

Raven ignored the commander's perusal, turning to survey their shelter.

Some of the soldiers had climbed the rickety stairs to the upper floor, leaving Borek and two of his men to guard Raven and Cara. She and Borek were the only ones with open eyes. The other vampyres rested at the far end of the room, eyes closed, giving the appearance of sleep.

Raven knew better. Vampyres never slept. But as William had confided in her, their minds needed time to process the tumult of the day.

She observed her sister, whose chest rose and fell with steady breath. Her expression was peaceful.

Raven leaned over her.

"I didn't mean for you to get hurt. Again." She cupped her younger sister's pretty face. "I'm so sorry."

"Sleep," Borek ordered. "Now is not the time for regret."

"I slept on the way here." Raven adjusted her injured leg into a more comfortable position. "Why aren't you resting with the others?"

"Someone has to keep watch." Carefully, he lifted the window shade a crack, peering out into the daylight.

He dropped the shade.

Borek was solidly built, with dark hair that fell to his broad shoulders. In appearance, he seemed to be in his twenties, but given his strength, Raven inferred he'd been a vampyre for some time.

"*Dan.*" The whisper came from Cara, who lay on the floor next to Raven.

"Cara?"

She whimpered, shifting her legs, and fell silent again.

Raven waited to see if she would stir, but Cara's breathing remained deep and regular. She was still asleep or unconscious.

Raven wiped at her eyes.

"You should join her." Borek's tone was pointed.

"I'll sleep in Rome."

"*Rome.*" His face grew thunderous. "If we make it there alive."

"One of the soldiers said we'd arrive tomorrow. I can last another day. How long have you lived in Florence?"

"Long enough."

Raven looked at him curiously. "Where are you from?"

His expression tightened, and he looked out the window again.

Raven turned back to her sister, placing a hand on her head and stroking the fine, blond hair.

"Russia," he answered at last.

"You don't sound Russian."

"I am," he rumbled.

Raven frowned. "Why did you leave?"

"Too many wars. And the Curia, always bringing death." He gave her a severe look.

She chewed at the edge of her lip.

"I'm sorry," she said gently.

Borek snorted. "Your lies mean nothing."

Raven lifted her chin. "It isn't a lie. I told Machiavelli the truth when we were in Florence: I'm against killing, even the killing of vampyres."

His hand moved to his sword. "Yet you threaten us with death."

"I'll do anything to protect my sister."

"You should save yourself."

"To save my sister is to save myself." She touched the top of Cara's head.

Borek closed his eyes.

For a moment, Raven thought he was resting.

He opened his eyes, his lips curling derisively. "How did a Curia spy end up a pet to the Prince of Florence?"

"Perhaps because I'm charming." Raven glared. "And what we were doesn't matter. He's dead."

"The price of treason." He gazed in contempt at her injured leg. "You must have gold running through your veins. Why else would the Prince risk his throne?"

"Maybe he loved me." Raven's temper flared. "Not everyone chooses a lover based on appearance. No wonder the Prince ruled you and your soldiers for so long. You're a bunch of empty-headed thugs."

"*Silence.*" Borek's raised voice drew the attention of the other vampyres. They sat up from their resting places, their hands reaching for their swords.

Borek gestured to them to return to their positions.

"The whore has teeth," he taunted her. "But teeth won't save you if the Curia decides you're no longer useful. Then I'll be the one spitting on your corpse."

Raven restrained the urge to curse him and turned her back, curling up next to Cara on the floor. She was so angry, her body nearly vibrated.

There were many who could be blamed for her predicament, including herself. But in that moment, lying next to her sister on the cold, hard floor of an abandoned building, she blamed William.

He should have fled the city when he had the chance and taken her with him.

Now he was dead. She and her sister stood on the very precipice of death, with only an angry, vindictive Russian to protect them.

Raven ran through the forest, searching for William. She called his name over and over. No answer came.

In her heart, she knew he was dead, but she would not give up.

"To arms!" Borek raised the alarm, interrupting Raven's dreams.

She moved slowly, shaking off sleep as the vampyres shouted at one another, descending the staircase from the upper floor.

Something smashed through the window, landing on the wooden floor and igniting into flame. A cloud of black smoke lifted to the ceiling before spreading through the room.

They were under attack.

Dim light shone from outside as the last rays of sun faded from sight. Two more fire bombs flew through the windows, engulfing the far end of the space in flames. They licked across the floor and climbed the wall.

"Grab your robes," Borek shouted. "Douse the flames!"

The soldiers followed orders, picking up fabric and throwing it over the fire.

Smoke billowed in Raven's direction, and she began to cough. She tried to shake Cara awake, but her sister merely murmured a few words and continued sleeping.

"There's only one exit." Stefan stood in the center of the room, gesturing to the front door. "We're trapped."

"Then get to work." A soldier threw a robe toward Stefan.

Borek moved beneath one of the windows, taking care to keep out of sight. He peered outside.

Somewhere nearby, a dog growled.

"Hunters." He swore an oath and moved away from the window. "At least ten. Maybe more."

Raven huddled next to her sister, fighting to stay calm. She remembered the hunters who'd cornered her in Florence. They'd felled Aoibhe with an arrow and tried to kill William. Even though she was of no use to their blood trade, they'd threatened her with death.

One of the soldiers approached Borek. "Give them the humans."

Borek boxed the soldier's ear with a meaty fist. "The hunters will kill them, and then the Curia will kill us. It would be better to throw you outside, Carlos."

"Pardon, commander," the soldier apologized, casting a baleful look at Raven.

Raven continued to cough as smoke filled the room.

Stefan gestured to the women. "The humans are a liability. Leave them."

Borek rounded on him. "And let them burn to death? Will you be the one to announce our failure to the new Prince? Or the Curia?"

Stefan scowled, pointedly turning his back.

Raven's coughing grew louder as she struggled for air.

"We must get the humans out now." Borek pointed at Carlos. "Take your sword and hold them off as long as you can. Your vest will block the arrows."

"Excuse my words. I was too hasty." Carlos began backing away.

Borek brandished his sword. "Step outside the door, or I'll toss you through it."

The other soldiers began to close ranks, moving behind Carlos with swords at the ready.

Carlos surveyed his brethren. Then, with a tight nod, he walked toward the door.

Borek gestured to two of the remaining vampyres. "Carry the humans. Keep clear of the skirmishes and head south. Those of us who survive will follow you.

"The rest of you, prepare to break through the back wall. Carlos will distract them."

"We're probably surrounded." Stefan grumbled.

"Then succumb to the flames." Borek glared.

"Be vigilant, all of you. They're armed with poisoned arrows and relics. Be sure you're wearing your vests." Borek nodded at Carlos, who cursed him before opening the door and stepping outside.

A group of soldiers began kicking and hacking through the back wall as the voices of the hunters rose from the front of the building.

As soon as the opening was large enough, the soldiers surged through, leaving Borek and the two vampyres carrying the women behind. Then they also leapt into the twilight.

Chapter Six

The hunters were mercenaries, not fools.

They'd tracked the vampyres to the abandoned house, lying in wait until just before sunset. It would be folly to force their prey into the light — the sun's rays would burn them to a crisp, destroying their valuable blood. Attack dogs prowled the perimeter, but the hunters restrained them, not wanting to alert the vampyres to their presence.

As soon as the first figure emerged through the front door, the hunters closed in.

An archer aimed at the vampyre's chest. He waited until he had the perfect shot, not wanting to waste one of his precious poison-tipped arrows.

But this vampyre was a trained soldier. He ran to face his enemies, avoiding the spray of holy water. Had each hunter not carried on his person a relic, the soldier would have felled some of them. Instead, he could only swing his sword and curse in frustration, edging toward the trees in hope of escape.

An arrow flew. It struck him in the chest but bounced off his Kevlar vest, falling to the ground.

The hunters murmured in shock.

One of them ran forward, holding out a cross. The vampyre retreated toward the building.

A Rottweiler bounded forward, snapping at the vampyre's legs and sinking its teeth into his calf. The vampyre cursed, slashing at the dog with his sword.

The animal didn't let go.

A garrote flew through the air, catching the vampyre around the neck.

He dropped his sword and tried to pull the wire away from his flesh.

It was no use. The garrote tightened with a loud clicking sound until it separated his head from his body.

Some of the hunters remained with the corpse to drain the blood, not wanting it to lose any of its magical properties. The others rejoined their gang behind the house, where they confronted the remaining vampyres.

Thrown over the back of a soldier, Raven had to rely on her ears rather than her eyes as they burst through a hole in the back wall of the building.

Arrows whizzed through the air, dogs growled and barked, and the panicked voices of hunted vampyres swirled around her.

The soldier who carried her wove from side to side, avoiding those in his path, until a German shepherd began to chase him, snapping at his heels.

Despite carrying Raven, the vampyre maintained his distance, but the animal would not give up. It began to jump, trying to catch Raven with its teeth.

She clutched her arms to her chest to avoid the snapping jaws.

Then she flew through the air and slammed to the ground. She lay on the damp earth, stunned, her right hand caught beneath her body. Pain lanced through her.

A few feet away, the soldier who'd been carrying her lay sprawled. He kicked at the snapping German shepherd, making contact with its muzzle.

The animal yelped and retreated, allowing the soldier time to escape. Unencumbered by Raven, he fled into the trees.

"Looks like someone abandoned his dinner." A male voice laughed.

With a great force of will, Raven began to crawl toward the trees.

Quick footsteps approached her. The hunter grabbed her by the hair, forcing her head back.

She looked up into dark, cruel eyes.

"How many are there?" he demanded.

"Go to hell!"

The hunter backhanded her, splitting her lower lip with the force of his blow. "How many are there?"

Raven made a show of wiping the blood from her mouth, while surreptitiously sliding her other hand down to her ankle.

"There are twenty vampyres. Ten inside the house and ten a short distance from here."

The man wrenched her hair, lowering his face so he could see her eyes. "There are more?"

She nodded, moving her hand beneath the hem of her jeans. "Ten more avoiding the daylight in a building to the north."

He hit her again. "You're lying."

She let out an anguished cry and tried to pull away from him. "I'm not; I swear it. We were supposed to meet the others after sunset."

"You will lead us to them." The man grabbed Raven's injured arm and pulled.

Before he could drag her to her feet, her fingers closed over the hilt of the dagger. In one swift motion, she withdrew it and plunged it into the top of his foot.

The hunter cursed and released her, his hands closing on the dagger.

Raven stumbled to her feet, cradling her injured arm and heading toward the trees as fast as she could manage.

Over her shoulder, she could see that several of the vampyres had been felled, and hunters were already gathered around their corpses. She couldn't see Cara or the vampyre who had been carrying her. Raven hoped they'd escaped.

Just as she approached the tree line, the hunter caught her from behind, wrapping his forearm around her neck. "You'll pay for that, feeder."

Raven scratched at his arm, gasping for breath.

He tightened his grip, and Raven felt her throat close. She continued to struggle, tearing his flesh with her fingernails and pulling at his arm.

"Release her." A voice drifted out of the trees.

Raven pounded the hunter's arm with her fists, straining for breath.

"I said, *release her.*" Out of the darkness a figure emerged, dressed entirely in black.

The fire from the burning building behind them illuminated the figure's face.

Raven looked straight into a pair of angry gray eyes.

Chapter Seven

"You wished to see me?" Father Jack Kavanaugh stood in front of the large desk, clasping his hands together.

The Director of Intelligence for the Curia was dressed in the robes of a cardinal, befitting his position. He peered up at the Jesuit, his dark eyes assessing. "Tell me about your trip to Florence."

"I met Raven, the young woman I wrote to you about. Two nights ago, her sister came to me with her fiancé. I gave them sanctuary, and we wrote to Raven, asking her to join us. She refused.

"This morning, one of our officers shared a report from Florence's police department, indicating that the fiancé had been murdered, and Cara and Raven are missing. It sounds as if the fiancé was killed by a vampyre."

The Director remained silent.

Slightly unnerved, Jack continued. "The Prince of Florence has been deposed by Machiavelli, who is sending Raven and Cara to us as a peace offering."

The Director blinked. "In your letter, you requested a squad of Curia soldiers so you could retrieve the women."

"Yes. I'm concerned for their safety."

The Director glanced down at the open file on top of his desk. "This Raven woman was the Prince's pet."

Jack grimaced. "I was unaware of that until I saw her in Florence."

The Director's eyes narrowed. "Did you write to the Prince, asking him to release her?"

"Yes. I've known her since she was a child. I've always protected her."

The Director rested his hand on top of the open file. "So you don't deny ignoring proper channels and compromising the Curia's mission?"

"Since when is an attempt to save a human soul a compromise?" Jack grew very red in the face.

The Director studied him.

"You Jesuits have a habit of asking for forgiveness rather than permission. We aren't all Jesuits, Father Kavanaugh, and that kind of thinking isn't tolerated here." The Director paused. "You were brought to Rome because of your service record. I will personally transfer you to Prague if you compromise our activities again."

"Prague?" Jack's eyebrows lifted. "But there aren't any—"

"Precisely."

Jack bowed his head to hide his anger. "Understood."

"It's fortunate Florence decided to accede to your weakness rather than to exploit it."

Jack lifted his head. "I don't consider caring for my parishioners to be a weakness."

The Director tapped one of his fingers on top of the desk. "We exist in order to protect humanity from evil. I wish we could save everyone. We both know that's impossible."

"I'm not asking to save everyone." Jack forced himself to keep his tone even. "I'm simply asking for support in protecting two young women, women who are like daughters to me."

"We have intelligence that they are being sent as a gesture of peace, but we have no idea what condition they're in or how many soldiers accompany them. It would be folly to send a squad outside our walls until we know more."

Jack leaned forward, placing his hands on top of the desk. "Raven and Cara are in danger, not just from the Florentines, but from ferals, mercenaries, other vampyres. They could be killed."

"You've already tipped your hand by writing to the Prince and expressing your attachment. Any movement of our troops will simply place a higher price on the women's heads."

"Then let me go. Alone."

The Director gave the priest a long look. "I admire your courage. But I'm not going to allow you to initiate a military engagement over two souls, one of whom is a pet."

Jack straightened. "Our Lord left Heaven to seek and to save those who are lost."

"I am well-acquainted with sacred scripture."

Jack leaned closer. "Then you must know the story of the Gadarene, who was a pet to various demons. Our Lord clothed him, fed him, and rescued him from his tormentors."

"If the women arrive at our borders, we will welcome them. But I won't allow you to walk into the arms of our enemies and be held for ransom. Nor will I send troops outside Vatican City, unless it's to lay siege to a stronghold we can overtake. We cannot tip our hand."

Jack gave the Director a long look. "Are there plans to invade Florence?"

The Director shuffled a few papers on his desk. "Since your protégé was a pet, she will have to be exorcised on arrival."

Jack touched the cross he always kept in his pocket. "I will see to it personally."

"I have already directed some of our agents to secure the body of the fiancé. We can't allow an autopsy to go forward, if he was killed by a vampyre." The Director made the sign of the cross. "You are dismissed."

Jack bowed and withdrew to the door.

"Father Kavanaugh." The Director's voice interrupted his movements.

He turned. "Yes?"

"The most recent intelligence out of Florence indicates that Machiavelli has been executed."

"Executed? By whom?"

"The Prince. It seems he survived the coup, executed his enemies, and is now in full control of the city, including the army."

"Raven," Jack whispered, his hand seeking the relic he carried in his pocket.

"The battleground on which we wage our war against evil is constantly changing." The Director turned his attention to the files on his desk. "Remember this when you are tempted to act without consulting your superiors."

Shaken, Father Kavanaugh bowed and left the office.

Chapter Eight

The hunter released Raven and pushed her to the ground. He withdrew something from his pocket, holding it in front of him.

He laughed.

"Oh yes, laugh." The Prince's gray eyes narrowed. "Trust in a trinket you aren't worthy to wield."

He approached the hunter, who extended the relic in front of his body as far as he could.

As William neared, the hunter's expression faltered. He lifted the relic higher, as if that could stop the angry Prince.

William's eyes grew strangely alight. He reached past the relic to fasten onto the hunter's wrist, pushing the man's hand back so quick and so hard that his wrist snapped.

The hunter screamed and dropped the relic.

"You touched what is mine." William grasped the much taller hunter by the back of his neck. "You made her bleed. Now you will pay for every mark on her perfect skin."

With a sickening sound, he wrenched the hunter's neck, breaking it. He shoved the body aside and wiped his hands on his black pants.

"Who laughs now?" he asked, kicking the corpse.

He turned, the firelight illuminating his handsome profile. His expression softened when he saw Raven sprawled on the grass. "*Cassita.*"

A shuddering sob escaped her chest. She covered her mouth with her hand.

William lifted her into his arms. "I'm sorry he hurt you."

"I thought you were dead." Raven burrowed her face into his neck, hugging him with all her might.

He pressed his lips to her temple. "Once you and your sister were safely outside the city, I was able to regain control of the army. Machiavelli is dead, and I am prince once again."

He nuzzled her face with his nose. "You're bleeding."

Raven wiped her mouth with the back of her hand, leaving a trail of blood across her skin. "Never mind about that. I thought I'd lost you."

"Little lark." He kissed her forehead. "I was only delayed. And for that, I'm sorry. Are you all right?"

"Yes." Raven dug her fingers into his shoulders. "But I'm so angry with you for sending me away. How could you do that?"

"I couldn't protect you and your sister and fight for the city at the same time," William said quietly.

"I don't care about the city!" She slammed her hand down on top of his shoulder. "I care about you. You promised!"

"*Raven.*" His tone was a warning.

She struck him again in frustration. This time he growled.

"You promised, William. You promised we would stay togeth—" Raven's words were cut off by his mouth.

He covered her, consumed her, swallowing her anger.

She wrapped her fingers in his hair, pressing herself against him.

He invaded her mouth, all sweetness and softness, a contrast to his branding kiss. He stroked his velvet tongue against hers, touching and tasting.

"May I?" He pulled back, his gray eyes darting hungrily toward her hand.

Raven was confused. But when William's tongue dipped to the injured portion of her lip, she understood.

She lifted the back of her hand and pressed it to his mouth.

His eyes locked on hers as he gave her a long, sensual lick. Then he was kissing her again, his tongue tracing the wound on her lip.

"The shedding of your blood is my fault," he whispered. "Forgive me."

"I'd shed more than this to keep you with me."

William's eyes blazed, and he kissed her again, all restraint giving way.

Raven responded, moving her tongue in concert with his.

Suddenly, she was on the ground, and he stood over her, sword in hand.

An arrow whizzed toward him, and he caught it in mid-air, flipping it around and throwing it like a javelin.

The arrow struck the archer in the abdomen. He fell down dead.

"An old one! Quick!" the leader of the hunters shouted in English.

The others closed ranks, abandoning their skirmishes to focus on the new prize. The surviving vampyres, with the exception of Borek, fled into the trees.

The commander gave the hunters a wide berth before approaching Raven from the side.

The Prince glanced at Borek and snarled. "Touch her and I shall kill you."

The commander bowed. "I swore to the new prince to protect her and deliver her to Rome."

The Prince's gaze returned to the hunters. "There is only one prince. She stays with me."

Borek stood still, sword drawn.

"Lay down your weapons, and I'll spare you." The Prince addressed the hunters, his voice echoing across the clearing.

The leader of the hunters laughed. "You may be an old one. But we are twenty. And we are all armed."

"Are you certain of your numbers?" William remained focused on the leader. "I count less. Perhaps your mathematical abilities are as lacking as your judgment."

"There is only way this will end—with your head on a stick and your blood in a bag." The hunter held out a relic, smiling.

Borek flinched and began to shake. He took two steps back.

"This is your final warning." William lifted his sword, and the blade shone in the firelight, as the building behind the hunters continued to blaze.

"Shoot him." The hunter lifted his hand, and the archers took aim.

Before a single arrow could be released, William closed the distance between him and his attackers and beheaded the leader. His body was a black blur as he raced from hunter to hunter, plunging his sword in their abdomens, withdrawing, and moving to the next victim.

Holy water and salt fell like rain over him, but he barely reacted, too busy knocking relics and garrotes out of the hunter's hands before ending them.

In less than five minutes, the hunters were destroyed, their bodies scattered.

It was a massacre.

Borek swore an oath. "Impossible."

Raven looked up at the commander. For the first time, she saw fear etched on his face.

William wiped his sword on the coat of one of the fallen men and tossed the garment aside. He strode toward Borek with purpose.

The commander retreated.

The Prince stopped once Raven was behind him, but he didn't lower his sword. "Machiavelli is dead. Florence is mine once again, as is the woman."

The soldier dropped to one knee, placing his sword in front of him. "Commander Borek, my lord, at your service."

"Commander Borek," the Prince repeated. "Your soldiers have deserted you, while you risked death to stay with your charge."

The Prince extended his hand to Raven, lifting her to her feet. "Has this one touched you?"

"No."

"How has he treated you?"

"He forced Stefan to examine Cara when he refused. He gave me a dagger for protection and told me to conceal it from the others. I used it on the hunter. It bought me time."

"Shall I kill him?"

Borek's dark eyes sought Raven's.

She shook her head. "No. The others would have thrown us to the hunters, but he protected us." She scanned the clearing, her heart racing. "Where's Cara?"

"She can't have gone far. I scented her on my approach." The Prince returned his attention to the commander. "Where is the other human?"

"With one of my detachment. He was told to flee south. We should be able to overtake them."

William gazed at Borek appraisingly. "Your bravery and attention to my pet has earned you your life. If you serve me well, you'll earn the right to return to Florence. If you don't, I'll kill you."

Borek bowed. "Yes, my lord."

"You may stand."

Borek stood, still gazing uneasily at the Prince.

"Where is Stefan of Montréal?"

"I don't know, my lord." Borek's sharp eyes took stock of the bodies scattered nearby. "I don't see his corpse."

"How unfortunate for him. The hunters would have been merciful." William lifted Raven into his arms. "You have seen some of my power, Borek; a glimpse I am sure you will keep to yourself."

The commander shifted his weight uneasily. "Yes, my lord."

"You're from Prague, as I recall. I am sure you wouldn't want the Curia aware of your true heritage."

Borek's eyes met Raven's. He looked uneasy.

"Serve me well, and your secret will also remain secret." William turned and ran into the woods, carrying the woman he loved.

Chapter Nine

"You aren't wearing Kevlar." Raven's hand had slipped inside William's shirt, making contact with his cool skin. He carried her, moving at a high rate of speed through the trees.

"No, I am not."

"Your soldiers are."

"I am an old one, *Cassita*. I am faster and stronger than the others."

"I wish you'd wear it." She spoke against his chest.

William's expression was impassive. "Hunters are the least of my worries."

Raven sighed and withdrew her hand. "Borek told me he was Russian."

William glanced back at the soldier, who strained to keep up with him. "He's from Prague."

"Why did he lie?"

"The Curia laid waste to the covens in Czechoslovakia. No vampyre dares live within its borders or lay claim to its heritage. No doubt Borek was afraid the Curia would kill him if they discovered the truth."

Raven shivered. "So much death. So much killing. I don't know how they live with themselves."

William snorted. "They baptize their actions by claiming God is on their side."

"Are they really so blind? There must be some way for them to combat a vampyre take-over of the world without killing."

"If there is such a way, they aren't interested in finding it."

"I thought you were dead." Raven's voice grew small. "I agonized over it. You promised we'd stay together, and you broke that promise."

"*Cassita*, I—"

"How could you send me away?" She squeezed his shoulder, her green eyes fixed on his face.

William slackened his pace.

"You could have been killed. Or worse, you and your sister could have become pets to anyone. Do you understand what that means?" His tone revealed the simmering anger that swirled in his chest.

"Machiavelli wasn't interested in us."

"Someone would have been. The best decision was to make everyone think the Curia wanted you and to have you escorted outside the city."

"I was nearly killed by a feral. A hunter grabbed me. I could have died not having—not having—"

William interrupted her. "I swear by the name of my teacher that I will never send you away. But if your priest persuades the Curia to take you from me…" He trailed off.

"I will persuade Father Kavanaugh to let me stay with you."

"I've always admired your optimism, Raven, but I cannot share it." He increased his pace. "Still, I have one ally left."

"Good." Fatigue overtook her, and she closed her eyes, resting her cheek against his shoulder.

It was easier like this—to close her eyes as they whipped past the scenery. The speed made her dizzy, and jostling gave her a headache. But the tender, tight embrace of her beloved comforted her. He would protect her, even with his life.

William was much, much faster than Borek, even with her in his arms. Twice he had to slow his pace so the commander could catch up.

At length they approached a hill and quickly climbed toward the summit. But before they crested the top, William halted.

"My lord?" Borek's voice was tight as he caught up.

William nodded toward the peak. "Your men and the other human are up there. But they are not alone."

Borek inhaled slowly. "Not hunters."

"No." William's jaw tensed. "Vampyres."

Chapter Ten

The Prince tested the wind, making sure it wouldn't betray them to the vampyres who'd assembled on the hill.

He gestured for Borek to follow him, and they slowly crept up to the top. As they approached, they could hear voices.

"But couriers were sent!" Stefan sputtered. "The new Prince of Florence sent a message to your princess, explaining that we needed to pass through her territory on our way to Rome."

"I know of no such message." The male voice was harsh. "You're trespassing. The price of trespassing is death."

Swords rattled, and the sound of heavy footfalls rang out.

William placed Raven on her feet and sprang forward, sword drawn.

"Stop!" he commanded, striding in between the Umbrian captain and Stefan.

William swiftly surveyed the situation, noting that the captain was accompanied by ten soldiers, seven male and three female. He noted with satisfaction that one of his own soldiers held Cara some distance away, while two others flanked them for protection.

"Your highness." The captain inclined his head respectfully.

The Prince returned his nod. "Your name, soldier."

"Julius, highness. We've met before. I'm captain of the princess's guard."

"Yes, we've met before." The Prince forced a small smile. "I see you've come across my detachment. I can verify that they're on official

Florentine business, tasked to deliver two human females to the Curia in Rome."

The captain's expression grew troubled. "We have no desire for conflict with the Curia. But with respect, your highness, we cannot allow you to pass."

"Your princess is a friend to me and I to her." The Prince's tone was firm.

The Umbrian shifted his feet. "Yes, highness. For that reason, I would prefer not to engage you. But we cannot allow you to pass through our territory without the princess's approval."

William scowled. "I sent couriers a day ago."

"As I said to one of your citizens, I know of no such couriers." The captain's eyes moved to the soldiers who were closing ranks behind their Prince. If they felt surprise at the sight of him, they chose to hide it.

"There are hunters about. We just battled twenty not far from here."

"And ferals," Borek added.

"We shouldn't tarry, then." The Umbrian captain lifted his sword.

The Prince measured him. Then his eyes met Raven's.

The Prince sheathed his sword. "Very well. Take us to your princess. She and I will discuss the matter. We will come peaceably, provided there is no provocation."

"No provocation from me or my guards, highness." The captain whistled to his soldiers, and they moved to surround the Florentines.

The Prince locked eyes with Stefan, who'd been cowering behind another soldier. "Hand me the missive."

The physician fumbled in his pocket and held out the letter with trembling hands.

The soldier in front of him passed it to the Prince.

"You shall be dealt with, *traitor*," the Prince hissed.

William turned his back on the physician and crossed over to Raven, while the Umbrians stood aside to let him pass. He picked her up and nodded to the captain.

"Proceed."

With another whistle, the Umbrians marched down the hill, heading north toward Perugia.

Chapter Eleven

"Why didn't you fight?" Raven whispered in William's ear. "The princess is an important ally. And the night has too many eyes." He gave her a significant look.

Raven bristled at his description of the princess, for it reminded her of William's description of Aoibhe.

"What about Cara?"

"She sleeps. When we arrive in Perugia, I will attend to her."

"What's in Perugia?"

"The princess." William kissed her lightly, never slackening his pace. "Rest. You have a bruised face and an injured arm. Simonetta will be curious about you, which means we need to be alert. It will be best if we feign indifference to one another."

"You may as well ask the sun not to shine."

William smiled and took her lips once again.

She closed her eyes, a feeling of disquiet growing within her.

"We have arrived." William's low voice broke through Raven's slumber.

The underworld of Umbria was, in appearance, very similar to the underworld of Florence. It consisted of a network of hidden passages lit by torches and large, cavernous rooms hewn out of stone.

The Florentines were escorted into what looked like a council chamber, dominated as it was by a gold throne that sat elevated at the far end of the room.

Without explanation, William placed Raven on her feet near the door and stepped forward until he stood squarely in front of the throne.

He adjusted the sleeves of his black dress shirt, the gold of his cufflinks shining in the torchlight.

As if on cue, the captain of the guard withdrew through a side door.

Suddenly, and without warning, a woman's scream filled the space.

Raven turned and saw her sister scratching and pummeling the soldier who held her.

The soldier cursed, but he would not strike her. Instead, he dropped her.

Cara fell roughly to the floor and kicked at his feet, cursing loudly in English. "You bastard! Don't touch me!"

The vampyre growled, baring his teeth.

"Cara, stop!" Raven limped toward her, but was surpassed by Borek, who placed his hand on the other vampyre's chest, propelling him backward.

"Enough," he commanded in Italian.

The angry vampyre spat a curse at Cara and moved away.

She peered up at Raven and Borek, brushing her long, blond hair away from her face. "Raven? What are you doing here?"

"Get control of her." Borek gave Raven a thunderous look.

Raven was about to challenge Borek, knowing that William was watching, but a door slammed at the front of the hall.

All eyes moved to the beautiful vampyre who floated across the floor to the throne, where she seated herself, adjusting her flowing azure silk dress.

"Simonetta," Raven whispered, eyes wide.

In front of her sat the personification of Venus from Botticelli's painting. Raven recognized the face and eyes immediately, as well the long, flaxen hair that fell to her hips.

As a vampyre, La Bella Simonetta was even more exquisite than she'd been in life. Raven felt her very legs shake in the muse's presence.

Cara tugged on Raven's sleeve. "Where are we? Where's Dan?"

"Quiet." Raven helped her sister to her feet and drew her to the back wall. "We're in danger here. Keep quiet. I'll explain later."

Cara muttered to herself, but was interrupted by a loud, musical voice.

"This is unexpected." The princess turned cool blue eyes on the Florentines.

The Prince gave an exaggerated bow. "You cannot condemn me for wishing to gaze on your beauty once again, La Bella."

The female vampyre's rosy lips turned up into a smile. "You flatter me."

"I apologize for interrupting your day. I trust my couriers delivered their message?"

"They did." She fussed with her robes, losing eye contact with the Prince. "My captain was sent out on patrol before the couriers arrived."

"A thousand apologies." He bowed once again. "Perhaps the patrol had something to do with the Umbrian army that stands on the border of Tuscany?"

The princess fixed her gaze on his face. "I heard rumors of your demise at the hands of our old friend Machiavelli."

"Those rumors were exaggerated."

"Indeed." Her clear, light eyes moved over the Florentine soldiers, coming to rest on Cara and Raven. "I don't suppose the humans are a gift?"

"I'm afraid not, princess. These are the humans spoken of by my couriers."

Simonetta regarded him shrewdly. "Since when does Florence give gifts to the Curia?"

"With respect, princess, since when does Umbria threaten to invade Tuscany?" The Prince's tone grew sharp.

She was quiet for an instant and then laughed, the musical sound echoing in the large chamber.

"Who's that?" Cara whispered, holding tightly to her sister's arm.

"That's the Princess of Umbria." Raven strained to hear the exchange ensuing between the two heads of state.

Cara frowned. "I didn't know Umbria had a princess."

Raven silenced her sister with a look.

"I assembled my army at the border simply as a precaution. As you know, Machiavelli and I have not been on the best of terms. Now that I see my closest ally is prince once again, I shall order the troops to withdraw."

The Prince nodded. "Thank you."

"With respect to your couriers, I prefer to be given the opportunity to respond to a request, rather than having my acquiescence assumed." The princess frowned.

"Of course." The Prince adopted a contrite expression. "A thousand apologies."

"Your apologies are noted, but not yet accepted." She smiled. "Let us retire privately, where we may discuss the matter further."

She stood, and everyone bowed.

Simonetta lifted her voice. "The Prince and I have private business to attend to. We shall return, in time."

"If I may, princess." The Prince stepped forward.

She nodded imperially.

"I regret I must trespass on your hospitality. My soldiers were set upon by hunters. They need food and other amenities, as do the humans."

Simonetta lifted her hand. "Julius, see to it that the humans have what they require, and give them a room in which to rest. The Florentines are to be given sustenance, but they are to remain in this chamber until we return."

"Allow me to post my own captain and his second outside the humans' door," the Prince pressed. "I would also appreciate it if you would detain Stefan of Montréal, the former physician of Florence. He is not to be trusted."

The physician sputtered his protest, but Simonetta was already nodding at her guards. Two of them walked over to Stefan and dragged him from the hall amidst his loud pleas for clemency.

The princess ignored his cries, extending her hand to the Prince.

He kissed it before placing it in his grasp. He and the princess exited through a side door.

Cara exhaled her relief. "Now what?"

Raven didn't hear her question. She was too busy staring after William, who'd left without a backward glance. He'd been so solicitous with the princess, so attentive.

She'd never seen him behave that way before.

Simonetta must be more powerful than she thought.

Julius, the Umbrian captain, interrupted her musings. "This way." He gestured to the door behind them.

Raven and Cara had no choice but to follow, with Borek and another Florentine at their sides.

Chapter Twelve

"Are you trying to get me killed?" Aoibhe's hands went to her hips as she discovered her lover reclining on her bed.

Ibarra smiled and rolled to his side. "Is that any way to greet an important ally? I seem to recall saving your life."

"As I saved yours, Basque. We are even." She bent to pick up his discarded clothes from the floor.

"Get dressed and get out." She tossed the clothes in his face. "There's a hunting party after you. If someone traces your scent here, the Prince will kill me."

"You didn't know I was here until you entered the room." Ibarra rested his chin on an upturned hand. "The Prince has barricaded himself in his impenetrable fortress. Not even he has spies in every corner of the city."

Aoibhe moved to the windows and drew the curtains. "Don't be a fool. You were head of security. You know some of the humans are in his service."

Ibarra waited until he had her full attention before removing the sheet from his body. "Very well, I'll leave. But I'd like to know how the Prince survived the last of the Medici and Machiavelli in a single evening."

Aoibhe leaned wearily against one of the bed posts. "Many of the brethren are loyal to him. Gregor rallied his supporters and came to his aid. When it looked as if the tide might shift, the army sided with the Prince."

Ibarra swung his legs over the side of the bed. "There are whispers the Curia has taken an interest in Florence."

Aoibhe lifted her long red hair. "The Prince sent his pet to them as a peace offering. Apparently, they want her."

"Is that envy I see on your face?"

She turned away, fussing with the skirt of her long, crimson dress. "I envy nothing, save the throne of Florence."

"Then I shall have to secure it for you. Come, Aoibhe." His tone gentled, and he extended his hand to her. "We have the entire day to enjoy ourselves. Love me a little."

Ibarra's body was aroused; it was obvious. But the expression on his face belied another, perhaps deeper, desire.

Aoibhe stared, her dark eyes calculating.

She unfastened her dress and pulled it over her head, dropping it onto a chair.

Chapter Thirteen

"You're crazy." Cara rounded on her sister as they entered a lavishly decorated room located off one of the many serpentine passages in Perugia's underworld.

The room itself was rectangular, furnished with a large, plush sofa and several high-backed armchairs. An open door on one end revealed a bedroom. A corresponding door in the opposite wall revealed a bathroom.

Exhausted mentally and physically, Raven collapsed on the sofa, cradling her injured arm. Bruises had blossomed on her pale skin, and the flesh beneath was tender.

She grabbed a fur throw and wrapped it around herself. Damp coolness radiated from the stone walls, and her teeth chattered. "I'm telling the truth. They're all vampyres."

"I knew it." Cara came closer. "When you called me about David, I knew you were cracking up. You've been carrying that shit so long you finally broke."

"If I was going to break, I would have done it a long time ago." Raven looked up at her sister. "Have you seen what they can do? Have you noticed how strong they are?"

Cara plopped down on the sofa. "It's a fricking Renaissance fair, complete with toy swords. Where's Dan? Don't tell me they tried to recruit him. He used to do community theater."

"He's in Florence. When you came to my apartment, a vampyre attacked us. We were brought here, and Dan was left behind."

Cara turned to face her. "Is he hurt?"

Raven hesitated. "I don't know. He was knocked unconscious."

"Unconscious?" Cara's face grew pale. "And you left him?"

"I had no choice. We were attacked and carried off. Someone called an ambulance before we left. That's all I know."

Cara bolted to the door. "We have to go. We have to get back to Dan."

"We aren't going anywhere until the princess releases us."

In defiance, Cara opened the door. Four soldiers stared back at her, two on each side.

She closed the door and leaned up against it. "There are guards in the hall."

Raven sighed. "Of course there are. Vampyres are extremely territorial, and we're trespassing. We can't leave until William persuades the princess to let us go."

Cara approached her sister again, standing in front of the sofa. "Forget about the vampyre bullshit, how come I don't remember being attacked?"

"You were thrown against a wall." Raven's voice wavered. "You had a head injury. You've been unconscious."

Cara touched her head, running both hands over her scalp. "I don't have a headache."

"William healed you."

"Who's William? Did he attack Dan?"

"No, he rescued us. He was the one in black talking to the princess. He's the Prince of Florence."

Cara rolled her eyes. "Everyone around here is a prince or a princess. What are you? The Princess of Portsmouth?"

"Very funny."

"Why would that guy help us?"

Raven looked at her sister defiantly. "We're together."

"You have a boyfriend? Why didn't you tell me?"

"Because he's a vampyre. He's the only reason we're still alive. We were attacked, and William saved us."

Cara turned on her heel and marched into the bathroom. She examined herself in the mirror. "I look okay."

"That's because he gave you…" Raven cleared her throat. "Never mind."

"Gave me what?" Cara emerged from the bathroom.

"They brought us food." Raven gestured to the lavish table set up on the far side of the room. "Why don't you have a shower and get cleaned up? Then we can have something to eat."

"These people call themselves vampyres, and you're sleeping with one of them." Cara scrubbed at her face. "Is this some weird fetish thing?"

"Cara, come here." Raven held out her hand.

Her sister took it reluctantly, allowing herself to be pulled to a seated position.

"You don't have to believe everything I say, but you need to hear me. These people, all of them, are dangerous. They view us as food, and they have no problem killing."

Cara grimaced. "Including William?"

"He's different."

"How different?"

Raven made eye contact with her sister. "He's the one who captured David and threatened to kill him."

"What?"

"I told him what happened to us when we were children. William was disgusted that David got away with it. He wanted him to pay."

"Did he kill him?" Cara squeaked.

"No. He wanted to, but I wouldn't let him. William turned him over to the police in California."

Cara stared at her sister, her expression blank. "We need to get to Florence. Dan is hurt, and he needs our help."

She strode into the adjacent bedroom, dismayed to discover it too was absent windows or any other visible egress.

"You aren't listening," Raven called. She waited for her sister to emerge from the bedroom. "When William comes back, we can ask him about Dan. But we aren't going anywhere."

Cara's blue eyes narrowed. "Yeah, your new boyfriend is a real prince. He drinks blood, hangs around with re-enactors, and kidnaps your stepfather."

Raven leaned forward. "If you don't believe me, ask Father Kavanaugh. He knows exactly who and what these people are. That's why he wanted me to come to Rome, to get me away from William."

Cara lifted her arms in frustration. "Then for God's sake, Raven, why didn't you come?"

"Because Father is hiding his own secrets."

"That's obvious. He was acting weird when Dan and I went to see him, and he wasn't going to let us leave. We had to sneak out of the Vatican in order to see you."

"Exactly. He doesn't want me near vampyres, and he doesn't want you near them, either."

Cara walked over to the table and retrieved an apple, taking a large bite. She gave her sister a hard look. "Tell me everything. And start at the beginning."

Chapter Fourteen

Simonetta Vespucci's beauty was the stuff of legends.

The Prince of Florence was well aware of this. He'd known her in life, and he'd known Sandro Botticelli, the artist who immortalized her in such paintings as *The Birth of Venus*.

The beauty she'd worn in life had been compounded a hundred fold when she became a vampyre. Now she owned the face and form of a goddess.

During his tenure as prince, William had enjoyed her on more than one occasion. Simonetta was passionate but particular when it came to her lovers. The Prince was one of her favorites, which was why he followed her to her bedchamber on this occasion with more than a soupçon of concern.

The princess inhabited a stately villa in Perugia, which was so lavish it rivaled the Palace of Versailles. Her bedroom, in particular, boasted large floor-to-ceiling mirrors on every wall, a gilded ceiling, and heavy, ornate furniture upholstered in crimson velvet.

Although one might have expected Simonetta to spend most of her time gazing at herself, she rarely did. The mirrors were installed primarily for her lovers, so that they could admire themselves as they consorted and fornicated with a goddess for hours on end.

There had been a time when the Prince was untroubled by the decadent furnishings, when he'd enjoyed the mirrors that reflected the large and stately bed, and the female striding toward it.

Now the sight repelled him.

"Given your trouble with Machiavelli and the Curia, I'm surprised you left Florence." Simonetta ushered the Prince to a large sitting area at the far end of the chamber, mere steps from her imposing bed.

"Machiavelli sent the detachment without my authority, and he neglected to send couriers first. I came to rectify the error and to apologize for the insult," the Prince lied smoothly.

She smiled. "I can always count on you to respect propriety. Shall I arrange for a feeding? You must be hungry."

"Your hospitality is appreciated, but a feeding is unnecessary. I am eager for the detachment to reach Rome before sunrise."

"I'd offer transportation, but since the Curia is involved, I prefer to remain neutral." She pulled a length of cord that fell from the ceiling. A knock sounded from behind one of the mirrors.

"Enter," she commanded.

The mirror moved, revealing a hidden door. A servant stood in the opening, bowing low.

Simonetta addressed him with detachment. "Fetch a bottle of our finest vintage, and be quick about it."

The servant bowed and withdrew, replacing the mirror.

Simonetta walked over to a low couch and sat on it, arranging herself to best effect. She cast a stunning figure with her long, gold hair and azure dress against the crimson velvet. And she knew it.

But the Prince's thoughts were otherwise engaged. Indeed, all he could think of was Raven and how much he wanted to return to her side.

He'd gone to Santa Maria Novella to beg his teacher for intercession. Perhaps the saint had hearkened to his request, perhaps not. At least he and Raven were together now.

Raven wasn't flawless in appearance as Simonetta was. But the nature of her soul, the strength of her virtue and character, made her unspeakably beautiful. With such thoughts in mind, William gazed on the princess's face and watched as the pearl of her legendary beauty lost its luster.

Simonetta invited him to sit beside her. When he did, she extended her hand.

He kissed it briefly. "I respect Umbria's desire for neutrality, but you must know a war is coming."

"Why should we have war now, after all these years? We aren't Prague or Budapest."

He released her hand. "The Curia is on the move. They are eying my principality, waiting for an opportunity."

"The Roman would never allow it."

"Treaties are made and broken; traitors abound." His gray eyes met hers. "I say this as an ally, Simonetta: be wary. Be vigilant."

Her pale eyes grew sharp. "What aren't you telling me?"

"I tell you what you already know — the Curia stood by while Venice and Florence went to war, hoping we'd destroy one another. When that didn't happen, they turned their eyes on my city. My detachment travels to Rome to try to negotiate a peace. But I have no confidence such peace will last."

The servant re-entered the chamber, delivering an opened bottle and two ornate goblets on a tray. He served the vintage and withdrew.

The two vampyres clinked glasses.

Simonetta inclined her head, watching as he drank. "If the situation is as fraught as you say, why leave Florence?"

The Prince swirled the blood in his glass. "As I said, I was cleaning up Machiavelli's mess."

"I thought that's why we had servants." She sipped the blood delicately.

"Servants can be incompetent. I need to execute Stefan for that reason. May I have your permission to do so here?"

"You're welcome to use our torture chamber, if you wish."

"That won't be necessary. All I require is your aid in having the head and body burned. I shall execute him personally." The Prince's attention returned to his glass, and he stared into the blackish depths.

"Of course." Her eyebrows drew together. "If news were to reach you that the Curia desired Umbria, would you tell me?"

"Yes." He looked at her carefully. "Can I hope the same from you?"

"As always. You have been an excellent ally and neighbor. Would that all the royals in Italy were the same." Her rosy lips pouted. "The last time you visited me, you kept me at arm's length."

"I was hunting." He drained his glass.

"Yes, an American family. My spies tell me you drove them out of Umbria, but you didn't kill them. I find that curious."

The Prince rose and placed his glass on the tray. "With respect, princess, I am eager to dispatch the detachment to Rome. I am grateful for your friendship, as always. I promise friendship in return."

Simonetta put her glass aside and stood, her long, flaxen hair slipping over her pale shoulders. "Surely your departure can be delayed.

"Come, William. Send the detachment, and I'll order one of my patrols to accompany them to the southern border. We can entertain one another in the meantime. I've missed you." She reached for him, but caught only air.

He bowed to cover his evasion.

"Your offer of support is appreciated, but it's best if the detachment departs as soon as possible, unaccompanied.

"As to your other offer, you honor me with your attention, but I must take my leave. Florence needs me."

Simonetta lifted her hand and placed it against his cheek.

She studied him.

"There was a time when you leaned into my touch." She stroked his cheek with her thumb and withdrew her hand. "Something has changed."

He forced a smile. "You are a delight to look upon as always, Bella. But I am in haste."

"Let us not lie to one another. Not about this." She returned to her couch. "I don't suppose Aoibhe is the reason for your indifference?"

William straightened. "I am hardly indifferent." He forced his gaze to wander over her comely form.

"Ah, my old friend, that was a lie.

"I've seen you distracted, but this is something else. One might almost think you're in love." Her beautiful face grew grave. "I know our kind only too well, William. We don't love. Even if we enjoy a fascination for a time, all good things for us must end."

She paused, as if waiting for him to respond.

He simply stood, worried he'd given too much away.

She gestured toward the door. "Execute your physician, send your detachment, and take your leave. May your beautiful city remain safe, and may we always be allies."

William's face grew grim. He retreated, pausing in the doorway. "Thank you, princess."

SYLVAIN REYNARD

She waved her fingers at him and returned her attention to her goblet of blood.

As William exited the doorway, he realized he had been the only one to gaze into the mirrors, noting their reflections. Simonetta hadn't bothered.

Instead, she'd sat like a bird in a gilded cage, watching his reactions.

He felt a good deal more than uncomfortable at the realization.

Chapter Fifteen

Ispettor Sergio Batelli ascended the staircase from the crime scene to Raven Wood's apartment, muttering curses.

The body of an American man had been found inside the door to Signorina Wood's apartment building by paramedics, who had been called to the scene by someone claiming to be a neighbor. Once they arrived, they'd tried to resuscitate the victim, but to no avail.

The investigating officer had written in his report that the victim suffered blunt force trauma to the head. Before an autopsy could be performed, someone from the American consulate had appeared, demanding the body. The local police refused. The autopsy had been postponed while superiors on both sides of the conflict argued.

Batelli's colleagues had already searched Signorina Wood's apartment. He tore through the tape that sealed the door and opened it. He risked the ire of his superiors, as well as that of the officer in charge, but he didn't care.

He flicked the light switch.

The apartment was clean, exceptionally so. Scents of lemon and orange filled his nostrils. But the apartment was empty.

In the police reports, which a fellow officer had shown him, neighbors claimed not to have seen or heard anything suspicious before the body was found. They didn't even know Signorina Wood was moving out.

A quick telephone call to the Uffizi Gallery revealed that her employer had no idea of her whereabouts; she was on holiday like the rest of the restoration team until September.

Batelli stood in her empty bedroom, staring at what appeared to be part of a cane that was embedded in the wall.

There was something ominous about the object. Batelli had no idea what it represented, if anything.

The victim they'd found downstairs wasn't a relative of Signorina Wood, and he wasn't the lover Batelli had observed from a distance entering and leaving the building.

Batelli trusted his gut. Right now, his gut was telling him Raven was somehow connected to the corpse. The homicide investigators were waiting on the American consulate to provide them with details about the corpse's identity.

Batelli hadn't given up on solving the mysterious theft of Botticelli illustrations from the Uffizi, despite the fact that their owner, Professor Gabriel Emerson, had given up hope of recovering the items and returned to America.

And Batelli hadn't given up his active pursuit of the mysterious and untraceable William York, who had been named by Professor Emerson as a suspicious person connected to the gallery.

Batelli's investigation had quietly yielded the record of a transfer of funds from a bank in Geneva to the Uffizi, a donation attributed to William York. Although Dottor Vitali, the director of the Uffizi, seemed to have no memory of William York or his extravagant donation, Batelli believed he had gifted the money for the purpose of securing an invitation to the private reception accompanying the unveiling of the Botticelli illustrations. Professor Emerson had corroborated the donation and York's presence at the unveiling.

Of course, the bank in Geneva refused to offer any information about the funds, apart from confirming that they had transferred the money from one of their institutional accounts at the request of a client. They refused to identify the client or to confirm whether he, she, or they held Italian citizenship.

Batelli thought it was interesting how all roads led to Switzerland. The illustrations had been sold to the Emersons by a Swiss family in Cologny, a suburb of Geneva. The car Raven Wood's lover drove around in was registered to a Swiss diplomat. A Swiss bank had transferred thousands of Euros to the Uffizi just prior to the opening of the Botticelli exhibition.

More puzzling still, there were no records of a Swiss resident or national named William York.

But the police had possession of his Mercedes, or what appeared to be the Mercedes Batelli had observed Raven Wood and her lover using. The car had been abandoned a short walk from her apartment. Earlier that day, the forensic specialist had combed it for evidence.

Batelli's cell phone chirped with an incoming text.

He was surprised to be receiving a message, as it was long past midnight.

The text was from an unknown number.

Find the underground club on Via Ghibellina.

Batelli was intrigued.

He shoved his phone in his pocket and quickly searched the rest of the flat. When he was finished, he turned out the lights and painstakingly repaired the tape sealing the apartment.

Perhaps the text was a joke. Perhaps it would lead nowhere. But he descended the stairs with the intention of finding the underground club.

Chapter Sixteen

"We are departing for Rome. Assemble the men, and don't bother trying to find Stefan. The traitor has been dealt with." The Prince addressed Borek, who bowed and marched away, taking the other Florentine soldier with him.

The remaining Umbrian soldiers departed also, following the instructions of the princess's lieutenant.

William exhaled his relief.

He opened the door to the chamber and hastily closed it behind him. Raven's scent assaulted him.

"William?" She sat up sleepily on the couch, rubbing her eyes. "What's happening?"

"We need to reach Rome before sunrise." He surveyed the dimly lit room. "Where is your sister?"

"In the shower." Raven pointed to the closed bathroom door.

"Can you be ready to leave in a few minutes?"

"I think so." She went to him and buried her face in his chest. "You were gone a long time."

He tensed in her arms. "Protocol is never swift."

She lifted her face. Without words, she pressed her lips to his.

He reciprocated, albeit briefly. "We don't have much time. I am sorry."

"I need you."

If William felt surprise at her declaration, he hid it. His gaze flickered to the bathroom door. "What about your sister?"

She squeezed his middle. "There's a bedroom. It has a door."

"After so much death, you still desire me?"

She pressed her body to him. "I thought I'd lost you. I'm so relieved you're all right." Her voice grew throaty. "I need you."

William didn't hesitate. He lifted her to the bedroom and kicked the door closed behind them.

"We aren't safe, but we will be. I swear it." His gray eyes burned into hers.

"I'm just grateful you're alive."

"As alive as a vampyre can be." He gave her a half-smile. "We don't have time for words, if coupling is what you truly want."

She stroked his jaw. "Yes."

He placed her on the large, four-poster bed, taking a moment to light a candelabra on one of the side tables. Then he reclined on his back and pulled her atop him.

"I can't," she whimpered.

William's face was stricken. "But I thought—"

She cut him off. "It's the position." She gestured to her injured leg. "I'm in pain. I can't be on top."

Understanding washed over his fine features.

A high-backed, armless chair stood nearby. William gestured to it. "Would that be all right?"

"We can try." She looked up at him shyly.

He carried her to the chair and sat, adjusting her on his lap so her legs were suspended on either side of his. His hand went to her injured leg. "And now?"

"Whatever you do," she breathed, "don't let go."

His hands gripped her hips. "Give me my name."

"*William*," she breathed.

"My lover, my *Cassita*. I shall never let you go."

She kissed him, her fingers combing through his short, blond hair.

It was easy enough to shift forward on his lap, feeling him rise between her legs. Raven's movements grew impatient, teasing the inside of his mouth with her tongue as she slid against him.

William touched the arm she'd injured in her altercation with the hunter. "Does it hurt?"

"Not anymore."

His eyes glittered in the candlelight. He traced her still-swollen lip with his thumb. "And here? Where that fiend struck you?"

"I only feel you," she whispered, nipping at his thumb.

"Look at you, your eyes, your breasts, your skin." He wrapped a hand around her neck. "You are magnificent."

She closed her eyes. "After seeing Simonetta in all her glory?"

William pulled her toward him, and his lips found her ear. "Not even Simonetta in all her glory can compare to you," he whispered. "I have no desire for her."

He kissed her urgently and divested her of her shirt and bra. He lifted her in order to remove her jeans and underwear. Now she was naked.

He gazed at her full breasts, wetting his lower lip in anticipation.

"Please," she whispered, rocking.

He peppered her round flesh with kisses, supporting her with cool hands. "Your skin smells of rain. It reminds me of home."

She kissed him reverently, leaning into his touch.

His mouth fastened on a nipple, drawing a moan from her mouth as he licked and sucked. He feasted on her for some time before drawing back and passing his thumbs over the sensitive tips.

"I want to feed from you." His lips fluttered to her throat and slid up the arch of her neck.

"Yes."

"Set me free." He licked a patch of skin beneath her ear.

She reached down to his trousers, shifting so she could work the zipper. She took him in her hand. He was already hard.

She moaned as he lifted her and slid her down on top of him.

Her heart beat frantically, the sound like a drum to his ears.

For a moment, she was still. Her skin burned against the coolness of his touch, a bead of perspiration sliding between her breasts.

William caught it with the tip of his tongue.

With a gasp, she began to move up and down, his fingers digging into her hips.

Perhaps it was the position. Perhaps it was the urgency or the darkness. Raven was tense, too much in need to prolong the seductive culmination of so much want.

She angled her neck, presenting the artery to his mouth, wrapping her arms around his shoulders.

She moved more quickly, his strong hands pushing and pulling.

Her hair billowed around her shoulders as her orgasm rocketed through her.

"Look at my lark fly," William whispered, his voice tinged with admiration. "Fly, *Cassita*."

He kissed her neck as she vibrated around him, tasting the skin before sinking his teeth into her artery.

Raven's orgasm crested, and William continued to move, thrusting into her while drinking.

She kept expecting the orgasm to wane, but it didn't, like a long, sustained note played in concert by an orchestra.

"I can't," she rasped. "It's too much." She slumped forward, mindless with pleasure.

William emptied himself into her before swallowing her blood. He licked the imprint of his teeth and kissed it.

"*Je t'aim.*" He buried his face in her mane of hair. "You are part of me, now and forever."

Raven crashed against his chest.

Chapter Seventeen

"It took me forever to finger-comb my hair." Cara swept from the bathroom into the living area. "You're lucky you showered first.

"Whoa." She stopped short, catching sight of William, who held her sister in his arms. He stood next to the couch; Raven cuddled against his chest with a blissful expression on her face.

Raven lifted her head and smiled. "This is William. William, this is my sister, Cara."

Cara took a step closer. "He doesn't look like a vampyre."

A deep growl sounded from William's chest.

Cara took a very large step back. "Do vampyres growl?"

"That's enough." Raven extricated herself from William's arms and sat on the couch.

His eyes fixed on Cara. "If we are to reach Rome before sunrise, we must leave now."

"Rome?" Raven caught his hand. "Why Rome? We need to go back to Florence. Cara's fiancé was hurt."

A muscle jumped in William's jaw. He switched to Italian and dropped his voice. "I'm sorry, *Cassita*."

"Sorry?" Raven repeated, also in Italian.

"What is it? What's he saying?" Cara approached the couch.

William pursed his lips. "His injuries were severe."

Raven's hand went slack. "How severe?"

"I'm sorry," he whispered.

Raven's eyes widened. As the realization slowly sunk in, her gaze shifted to her sister.

Raven blinked back tears.

Cara crossed her arms. "Seriously. You're both being rude."

"Cara, please," Raven stammered. "Give us a minute."

William squeezed Raven's hand. "I shall tell her gently, I promise."

"No." Raven swallowed hard. "I need to do it. Just—just give me time to figure out how."

William winced. "I failed to protect you both. I am sorry."

"But we don't have much time. The Curia will have heard about the attempted coup. I need to prevent them from marching on my city."

"How?"

"By asking for the support of the one person the Curia won't wage war against."

"Who's that?" Raven asked.

"The Roman."

Raven passed a hand over her eyes. "What about Cara?"

"The sooner she returns to America, the better." William turned to Cara and switched to English. "We are going to Rome."

Cara rushed forward. "I need to go back to Florence to find my fiancé. I don't have time to go to Rome."

"We are leaving now." William's tone brooked no argument.

Cara gave her sister a challenging look.

"We can't travel back to Florence by ourselves; William needs to go to Rome." Raven stood unsteadily.

The Prince wrapped his arm around Raven's waist, since she was without her cane, and helped her to the door. Cara followed them into the hall.

As they moved down one of the darkened passages, he spoke to Raven again in Italian. "I don't think the boy suffered."

Raven peered back at her sister, who eyed the two of them curiously. Her heart sank.

"He was good to her. She loved him."

William gazed down at her in distress. "You mourn him."

"I do. He was her world. She'll be devastated."

"What are you saying to each other? What's going on?" Cara crowded them.

William ignored her, still speaking Italian to Raven. "If your priest is as good as you say, he could help your sister return to America."

Raven tripped over her feet, stumbling in the darkness.

William lifted her into his arms.

"I can walk," she protested in English.

"We are in haste, and you're without your cane." William increased his pace down the dark corridor.

"She's not an invalid." Cara trotted after them. "And I'm still waiting for someone to explain what's going on."

"Just a minute, Cara." Raven turned to William, addressing him in Italian. "You want to hand my sister over to the Curia?"

William stopped, his expression dark. "I was hoping we could make arrangements to take her to your priest. If what you believe about him is correct, he will protect her. While she's with the Curia, she won't be prey to vampyres."

Raven searched his eyes. "But you told me they erase memories."

William continued walking. "They erase memories having to do with vampyres."

"But what about—"

"Your priest wants both of you. I'm more than willing to deliver your sister, but he won't be satisfied with that. I need to ask the Roman to support my decision to keep you."

Raven drew a shaky breath. "What if the Roman refuses?"

"Then it will be up to you."

"I won't leave you."

William's expression was grim. "If we lose the Roman's support, nothing will prevent the Curia from marching on Florence."

Raven grabbed his shoulder. "Then we run away. We go somewhere they can't find us."

"You are a lark that deserves to be free. Not a fugitive."

Raven placed her hands on his cheeks, forcing him to look at her. "I want to stay with you. No matter what."

He searched her eyes. "I cannot abandon my city. I've seen the devastation of Prague. I can't allow that to happen to Florence."

"No one wants a war. There has to be a way to avoid it."

"I wish I could believe that." William captured her lips with his.

"Okay, if you guys would stop kissing, we could get this show on the road." Cara sounded impatient. "And speak English."

"William is doing his best to protect us. I need to talk to you." Raven paused, struggling with the weight of the news about Dan.

At that moment, an Umbrian soldier materialized through one of the doorways.

William snarled, and the soldier made a hasty retreat.

Cara scowled at her sister. "Your boyfriend is an animal."

Raven sighed. "You have no idea."

Chapter Eighteen

"Cara." Raven took her sister's hand. "There's something—"

"You really think they're vampyres?" Cara interrupted, scanning the supernatural figures that stood several feet away.

The detachment had taken a short rest just outside of Rome, so the sisters could speak privately. Earlier, William had dispatched one of the soldiers for Florence, ordering him to notify Gregor that the Umbrian army stood on the border. The soldier was also instructed to conceal William's whereabouts.

"Yes, I do." Raven sandwiched her sister's hand between both of hers. "Cara, I—"

"They look human. Obviously when they picked us up and started running, I realized they weren't. They can't all be Olympic sprinters." Cara looked at her sister curiously. "How exactly does one become a vampyre?"

Raven's gaze flickered to William, who was engaged in an intense conversation with the others.

"He explained it to me once. Dark magic is involved, but it's like transubstantiation."

"Good grief. As if anyone can understand that." Cara flopped on her back underneath a tree. "You say your boyfriend is the one who kidnapped David?"

"Yes, I explained that already. Cara, you need to listen to me. I—"

"Why would he care about David?"

Raven moved closer, lowering her voice so the soldiers wouldn't hear. "He loves me. I told him what happened to my leg, and he was angry. He said he'd give me justice."

Cara's eyebrows shot up. "Is he a vigilante or something?"

"Something like that." Raven rubbed her forehead distractedly. "Didn't you hear about what happened to David? Mom said it made the news in Miami."

"You talked to Mom?"

"I was worried about you. You weren't answering the landline at your house, so I called Mom. She said David's arrest in California made the news."

"I don't remember." Cara closed her eyes for a few seconds. "It must be lack of sleep. And I have a splitting headache."

Raven touched her sister's face, smoothing the hair back from her forehead. She knew Cara's loss of memory was related to ingesting Aoibhe's blood. But she didn't have the heart to tell her.

She changed the subject. "I wanted you to make the decision about what to do with David. After we fought, I told William to send David back to California. He was arrested and led the police to a pedophile ring."

"*Back* to California?" Cara rolled to her side. "So David was here? In Italy?"

"Yes."

"That must have scared the crap out of him." Cara paused, running her hand along the grass. "If I'd asked for a different outcome, what would you have done?"

"I would have given it to you."

"Anything?"

"Anything," Raven spoke without hesitation.

"Why?"

"Because I love you. Because you're my sister."

The words hung in the air between them.

At length, Cara broke the silence. "I wonder if I would have behaved the same way if I were the older sister."

"Of course."

"Not *of course*." Cara flipped her long, blond hair behind her shoulder. "Most people only worry about themselves. You've always worried about everyone else."

Raven avoided her eyes.

Cara continued. "I've always known that if I was in trouble, you'd help me. Apart from Dan, you're the only person I trust."

"Thank you." Raven's voice cracked, her eyes filling with tears.

"Don't cry, sweetie." Cara smiled and touched her sister's face. "I'm sorry I flipped out on you. Dan is sorry, too. That's why we came to see you. I don't understand why your vampyre boyfriend won't let us go back to Florence to help Dan."

"That's what I've been trying to tell you. William had news."

Cara sat up. "Of Dan? Is he okay?"

"He was badly injured."

"I know that." Cara dusted grass off her clothes. "That's why I need to get to him."

"Cara, Dan's injuries were really severe. When the ambulance arrived, they tried to revive him and—"

Cara interrupted. "Said who?"

"William. That's what he was telling me in Italian, back in Perugia. I'm so sorry." Raven shook her head.

"No." Cara stood, placing her hands on her hips. "It must be a mistake."

"I wish it were." A tear fell on Raven's cheek.

Before Raven could rise from the ground, William was at her side. "*Cassita?*"

"You don't know him." Cara whirled on William. "You don't know what he looks like. You could be mistaken."

William offered Raven his hand and helped her to her feet. "I never met him, but my sources are reliable. His body was found in Raven's apartment building."

"I don't believe that. I would have felt something. I would have known." Cara looked around wildly. "We have to go back. No one knows him there. He's probably in the hospital, unconscious."

"Cara, listen to me." Raven tried to put her arms around her sister, but she pushed her away.

"We have to go back." Cara grabbed William's arm. "We have to go now!"

Raven inhaled loudly at the sight of her sister grabbing the Prince of Florence.

William merely inclined his head to look at Cara's hand, wrapped around his bicep. His expression was illegible.

"Cara, let go," Raven whispered.

"She's grieving." William spoke Italian, and his eyes sought Raven's. "Am I going to have to use mind control?"

"She's been through enough," Raven replied, also in Italian.

"If she becomes hysterical, I shall have no choice."

Cara pulled on William's arm. "I want to go back to Florence. I want to see my fiancé. *Please.*"

William regarded her for a long moment. His expression softened. "You are correct; I didn't see the body. And of course, you weren't there to identify him."

"See?" Cara released William's arm and gave her sister a hopeful look. "It's mistaken identity."

"I can take you to your priest in Rome," William offered. "He can contact the Florence police and make enquiries. It's too far to travel to Florence tonight. Others of my kind might attack us, and there are hunters who would like nothing more than to kill us—all of us, including you and your sister."

Cara's eyebrows crinkled. "Is Italy really that dangerous?"

The Prince ignored her question. "Our best course of action for you and your fiancé is to depart for Rome immediately."

"William," Raven's voice was a plea.

"Let her have her denial," he responded in Italian. "The truth will confront her soon enough."

Cara dusted off her jeans again. "The sooner we get to Rome, the sooner we can see Father Kavanaugh and head back to Florence. Let's go."

Raven turned her back on her sister, furiously wiping away another tear.

"*Cassita.*" William placed his lips to her cheek. "Trust me to treat your sister with care."

She nodded, stifling a sniffle.

William lifted his voice to address the detachment. "We depart for Rome. From now until we return to Florence, assume all your words will be heard by our enemies. Say nothing that will compromise our purpose." His eyes fixed on the women as he switched to English. "That includes you, as well. Say nothing of your priest. Say nothing of your fiancé."

He lifted a distressed Raven into his arms and led the detachment toward Rome.

Chapter Nineteen

"We have arrived." The Prince halted the detachment just outside the city.

"*Cassita*," he said gently.

Raven jolted awake, and he placed her on her feet.

Borek deposited Cara next to her, and the two women leaned on one another, blinking away sleep.

Cara squinted at the lights of the city, visible in the distance. "We aren't at the Vatican."

Raven shushed her. "We need to make a stop first."

"A stop?" Cara looked around. "Why?"

"*Silence*." William's tone was a commanding whisper.

"Would you like me to act as courier, my Lord?" Borek bowed.

The Prince turned his face downwind. "They know we're here. They've been tracking us the past seven miles."

"Why aren't we at the Vatican?" Cara approached William with two quick steps. "I thought we were going to see Father Kavanaugh."

The Prince wrapped his hand around her neck, forcing her to look at him. "Silence. You will stay silent until I give you permission to speak. I am your master now."

Cara's eyes glazed over, and she closed her mouth.

"No!" Raven cried, limping toward her sister.

As if on cue, an armed company of soldiers materialized from the direction the Prince faced. They encircled the Florentines completely.

The Prince released Cara and placed her and Raven behind him.

Raven tucked her sister into her side and murmured comfortingly in her ear. But before she could demand that William release the mind control, the leader of the company of soldiers stepped forward, sword drawn.

"This is the border of the principality of Rome. You're trespassing."

The Prince arched an eyebrow.

Raven noticed a slight shift in the leader's expression when William didn't respond.

The leader examined him with narrowed eyes.

"Since we are standing outside the border of the principality, we are not trespassing." The Prince's gaze moved to some invisible line that lay to his right.

"State your business," the leader snapped, brandishing his weapon.

The Prince rumbled, deep in his chest. "I am the Prince of Florence."

The leader's frown deepened.

The Prince lifted his arm to display the signet ring he wore on his right hand.

"Beg pardon, your highness." The leader inclined his head slightly. "We had no notice of your arrival."

"Unfortunately, it appears my couriers were killed before they arrived. Hunters.

"I am accompanied by my personal guard, along with two pets. I'm here to speak with Lieutenant Cato on urgent business." The Prince gestured toward the leader. "And you are?"

"Captain Gaius." His gaze moved from Florentine to Florentine, as if measuring their threat. "It's almost sunrise. Lieutenant Cato will not be receiving guests at this hour."

"Then we shall wait until a more reasonable hour, inside the palace."

Gaius scanned the detachment once again. "I can't escort you to the palace without approval of the lieutenant."

The Prince appeared irritated. "Then I shall escort myself. If you're old enough to be captain of a company, Gaius, you're old enough to know of my loyalty. I sent an emissary to speak with the lieutenant only recently. Now I have decided to speak with him myself."

"I meant no disrespect, your highness, but I must obey orders."

"The location of the Roman palace isn't a secret to me. Escort us to the Forum and allow us to wait while you secure approval. But be advised I will not be caught out of doors after sunrise." The Prince's tone held a warning.

Gaius hesitated.

He turned and barked an order to one of his soldiers, who took off at high speed.

Gaius replaced his sword in its scabbard. "We shall escort you to the Forum, your highness, while my courier sends word to the lieutenant. But your detachment must disarm."

"No."

The leader stared into the Prince's eyes, and his own eyes grew unfocused.

He broke eye contact abruptly and turned on his heel. "This way."

"Jedi mind tricks," Raven muttered as the Roman soldiers began to march toward the city.

"Look sharp," the Prince whispered to his soldiers as they followed the Romans. "Keep hold of your weapons, but be discreet."

Raven contemplated arguing with William about what he'd just done to Cara, but elected to wait. They were in a precarious position, one she would not worsen by drawing attention to herself.

William gestured to Borek to carry her, while one of the other soldiers carried her sister.

When the Czech lifted her over his shoulder and strode after the Prince's departing back, Raven couldn't help but feel punished.

Cara hadn't uttered a sound since the Prince had silenced her.

The Roman guard led them on a circuitous route through the city. Finally, they arrived at the Forum, stopping under the arch of Septimius Severus.

Gaius addressed the Prince. "We will await word from the lieutenant here. If the lieutenant tarries, there's a hiding place nearby."

The Prince stared over the captain's shoulder at the Palatine Hill. He nodded imperially.

Sunrise was fast approaching, and the landscape was changing. No one would risk being destroyed by the sun's rays.

Mercifully, the captain's courier returned quickly.

He whispered a few words in the captain's ear and stood back.

The captain bowed. "Lieutenant Cato welcomes the Prince of Florence and offers greetings and hospitality. We shall escort you into the palace. But the pets must be blindfolded."

The captain gestured to the courier, who held out two lengths of red silk.

The Prince nodded at Borek, who retrieved the silk and quickly blindfolded Cara and Raven.

Raven shifted her blindfold discreetly, hoping to catch a glimpse of their destination.

"Careful," Borek growled in her ear. "You'll get yourself killed."

She dropped her hand. Still, if she positioned her head at a particular angle and looked straight down, she could see what lay beneath her.

"Forward, march!" The captain led the party down the Via Sacra and through the Roman Forum.

The vampyres, as always, moved at an inhuman pace, even over uneven ground. The ride on Borek's shoulder was incredibly bumpy. Raven clutched at his shirt, terrified he would drop her.

Shortly, they halted at the base of the Palatine Hill.

The captain led them into a dark passage that had been carved into the hill itself. The scent of damp earth filled Raven's nostrils.

A loud scraping noise, like the sound of iron against iron, echoed and reverberated. Raven heard the groan of what sounded like metal hinges and the low whistle of something moving through air.

The detachment moved forward, marching and turning through a labyrinth of passageways only dimly lit with torches.

Raven held her breath as the palpable feeling of danger pressed in from all sides.

Chapter Twenty

Raven had felt fear before. She'd been afraid of her stepfather when she was young, she'd been afraid of the dark when she lived in foster care, and she'd been afraid when she first entered the Prince's world. She disliked being in the underground of Florence. She disliked being blindfolded.

But in the underworld of Rome, something even more sinister hung in the air. Icy tentacles of fear crept over her skin, despite being suspended on Borek's shoulder, surrounded by the rest of the detachment.

Music reverberated, as if from a distant dance club, the bass line shaking Raven's body. She found herself clinging to Borek's shirt amid the punishing, relentless rhythm.

The music grew fainter as they marched. Screams and harsh laughter exploded from places unknown, along with orgiastic cries. Sobbing and moaning could be heard — now near, now far — throwing Raven's senses into confusion.

If there were a hell, it would sound like this, she thought.

She pressed an ear against Borek's body and covered the other with her hand, trying to block out the cacophony.

"Calm yourself," he hissed. "Everyone can smell your fear."

"Where's my sister?" She tried to catch a glimpse of the soldier who held Cara.

Borek's large hand flexed over the back of her legs, a move calculated to silence her.

"She's in front of me," he whispered.

Raven stopped struggling, but her heart beat a furious pace. What if they were separated from the group? What if one of the Romans decided to take Cara?

She couldn't breathe. Panic ensued as she gasped for air.

Something cool touched her hand.

Raven jerked her hand away, but the coolness followed; a hand gently covered hers. A thumb stroked her palm.

William.

She couldn't see him, but she could feel him. A measure of calm washed over her. William would stand between her and the darkness. Always.

She moved her hand, questing for his fingers. She wished she could speak to him. She wished she could beg him to get her out of this terrible place. But he was on a mission, and the protection of the Roman must be worth the risk of descending into what seemed like perdition.

William traced a pattern on her palm and withdrew. Raven focused on the memory of his fingers and drew a very deep breath, willing her heartbeat to slow.

The detachment of Florentines ascended a staircase that seemed to spiral in a never-ending circle. The music dulled to a low thud, as if it were far below them.

Eventually, they halted.

Raven moved her head and was able to discern that they were gathered in a narrow passage, lit by torches.

Captain Gaius announced that they were to wait inside the rooms provided until Lieutenant Cato sent for the Prince. The captain gave no indication of how long that might be.

The Prince had a short exchange with the captain, which was studiously formal. Raven knew from William's tone that he was angry at being delayed. But he eventually acquiesced to the captain's instructions.

The Florentines were ushered through a door, and the Roman escort withdrew. She heard the sound of a door closing.

William undid Raven's blindfold, pointing her and her sister toward a lavishly decorated sitting room. He remained with the soldiers, who cloistered themselves in the adjoining space.

"You are confined to these quarters until I order otherwise. Commander Borek, I leave you in charge. I will see to it that bottles of blood are delivered to you for feeding."

The Prince crossed over to the sitting room and closed the door between the two spaces, closeting himself with the women.

"Release her." Raven's arm was around her sister's shoulder, while Cara stared unseeingly into space.

"No."

"William." Raven's voice edged past reproachful into angry.

"Remember how you felt walking through the palace halls?" William's gray eyes were knowing. "You were right to be afraid. Even though the Roman is my ally, like all vampyres, he is capricious and not to be trusted. We are surrounded by potential enemies. The smallest unguarded word from your sister's lips could mean the death of all of us."

Raven's green eyes grew round. "But—but the Roman would never kill you."

"Even I have executed allies."

Before Raven could respond, he gestured to the twin couches that stood in the center of the room.

"Rest. I shall arrange for food and drink to be sent down. But don't leave this room." He paused, his eyes moving over her face. "We may be here for some time."

Chapter Twenty-One

The Prince was on a mission.

Even now, the Curia could be storming his city. Ibarra and Aoibhe were likely colluding against him. Indeed, they could have usurped his throne in the hours he'd been absent.

He did not have time to wait until the lieutenant tired of his current pursuits and decided to grant him an audience.

The Prince arranged for his soldiers to be fed and for human food to be delivered to Raven and her sister. He insisted he be allowed to wait outside Lieutenant Cato's audience room until the lieutenant agreed to see him.

Captain Gaius had ordered the Prince to return to his quarters, but William simply used a mild form of mind control on the captain, and he'd relented.

The Prince was surprised that a captain in the Roman guard would be so susceptible to an old one's influence. He made sure to keep his mind control subtle, so as not to attract attention.

Now he waited on Cato, his body and mind restless.

He'd forgotten what life was like in the Roman's palace, but was reminded by the citizens who used the antechamber as their pleasure den. Vampyres drifted in and out of the room, fornicating and feeding on human beings and each other.

William's sensitive ears pounded with music that emanated from the large central hall on the ground floor of the palace.

From time to time, a citizen's eyes would stray to William's, and he or she would beckon him. William merely shook his head, too disgusted to exchange words.

Eventually, Gaius drove the revelers away, ordering them to pursue their orgy elsewhere.

The Prince closed his eyes in relief.

Much ink had been spilled on the decadence of ancient Rome. But the decadence of vampyric Rome was surely a rival. How he longed for the order and dignity of Florence. How he longed to retreat to his villa and hold Raven in his arms, blotting out the stark depravity of his brethren.

These thoughts plagued him as the lieutenant kept him waiting, minute after minute and hour after hour.

The slight was intentional. However, the Prince was shrewd enough to hide his ire. When he was finally escorted into the audience room, just before sunset, he forced himself to greet the lieutenant with deferential respect.

Cato was an Italian and at least two centuries away from becoming an old one. Nevertheless, he dressed as the Roman himself, in the purple imperial toga of ancient Rome.

The Prince was surprised. Only the Roman himself wore purple, while his lieutenant was usually restricted to wearing white.

William's eyes narrowed as he took Cato's measure.

"Welcome, your highness." The lieutenant inclined his head from his position on the throne. "I apologize for the delay. If we had had advance notice of your arrival, I would have arranged a more suitable welcome."

"Thank you, lieutenant." The Prince bowed his head perfunctorily. "Rome's hospitality is always suitable. Florence is at grave risk, which is why I arrived unannounced."

"I heard of the attempted coup." The lieutenant gazed at the Prince appraisingly. "You appear to have survived it."

The Prince stood tall. "I've come to see the Roman."

"I'm afraid the king is not receiving visitors."

The Prince frowned. "It is a matter of some importance."

The lieutenant offered him an indulgent smile. "The Roman has delegated affairs of state to me. I perceive that you know this since

SYLVAIN REYNARD

I was visited by your own lieutenant some time ago. Perhaps if you were to communicate your concerns to me, I may be of assistance."

"There is an issue with the Curia."

The lieutenant's gaze sharpened. "What issue?"

"An issue so great I have come to solicit the Roman's guidance."

"As I said, the Roman has delegated affairs of state to me. If you need guidance, I shall offer it. In consultation with the king, of course."

The Prince paused, struggling to keep his temper. "Your wisdom is not in question, lieutenant. But the Roman and I know one another personally. I come not only as a subject but as a friend."

Cato fingered the gold-embroidered edge of his toga. "The Roman has no friends."

"It appears you don't know me, Cato, but I know you. I know you came from Pisa in the sixteenth century. I know you have been a loyal subject to the Roman, and in return, you were elevated to lieutenant.

"But you are not an old one. Thus, you can be excused for not knowing that my friendship with the Roman began centuries before you were born."

The lieutenant gave the Prince a long look, his eyes beady, his face pinched.

The Prince gestured to the door. "Perhaps if you were to consult one of the old ones of Rome, he or she could corroborate my connection?"

The lieutenant smothered a smile. "Come, let me offer refreshment." He beckoned the Prince to sit in a nearby chair and began pouring blood into two ornate silver chalices that rested on a side table.

The vampyres saluted one another and drank.

"I know more about you than you might think, Florentine." Cato's expression grew accusatory. "You claim to be a friend of the Roman, but you haven't visited the city within my memory."

The Prince held the chalice loosely. "That is true, but our connection is of a unique nature."

Cato leaned forward, his voice taking on a salacious tone. "I did not realize your acquaintance with the Roman was intimate."

William pressed his lips together. He had mere seconds to decide if he was going to correct Cato's characterization. But on reflection, he realized it might offer an advantage. "It could be described thusly."

"Interesting," the lieutenant murmured, sitting back on his throne. He seemed to peer over at the Prince with new eyes.

"I repeat, perhaps one of Rome's old ones might corroborate my connection?"

"I am the oldest, next to our king." The lieutenant preened.

The Prince hid his surprise. There should have been at least three old ones still in residence in the principality of Rome, in addition to the king. He had not heard news of their departure or of any foul play having befallen them.

Something very strange was going on.

He schooled his features carefully. "It's clear the Kingdom of Italy is in capable hands. But my issue with the Curia is urgent. I must seek the Roman's counsel."

"Since you are an old one, you know that the Roman has had no dealings with the Curia since the treaty was signed. They pursue their goals, and we pursue ours."

"As it should be. But Florence is being threatened. It would be folly for me to enter into a new treaty without the Roman's counsel."

Cato lifted his head. "Florence entering into its own treaty with the Curia? That would be unwise."

The Prince replaced the chalice on the table. "Which is why I need the Roman's counsel."

"Rest assured, I will convey your concerns to the Roman personally. Now if you'll excuse me." The lieutenant continued drinking from his chalice.

The Prince stood. "The matter with the Curia is of some urgency. I must speak with the Roman today."

"And as I said," the lieutenant dropped his voice, "I will convey your concerns. That is all."

The Prince's arms moved to his sides, and his hands curled into fists.

He was more powerful than the lieutenant and could kill him easily, but only at great peril to his mission and to the women who rested obliviously in the guest chambers.

The Prince closed his eyes, his nostrils flaring like a dragon's.

He opened his eyes. "You are wasting precious time."

"I believe I should be the one making that claim, since I have offered my assistance repeatedly, only to be rebuffed."

"Given my most recent correspondence with the king, I believe he would welcome my presence."

"Correspondence?" The lieutenant laughed. "The Roman has engaged in no recent correspondence."

Now the Prince smiled. He did so slowly and with a dangerous, knowing glint in his eye. A glint the lieutenant could not overlook.

"Perhaps you did not see the king's addendum to the message I received from you recently. Do you remember that message, Lieutenant Cato?"

The Prince waited for an acknowledgement, toying with his enemy before lowering the noose.

"What of it?" The lieutenant eyed him grumpily.

"The message was hand delivered by Lorenzo, my lieutenant, after conflict ensued between Florence and Venice." The Prince retrieved a folded piece of paper from his pocket.

He held it out, the way a child dangles a bone in front of a dog.

Cato placed the chalice on the table. "The king doesn't engage in correspondence. That letter is a forgery."

"Ah, but it isn't a letter from the king. The letter is from you, in your own hand. You can scarcely deny it." The Prince prodded. "It's the addendum at the bottom you should be concerned about."

Cato lifted from his throne and snatched the paper from the Prince's hand. He unfolded it quickly. As his gaze alighted on the short message at the bottom of the page, his eyes widened.

He returned the letter to the Prince with a scowl. "I was not aware the Roman had seen that letter."

The Prince folded the paper carefully and placed it back in his pocket.

Cato began drumming his fingers against the armrest of his throne. "I did not know you were his son."

"I am the Roman's son, and as you have read, I am beloved of my father. I want to see him."

The lieutenant's hands went to his knees. His knuckles whitened. "I cannot promise an audience. The decision rests with the king."

"Just send word to the king that his son is here. I shall return to the rooms you've generously provided and await his response."

Cato scowled, adjusting his purple toga once again. "It's possible the king will refuse your request."

"No, he won't," the Prince's voice rumbled. "And Cato, if he is truly wise, will see that I have my audience."

"And if for some reason the king refuses?"

The Prince angled his head, his eyes threatening. "The king won't refuse me. I know this. You, Lieutenant Cato, are a different matter. But you must know now that it would be folly to oppose me.

"Someone intercepted your missive and delivered it to the Roman before handing it to my lieutenant. You were unaware of this fact until you read his words. Perhaps the Roman doesn't have as much confidence in you as you believe."

Cato sputtered something in protest.

The Prince interrupted him. "I have no quarrel with you, at least not yet. My concern is for Florence. Once my audience is concluded, I shall return to my city, and you shall have to deal with a palace full of the Roman's spies. But if I don't have my audience today, you and I will be having a very different conversation."

The Prince gave the lieutenant a hard look before withdrawing, leaving Cato seated uneasily on his purloined throne.

Chapter Twenty-Two

Perhaps it was Cato. Perhaps it was the Roman. The Prince was kept waiting by someone until after sunset. Only then did Gaius appear, announcing that the king, in his infinite beneficence, had granted the Prince a private audience.

The Prince followed the captain to the throne room occupied by the lieutenant, who had changed out of his imperial robes into a white toga. Cato joined Gaius and the Prince as they ventured through a series of passages until they came to an immense metal door, which was flanked by two sets of Praetorian guards, wielding spears.

"The Prince of Florence to see his excellency." Cato nodded in William's direction.

One of the guards opened the door while another escorted Cato, Gaius, and the Prince inside.

The Roman's throne room was smaller than the room occupied by Cato, but far more elaborate. The floor was covered with mosaic tile, and the walls and ceiling decorated with elaborate frescoes. The frescoes appeared to depict ancient Rome, populated as they were by men in togas and classical architecture. But on closer inspection, each scene included the same handsome, dark-haired figure, dressed in imperial purple.

Many of the images praised his exploits and his taste for young, beautiful men. William's own transformation was featured in one of the panels to the right of the door, complete with his likeness dressed in the robes of a Dominican.

The Prince glanced at it and looked elsewhere.

"The Prince of Florence, your excellency." Cato addressed the Roman in Latin, bowing deeply.

The room itself was completely dark, with the exception of two pillars of flame that flanked a short gold staircase ascending to an ornate throne.

The figure who sat on the throne was robed in purple, his head wreathed with gold laurel leaves. His eyes were closed, and he sat perfectly still, like a statue.

"You are dismissed." The Roman's voice was low, his accent ancient.

Cato bowed. "If I may, your excellency, I think that—"

"Now." The Roman's voice deepened, but still, he did not open his eyes.

Cato scurried to the door, still facing the throne, and exited with Gaius.

The Roman pointed a pale finger at the Praetorians, who lifted their spears in salute and departed through the door, closing it behind them.

William went down on one knee before the throne. It was only then that the Roman opened his eyes.

In appearance, he was handsome, with dark hair clipped close to his head and dark, fiery eyes. His nose was long and prominent, his cheekbones high, his jaw square. If one hadn't known he was a vampyre, one might have marked his age at about thirty.

"My son." The Roman adjusted his toga in order to bare his right arm.

William climbed the steps to the throne. The two vampyres clasped arms.

The Roman lifted William's chin and kissed him.

"Father," William whispered.

The Roman released his arm. "I was not expecting you."

"I apologize." William descended the steps to stand between the pillars of flame. "I should have sent word of my visit."

"Notice is not required. Not by you." The Roman gazed at him shrewdly. "But I perceive this is not a familial visit."

"I'm afraid not. My visit concerns the Curia." William withdrew a copy of the letter Father Kavanaugh had written to him. He held it out.

The Roman waved it aside. "Tell me."

"For some time the Curia have been watching Florence. Now they are threatening me and have ordered me to surrender my pet."

The Roman's eyebrows lifted. "The Curia concerned about a pet? What madness is this?"

"The pet in question is a daughter of sorts to one of the priests."

The Roman chuckled. "Ah, yes. The Church extols the virtue of chastity, but behind their walls there is no such practice. So you've taken the daughter of a priest. This is not without precedent."

William averted his eyes and folded the letter carefully, placing it inside his pocket.

"It is always a pleasure to be in your company, Father. I have stayed away too long. But you are correct. There is more."

"Proceed."

William cleared this throat. "The pet is a pretext. I believe the Curia desires to weaken your authority, and to do so, they have targeted Florence."

The Roman lifted his arms. "The Curia has desired to weaken my authority for centuries. Yet, here I sit. The solution to your problem is clear: remove the pretext and entrench your position."

William lowered his gaze. "Yes, Father. But if the Curia is successful in this matter, what is to prevent them from additional demands? Or an unprovoked attack?"

The Roman regarded the gold signet ring of Rome, which he wore on his right hand. "I grew tired of petty squabbles years ago. That is why my lieutenant oversees such matters."

"I apologize, Father." William tried very hard not to give expression to his agitation. "But I believe the Curia's tactic is to make an example of Florence, in order to bring the other Italian principalities to heel. If they can transform Florence into Prague, without your intervention, what's to prevent them from decimating the other principalities?"

"Our enemy has yet to move against an Italian city since we signed the treaty."

William made eye contact with his maker. "Let not Florence be the first."

"What is your recommendation?"

"I am approaching my last centuries. Father, I ask that you allow me to serve out my final years as Prince of Florence and that you defend us against the Curia."

The Roman's eyes searched William's.

"Are you asking as the Prince of Florence? Or as my son?"

William's fingers curled into fists. "Your son, if necessary."

The Roman frowned. "I have not seen you for some time. Now you appear, begging favors."

"Pardon, your excellency. I mean no disrespect." William appeared contrite. "Florence is a jewel and one that many of my neighbors covet. I have traveled little during my time as prince."

The Roman blinked. "You are a favorite of mine; it is true. As you say, Florence is a jewel. Are you certain your time is short?"

"You made me in 1274. My thousand years approaches."

The Roman hummed. "Centuries come, centuries go. When one has forever, the marking of time seems immaterial. Since I have escaped the curse and you are my offspring, perhaps you will escape the curse also?"

William shook his head sadly. "You are the great exception, Father."

The Roman hummed again, his brow furrowed.

At length, his expression brightened. "I had forgotten how much I enjoy your company."

"As I enjoy yours." William bowed.

"What were we discussing?"

William's brow furrowed. "We were discussing the Curia."

"What about the Curia?"

"The Curia is looking for an occasion to attack Florence, Father. They are demanding my pet."

"A ridiculous demand." The Roman smiled. "Promise you will visit your father more than once every few centuries."

"I promise," the Prince vowed quickly.

"Good. I see no reason for you to acquiesce to the Curia's commands. You are a prince and under my authority. You may decline their request for your pet, but do so with prudence. There is no need to antagonize them unnecessarily." The Roman exposed his teeth. "I admit you've made me curious. Tell me, is your pet beautiful? I should like to see it."

In an unguarded instant, William's eyes grew wide. He dropped his gaze to the stones at his feet. "I serve you, Father. Of course I could bring my pet to you. But I doubt you would find her appealing."

"*Her?* Ah, yes. I forgot." The Roman examined William's bowed head. "I take it you have a fondness for this one."

"I've had her but a short while."

"I wonder." The Roman adjusted the signet ring on his hand. "I have given you long life, power, wealth, and the jewel that is Florence. And I have never asked anything in return, except for loyalty. You are loyal to me, are you not?"

William lifted his gaze. "Without question."

"And you serve me in all things?"

"All things, your excellency."

The Roman leaned forward in his throne. "Then give me your pet."

The Latin words echoed in the throne room.

The room fell silent.

Despite his best efforts, William's heart beat irregularly.

"In comparison to everything I have given you, the request for your pet is very small." The Roman's nostrils flared, but his body remained still.

"Yes, Father." William hid his face by bowing.

"Excellent." The Roman leaned back in his chair. "Cato tells me your pet is here, in the palace, along with its sister. I want them both."

William's mind raced as he calculated how he could smuggle Raven out of the palace before the Roman realized the deception. It would be too risky to try to escape with both women. He'd have to leave Cara behind.

His innards twisted.

William genuflected and backed toward the door, hoping the Roman couldn't scent his anxiety.

He opened the door, and the Praetorian guards snapped to attention on the other side.

"William," the Roman's voice echoed in the hall.

The Prince turned, ever so slowly.

"You may close the door." The king motioned to William to approach the throne once again.

Confused, he did as he was ordered, then stopped before the steps and knelt.

The Roman's gaze flickered to William's hands before moving to his eyes. "I perceive strength in your attachment to me, Prince of Florence. But I also perceive weakness. How much do you value your pet?"

"She is but a pleasant diversion, Father."

The Roman closed his eyes.

William's entire body tensed. He could almost feel his bones bending beneath the strain of his muscles.

"Kiss me, my son." The Roman opened his eyes.

William climbed the steps and kissed his maker.

The Roman stroked his head, running his fingers through the short, fair hair.

"Here is my beloved son," he whispered. "Who would never betray me."

He released William with a short caress, and the Prince withdrew down the steps.

"I shall speak to Cato about our conversation. You are free to deny the Curia's request and to return with your pet to Florence."

"Thank you, Father." William knelt on the ground, relief coursing over him.

"You may inform the Curia that you consulted me, and I agreed with your decision."

At this, William lifted his head.

The Roman was staring at the fresco of William's transformation. "I have seen much since the second century. Kingdoms rise and fall; the strength of our enemies grows and wanes. But they cannot destroy me, and this they know."

The Roman's gaze sharpened as it fixed on his son. "Perhaps you will escape the curse. Perhaps not. Only time will tell.

"I have granted you this favor. You have pledged unfailing service. In the years you have left, I demand absolute obedience."

"Yes, Father."

"Good. Send Cato to me."

William bowed and retreated to the door, watching as the Roman glanced at the fresco once again before closing his eyes.

Chapter Twenty-Three

W illiam was tremendously disquieted.

He had to resist the urge to run through the palace corridors, pull Raven into his arms, and flee. But the eyes of the Roman were upon him, he was certain, so he forced himself to follow Gaius at a moderate pace as the captain led him back to the room where Raven waited.

He'd accomplished his goal. He'd secured the support of the most powerful vampyre in Italy, if not the world. But undoubtedly, it had cost him. The Roman might be weary of public life, but he was no fool. He'd noticed William's attachment to his pet. The sooner he was able to remove Raven from the palace, the better.

"Prepare to depart." William barked to his soldiers, sparing them not a glance as he crossed to the adjoining room.

He opened the door and noted the two sisters curled up together on one of the couches, asleep.

He closed the door and stood over them, like a dark angel.

He barely remembered his own siblings, and he couldn't imagine resting with them. He'd loved his family, especially his sisters and his mother. But family life in the thirteenth century under the tyranny of his father had not been warm or comfortable.

The bond between Raven and Cara was not something he understood.

He placed a light hand on Raven's head. "*Cassita.*"

When she didn't stir, he stroked her hair gently. "*Cassita.*"

Raven came awake with a start. "What? What is it?"

She pulled away from her slumbering sibling and sat up. Cara didn't move.

"The Roman has taken our side." William caressed Raven's face. "We must contact your priest as soon as possible and make arrangements to deliver Cara to him."

"Will she be safe?" Raven eyed Cara with concern.

"Much as it pains me to say it, she is more vulnerable to vampyres than to the Curia. The Curia won't kill her." William's expression hardened. "Your priest will be angry that I refuse to give you up. He may try to take you by force. We must be prepared."

"I'm not worried about myself; I'm worried about her," Raven replied. "She will have to deal with losing Dan. I suppose forgetting about vampyres will be a mercy."

"The Curia are not known for their mercy," William sniped. "But she is a victim to them, which means they will protect her."

"We must go. The sooner they know we have the Roman's support, the better."

"I have my cell phone." Raven retrieved it from the pocket of her jeans. "I'll call Father. But I want you to remove the mind control from Cara first."

"No."

"*William.*"

He crossed his arms over his chest. "I shall remove the mind control when she joins your priest, but not a moment before. It's too dangerous."

Raven's gaze dropped to his arms, to the muscles that contracted as his body tensed.

"I thought the Roman agreed to help us."

"He did."

She frowned. "Then why are we still in danger?"

As if by instinct, William glanced around the room. But he and the women were alone.

"The Roman seems to have taken an interest in my pet. He asked to meet you and your sister."

Raven shifted backward on the couch. "I don't want to meet him."

"No, you do not." William passed a hand over his mouth in agitation.

"Will he keep us here?"

"At the moment, we are free to leave. But we should arrange to deliver Cara to your priest as soon as possible."

Raven stood. She placed her hand at the back of his neck, drawing his forehead down to meet hers.

"Thank you."

He didn't respond.

"I love you," she pressed.

"*Je t'aim.*" He wrapped his arms around her, pulling her against his body.

"Thank you for protecting us." She kissed the corners of his mouth before centering her lips on his. "I trust you."

"You are the only trust that exists in my world." He spoke against her mouth. "I trust no one else."

He kissed her deeply, angling his head. Just as quickly, he released her, kissing her forehead. "We need to contact your priest."

"Okay." She lifted her cell phone, took a deep breath, and dialed a number.

The priest answered on the third ring. "Raven?"

"Father? I'm in Rome with Cara. We need to see you."

The journey from the Palatine Hill to the Vatican was not a long one, only about five kilometers. Gaius and a few of his soldiers accompanied the Florentines up Via della Conciliazione toward the border between Italy and Vatican City. Beyond this point no vampyre dared go, as the entire city state was built on holy ground.

Within this walled enclave, the Curia trained, plotted, and conducted its business in secret, protected by the public face of the Vatican.

It was a few hours before sunrise, and the city of Rome remained shrouded in darkness. The great Basilica of St. Peter shone like a beacon, while the *piazza* in front of it was only dimly illuminated. Unfortunately for the vampyres that approached on foot, the accompanying shadows were not large enough to conceal them.

The Prince sniffed the air, his gaze drawn to the rooftops of the buildings that rose on either side of the street.

"Curia," he whispered, pointing with his chin at their unseen enemies.

In reaction, Gaius barked, "Lift high the standard."

The standard bearer raised the flag of the Roman, which featured a ring of laurel leaves on a black background. A she-wolf stood in the center of the ring.

Gaius addressed the Prince. "Our presence should guarantee your safety. But my orders are not to engage, unless attacked."

"So noted." The Prince extended his arm in friendship, and Gaius clasped it, hand to elbow.

The captain and his soldiers fell back, standing by one of the buildings while the Florentines marched toward Vatican City.

About one hundred meters from the border, the Prince commanded his soldiers to halt, arms at the ready. They were exposed in this position, but he was determined to show strength.

He turned to stare at the standard of the Roman flying nearby, knowing his every move was being watched.

Gaius saluted in return.

The Prince took Raven and Cara by the hand, one on each side, and began to walk toward the border.

"Whatever happens, don't cross the line," he whispered to Raven. "I cannot tread on holy ground."

Raven's eyebrows lifted, for she knew his last statement to be a lie. But she nodded.

He stopped short of the border, occupying a space where the light was dim. He released the women's hands and took Cara by the shoulders. Fixing his eyes on hers, he spoke. "Cara, I release you. Your mind is your own again."

The young woman blinked, her blue eyes suddenly focusing on his face. "What? What are you doing?"

"Cara." Raven pulled her away from William. "We're here to see Father Kavanaugh."

"Good." Cara rubbed her eyes and yawned. "I can't believe we got here so quickly. I must have fallen asleep."

The sound of boots striking cobblestones pounded in the distance.

A century of soldiers dressed in black uniforms entered the *piazza* from the left side of the basilica. The soldiers wore crucifixes around their necks and carried swords.

"Black robes," the Prince spat.

Cara snorted. "What's with the army? I thought the Church was pacifist."

"Perhaps you should ask your priest about that." The Prince's voice was cold.

"Whatever." Cara rolled her eyes.

The soldiers marched toward the border and spread themselves out, one hundred meters inside the line. A lone figure emerged, walking in the direction of the Florentines.

Cara tugged on her sister's hand. "There's Father. Let's go."

"Approach slowly," the Prince commanded.

Raven limped with Cara toward the border, while the Prince hovered behind them. A few feet from the line, Raven stopped. "I'm going back to Florence with William. You go ahead."

"What?" Cara's voice grew shrill. "You have to come with me. We have to find Dan!"

"Father will help you. I can't leave William." She pulled her sister into a hug and kissed her cheek. "I'll see you soon."

"You have to come with me," Cara wailed. "I need you."

Raven looked toward the priest, who stood fifty meters from the line. "Father will help you."

"You can't leave me." Cara grabbed Raven's arm and pulled her closer to the border.

William clung to Raven's side, his hand ghosting over her elbow.

Just before they crossed the line, Raven planted her feet. "This is as far as I go."

"Don't you care about Dan? Don't you care about me? I came all the way from Florida. You can't ditch me for your boyfriend." Cara stepped nimbly across the line formed by a band of white between the cobblestones. "Come on."

Father Kavanaugh strode to Cara's side and embraced her as six Curia soldiers closed ranks behind them.

Behind Raven and the Prince, the Florentines closed ranks as well.

Father moved to the border and extended his hand. "Come, Raven."

"No." Raven glared. "I explained on the phone what was going to happen. I need you to look after Cara, but I'm not coming."

Next to her, the Prince growled. "She is my pet. I will not surrender her. The Roman supports this decision."

Ever so carefully, the Prince turned his head to look at the Roman guard.

The priest followed his gaze.

At that moment, a fine mist appeared, lifting as if from beneath the city streets. The mist rolled down the road that led to Vatican City and began to approach the border.

"Is this your doing?" The priest addressed the Prince, pointing to the fog.

The Prince remained impassive.

"Raven." Father turned his attention back to her. "Come here, my child."

She grasped William's elbow, leaning on him as she took the weight off her injured leg. She switched to Italian. "Maximilian killed Dan. I saw it happen. Cara doesn't believe me, and when she realizes what's happened, she'll be devastated."

"Maximilian has been dealt with," the Prince interjected, also in Italian.

Father glanced at Cara, who stood at his side, watching. He spoke to Raven in Italian. "We have the body. He will be prepared for burial once the autopsy is complete. Come with me now before something else happens."

"No," Raven repeated.

The mist had grown thick, standing as tall as William and cutting the Florentines off from the Roman guard that stood nearby. But it also shielded them from the Curia snipers.

Surprisingly, the fog traveled as far as William and Raven's backs, but did not venture to the border of Vatican City.

The priest withdrew a glass vial from his pocket and held it aloft. He fixed his eyes on the Prince's even as the fog swirled behind him. "You have no power here. I command you to release her."

The Prince snarled and bared his teeth, but did not retreat.

"Raven? What's happening?" Cara took a few steps in her sister's direction.

Father Kavanaugh gestured to two of the black robes, and they marched forward. They took hold of Cara's arms and began to escort her toward the basilica.

"Let me go!" Cara's voice lifted into a panicked cry. "Raven, help me."

"What are you doing?" Raven's anguish was directed at the priest. "Stop them! Don't let them hurt her."

"Come now." Father leaned across the line.

William's arm snaked around Raven's waist, his mouth finding her ear. "It's a trap."

"Raven! Help!" Cara shouted.

William tightened his grasp and continued to whisper, "If you follow her, I shall follow you. And they'll kill me."

"Then do something," she pleaded.

The Prince's gray eyes swung to the white-haired man who stood in front of them. "We came to you in peace. We surrendered the human at your request. This is how the Curia treats their charges?"

"Give me Raven, and we will have peace." Father leaned farther across the line, his hand mere inches from hers. "And send your cursed fog away."

"It isn't mine," the Prince remarked grimly, looking the priest squarely in the eye.

Raven watched as the soldiers continued to drag her sister toward the basilica. She saw Cara struggle, her shouts and screams echoing across the *piazza*.

"I trusted you!" She pushed Father Kavanaugh's chest. "Let her go. Right now!"

The priest grabbed her arm and began to pull.

William had her by the waist. He planted his feet.

A tug of war ensued, with Raven's body forming the rope.

The priest began reciting words in Latin, waving the relic he held in his other hand.

Both Curia and Florentine soldiers approached, keeping a healthy distance but wielding their weapons. The fog continued to swirl around the Florentines.

"Let go," Raven whispered, her eyes moving to the priest's. "I'm not coming with you. If anything happens to Cara, you'll regret it."

Father Kavanaugh ignored her, his gaze focused on the Prince and the relic's obvious lack of effect.

It was at that moment, quite by chance, that the priest lowered his eyes and saw William's foot resting over the line.

Chapter Twenty-Four

In a move so quick it could not be detected by human eyes, the Prince drew his foot back into the surrounding fog.

He pried Raven's arm from the priest's grasp, his body a blur, and shuffled her behind him.

Father Kavanaugh froze.

"You asked for the lives of two humans." The Prince glanced behind the priest to see Cara being taken up the stairs that led to the massive doors of the basilica. "I delivered one of them to you, unharmed and unspoiled. The other belongs to me."

"Impossible," the priest whispered, fear causing his face to pale beneath his white beard.

"The Roman supports me, the Prince of Florence, and the assertion of my right to keep the pet of my choice. You have our answer." The Prince lifted Raven into his arms and disappeared into the fog, the Florentines following hard on his heels.

Father Kavanaugh seemed to shake himself out of his reverie. "Raven! Raven!"

The Prince and his soldiers flew in the direction of the Tiber, the fog accompanying them. Once they reached the river's edge, the fog lifted. They turned north and raced out of the city.

Chapter Twenty-Five

Father Jack Kavanaugh paced the hallway outside the Superior General's office in the Vatican, praying nervously.

As soon as he'd left the *piazza*, the head of the Curia had summoned him. He'd barely had time to issue instructions to the soldiers guarding Cara. She'd been transferred to the infirmary, where medical officers would examine her for signs of trauma.

Jack was fearful of what they'd find.

He should have been grateful that the General had afforded him a face-to-face meeting. The General kept a punishing schedule that was filled with intelligence briefings and assemblies from dawn until well into the evening. He rarely, if ever, met with anyone individually, other than those in the highest positions inside the Vatican. Jack was not one of them.

However, nothing like gratitude lifted from his heart, only whispered supplications. He was worried about Raven and already formulating a rescue plan. He simply needed the General's permission.

The door to the General's office swung inward.

"*Ave.*" The General's secretary, a high-ranking Curia member, called out in Latin.

"*Maria,*" Jack responded, accepting the invitation to enter.

The room was simple and unadorned, save for a large medieval crucifix hung on a side wall. Beneath it was a bench on which the General could kneel and pray, eyes lifted to the savior.

The secretary ushered Jack inside and toward an empty chair in front of the General's massive desk.

The General, dressed in black robes, was seated behind the desk, which was piled high with paperwork and files. He was a Spaniard, a priest in his sixties who had worked in intelligence for most of his career before being elevated to the position of Superior General three years before.

He peered at his secretary over the rims of his spectacles.

The secretary bowed and exited through a side door.

"Father Kavanaugh," the General addressed him, his Spanish accent thickening on the English words.

"Your eminence."

The General extended his hand, and Jack took it. "You came to us from America. I trust you are finding your way."

Jack shifted in his chair. "I am, thank you."

"Good." The General sat back. "Describe what happened in the *piazza*."

Jack switched to Italian, the language of the Vatican. "Two young women, who I have known since childhood, have fallen under the influence of the Prince of Florence.

"The younger woman traveled to Florence with her fiancé in order to persuade her sister to come to me here. The sister is the Prince's current pet. Tragically, the fiancé was murdered by one of the Prince's council members. For some reason, the Prince himself brought the women to Rome yesterday."

"Not *for some reason*," the General interjected.

"Pardon?" Jack's eyebrows shot up.

"The Prince brought the women in response to your letter." The General looked pointedly at a closed file in front of him.

Jack tapped his foot in agitation. "Yes."

"I know the Director of Intelligence has already spoken to you, my son. I must stress that your action has placed a number of our operations at risk."

Jack was stricken. "Forgive me. I didn't know."

The General's dark eyes met his. "You are forgiven, but forgiveness is not license."

"Yes, your eminence."

The General's expression grew less severe. "My intelligence officers report that the Prince visited the Roman and sought his counsel before appearing here. The Prince surrendered the younger sister to you but refused to turn over his pet, despite your insistence."

"That's true. He claimed to have the Roman's support."

"Do you believe him?" The General's tone was relaxed. Perhaps too relaxed.

"The Roman's standard bearer and a small group of soldiers stood in plain view, watching. Their presence seems to indicate an alliance."

"We are skeptical of the Prince's claim. There's been no direct communication from the Roman. The presence of soldiers and a standard indicate nothing. They could be Florentines masquerading as Romans."

Jack wiped his palms on his trousers, for he was beginning to sweat. "A strange fog appeared, but did not cross the border. The Prince declared it was not of his doing. Who else but the Roman could have done such a thing?"

"There are multiple forces of darkness." The General seemed unaffected by Jack's insinuation. "What of the woman surrendered to you?"

"She is being examined by the medical officers."

"Yes, I know. How did she appear?"

"She appeared healthy. She didn't know her fiancé was dead, which means she's probably been under mind control."

"Once she's healed of any injuries, her memories will be adjusted. You are to escort her and the body of her fiancé to America. The intelligence office is ensuring that an approved report is released to the media by the police."

"Yes, your eminence." Jack's hand went to his Roman collar, which seemed to be suffocating him. "What about the other sister?"

"She and the Prince have left Rome. We are tracking their movements."

"She's in danger." Jack rummaged in his pocket and closed on a glass vial. "I have in my possession a relic of St. Teresa of Avila. I carried it with me into the *piazza,* but it seemed to have no effect on the Prince." He paused, as if fumbling for words. "The Prince laid his hand on my arm in order to free his pet. He also set foot on holy ground."

The General scowled. "Impossible."

Jack withdrew the relic and placed it on the General's desk. "With respect, your eminence, I saw with my own eyes. The Prince's foot crossed the border."

The General sat back in his chair. "This ground is holy. Vampyres and other demons cannot pass."

"I know what I saw." Jack pointed to the relic. "He should not have been able to touch me; not with the blood of St. Teresa in his face."

The General's eyes focused on the relic. "Intelligence officers monitor the *piazza* constantly. No one saw the Prince set foot in Vatican City."

"The fog," Jack sputtered. "How could they have seen anything?"

"I viewed the video myself."

"Then you must believe what I say." Jack stood, placing his hands on top of the desk, next to the relic.

The General's gaze shifted to the crucifix and then back to the Jesuit. "Be seated, Father."

Jack replaced the relic in his pocket and returned to his chair.

The General removed his spectacles and rubbed his eyes. In that moment, he looked aged and worn and very, very tired. "In science, as in life, there are anomalies. Sometimes an anomaly is merely an illusion, a fault with the observer.

"Sometimes an anomaly recurs. It's the recurrence that challenges a scientist to re-examine his theory.

"The Roman appears to be an anomaly. He continues to outlive his thousand-year lifespan. And we have no idea why."

Jack stared in shock. "How is that possible?"

The General pursed his lips. "*We battle not against flesh and blood.*

"God enabled our forefathers to restrict the lifespan of vampyres. Through earnest prayers and through grace, judgment was passed on our enemies, and they ceased being everlasting. From that moment on, every vampyre has slowly gone mad as he or she approaches the thousandth year, and then they eventually expire. The Roman is an exception.

"According to the records, he was turned in the second century. By the time of the judgment, he was already a thousand years old."

"Is that why he escaped death?"

The General replaced his spectacles on his face. "An interesting hypothesis. But legions of vampyres his age or older were struck down immediately.

"For centuries we have waited, convinced he would succumb to madness. He has taken little interest in affairs of state, choosing to delegate much to his lieutenant. We interpreted that as a positive sign. If what the Florentine says is true, the Roman's renewed interest in his principality is cause for concern. More troubling is the possibility that the Roman's anomaly has recurred in the Prince."

"But General, my understanding is that the Prince is well within his thousand years."

"Yes, but if—as you say—he was resistant to your relic and able to tread on holy ground, we have another powerful anomaly to worry about. An anomaly that is much more worrisome given the fact that the Roman is his maker."

Jack closed his eyes momentarily. "I was not aware of that."

"Neither were we. The connection between the two was concealed from us. But we know it now. Should the Roman and the Florentine join together and generate a new race of anomalies..." The General closed his mouth.

"They would destroy us."

The General shook his head vigorously. "We have God on our side. I cannot believe he would have protected and preserved us this long only to hand us over to our enemies. But we must discover precisely what the anomalies are, who possesses them, and how we can defend ourselves against them before we engage in armed conflict."

"Forgive me." Jack looked down at the floor. "When I wrote to the Prince, I did not foresee the consequences."

"For now, we must watch Florence carefully. We must discover more about the nature and scope of the Roman's support. We must pray they don't form an army." The General foisted a severe look in the Jesuit's direction. "You must abandon your pursuit of the second woman. The Prince has her. You must accept that."

Father Jack leaned forward. "Is there no way to save her?"

"She made her choice when she gave herself to him. Perhaps he will tire of her. For now, you must leave her to her choice."

The General lifted his hand and made the sign of the cross, murmuring in Latin.

"You may speak to the woman you rescued and find out what she knows. You are to accompany her to America as soon as she has been healed. You may return here afterward."

"Yes, your eminence." Father Kavanaugh's shoulders slumped as he bowed and took his leave.

Chapter Twenty-Six

Ispettor Batelli stared at a series of blood droplets that led from Via
Ghibellina into an alley. The blood was old, not fresh, and seemed
to form a trail that ended in front of a rusty metal door.

The inspector scowled in the morning sun, searching for a means
of opening the door, but there was none. He curved his fingers around
the edge, trying to pry it open.

He had no idea what was behind the door. It had taken some
time to follow up on the mysterious text he'd been sent. No one in
the *carabinieri* seemed to know anything about an underground club
on Via Ghibellina. He'd searched in vain for two days.

Now he'd found blood.

Batelli removed his cell phone from his pocket and called his
supervisor. Perhaps the blood had nothing to do with Raven Wood
and William York. Perhaps it had everything to do with them.

As Batelli explained what he'd found, he was completely unaware
of the vampyre watching him through a security camera.

Chapter Twenty-Seven

Raven slept like the dead. There really was no other description for it.

William left her side for a few hours to check on his principality and meet with Gregor, the newly minted head of security.

Ispettor Batelli's presence outside Teatro had caused Gregor a good deal of anxiety, especially since he'd witnessed the execution of two heads of security in the past few years.

But the Prince reacted to the news calmly, instructing Gregor to order their contacts within Florence's police force to protect the secrecy of Teatro and bring Batelli to heel. The Prince then registered his displeasure at the hunting party's inability to locate and destroy Ibarra.

Gregor promised to double the party's numbers, privately planning to use some of his almost non-existent liberty to hunt the traitor personally. The Prince indicated Gregor's solution to be satisfactory, for the moment.

The sun was beginning to set as William returned to the villa. He drew the curtains in his bedroom and threw open the balcony doors, letting in a refreshing breeze.

Raven stirred.

William sat at her side, watching. She looked so young, so beautiful, her cheeks rosy with sleep and her long, black hair alluringly mussed.

He pushed a lock back from her face and her green eyes opened.

"Good evening," his rich voice rumbled. He bent down to taste her lips. "Did you rest well?"

"Yes, but I'm still tired. And sore." She winced as she extended her legs under the covers.

"I can fix that."

She smiled crookedly. "I just need a hot bath."

William pulled back the covers and moved over her. Her body was soft and pliable beneath his. "I have an alternative."

He cupped her face with both hands and kissed her, lightly at first, and then more urgently.

Raven returned his embrace, her tongue entering his mouth.

They kissed until William's lips trailed to her neck. He grazed the flesh with his teeth.

Raven stiffened. "No."

"Why not?" He sucked her neck without breaking the skin.

Her hands dropped to his shoulders. "Because I'm filthy. And sad."

"You aren't filthy." He nuzzled the path of her carotid artery. "You smell delicious."

She pushed his shoulders.

William's brow furrowed. "We are home. We are safe. We should be celebrating."

"My sister." Her whisper was anguished. "I stood there while they carried her away. I shouldn't have left her."

William looked puzzled. "You had no choice."

"I did, actually. I chose you."

William blinked. "Is that choice so terrible?"

"She's my sister."

The vampyre prince dropped his mask, but only for a moment. He released her and sat upright, distancing their bodies. "I didn't realize you regretted your decision."

"I didn't say I regret it," she said quietly. "But being forced to choose between my sister and my lover was painful. Even more so because I knew that if I went after her, it would mean your destruction."

William's features remained blank. "I'm sorry. I thought you chose to be with me out of love, not out of your usual commitment to protecting people."

Raven flinched.

The Prince avoided her eyes and stood. "I shall leave you to your bath. Good evening."

He turned his back.

She lifted to her knees and reached for him. "William."

He glowered at the hand that grasped his elbow.

"I love you, William. I also love my sister. She came to Florence for me and lost the love of her life. Can you imagine how that feels?"

"Yes, I can." His words were clipped.

She sank back on the bed.

"I know you lost Alicia. I'm so sorry." Raven released him. A tear spilled over her dark lashes.

William cursed in the language of his youth.

He reached out a finger to catch her tear. "Don't weep."

Two more tears welled in Raven's eyes and dropped to her cheeks.

He wiped the wetness away with his thumbs. "From the moment I looked into those great, green eyes, it was you.

"Alicia wasn't the love of my life, you are. Please don't regret choosing me." William's voice was a pained whisper.

"I love you," she managed.

"You are my choice, my destiny, my blessing, and my curse. If I were to lose you, my life would be over." He kissed her forehead and sat down, drawing her into his arms. "Because of you, love has entered my cursed existence. In comparison with the great fire of my love for you, everything else is merely an ember."

He rested his chin on top of her head.

"We don't have spies within the Curia, but we have informants in Vatican City. I will inquire about your sister." He tightened his arms around Raven's body. "If I learn she's being mistreated, I shall intervene. You have my word."

"Thank you." She wiped at her face with her sleeve.

"You are my great love, *Cassita*. I hope, with the Roman's support, we will have peace."

"Me too."

They sat there for some moments, until Raven's tears had subsided and her body had relaxed.

Only then did William stand.

"I believe someone was in want of a bath." He kissed her forehead. "I shall go in search of your dinner."

He exited the room with a look of concern on his face.

Raven walked to the bathroom, her heart heavy and her mind full.

"You look like a river nymph."

Raven's eyes snapped open.

William lounged in the doorway to the bathroom, his lips turned up, his eyes intent and predatory.

She averted her gaze, her pale cheeks ripening. "I was just about to trade the bathtub for a shower and wash my hair."

"Allow me." He stalked toward her.

"You'd wash my hair?"

"I shall try."

"Do you know how?"

His brow crinkled. "I believe I am familiar with the general procedure."

He removed a pitcher from the bathroom counter and retrieved shampoo from the shower. He placed the items on the platform in which the immense bathtub was set.

"Please add more hot water." He gestured to the faucet.

Raven sat up and turned on the water.

William removed his clothes, folded them and placed them on the vanity.

There was something godlike about his appearance. His face edged from handsome into beautiful with fine features and an elegant mouth. His body was lean and well-defined, his muscles proportioned.

His perfection never failed to stun her. Even though she'd spent so many times naked with him, Raven could not help but gaze at him in wonder.

Without ceremony, he switched the water off and stepped into the tub behind her. Placing his legs on either side of her body, he coaxed her to lean back.

"You're going to wash my hair like this?" she asked.

He arranged her long locks behind her shoulders. "I want to touch you."

As if in demonstration, he lifted his knees, cocooning her between his hips. He pressed his hands to her shoulders and kneaded the muscles lightly before smoothing his palms down her back.

She shivered.

"Add more hot water." He rubbed her arms up and down.

"I'm not cold. Just…excited." Raven sounded shy.

William smiled, for her reaction pleased him. He dipped the pitcher into the bathtub and held it aloft. "Ready?"

"Yes." She closed her eyes.

William smoothed her hair down her back. Slowly and deliberately, he poured the warm water, his fingers following.

He scratched at her scalp. "Are you sure the temperature is right? I have difficulty discerning it."

"It's perfect," she hummed.

He chuckled and continued to wet her hair.

William used both hands to apply the shampoo and worked his fingers from her scalp to the ends of her hair as if it was his sole purpose in life.

"How does it feel?" He massaged her scalp using a firm, circular motion.

"Heavenly."

"Women are mysterious," he mused.

She laughed. "In what way?"

"They're a study in contrasts: soft and strong, fierce and gentle. They can do everything, of course, and yet one feels compelled to do everything for them."

"You sound as if you've just entered the Enlightenment, my friend. Welcome to the revolution."

He tugged gently at her hair, and she laughed again.

He continued washing, and after the final rinse, he carefully squeezed moisture from the long tresses. He rested his chin on her shoulder, covering her breasts with his arms.

Raven sighed heavily.

"What was that for?" He kissed her shoulder.

She lowered her lips to his arm. "I have you, and my sister lost Dan."

"You, of all people, know the world is unjust. Things are given, things are taken away. It's beyond our control."

"I should have found another way." She bowed her head.

"Maximilian could have killed her. She is still alive."

Raven didn't answer.

"Let me turn you," he whispered, his body tense behind her. "Then you will be safe, and we shall be together. Forever."

"No."

His grip on her loosened. "You didn't even consider it. Not for a moment."

"We spoke about this before. I don't want to live forever."

His mouth found her ear. "But you would be with me."

"I love you, William. I want to spend the rest of my life with you. But I don't want a thousand years of this world. It's riddled with loss and pain and guilt."

William released her.

She turned and placed her hand to his cheek. "You won't live forever. You know that. Your thousand years will end, and I'll be condemned to century after century without you."

His hand covered hers, his eyes strangely aglitter. "We would have more time."

"If it were just time with you, of course I'd want it. But that's not what we're talking about. We're talking about death and feeding and battles." She shook her head, her wet hair spilling over her shoulders. "I don't want that."

He laced his fingers with hers, pulling her hand to his mouth. "You would feel differently after the change."

"Are you so very different from William Malet, the Norman? Is your character completely changed?"

He opened his mouth to argue and shut it abruptly.

She placed her other hand atop their conjoined ones. "You, of all people, know the power of choice. You must respect mine."

"Think of what my life will be when you are gone." His eyes were pained.

"You have choices, too, William."

"This is not the life I would have chosen for either of us."

"Then don't ask me to choose it."

"No suicide," he murmured. "Promise me, no matter what, that you won't take your own life."

"I don't intend to kill myself. Why are you worrying about it?"

"You don't believe in an afterlife, but I do. And suicides…" His body shuddered.

"I promise. But you're worrying about something that doesn't exist."

He hummed in her ear but did not acquiesce. "I pray my teacher will continue to watch over you." He breathed a resigned sigh against her skin before burying his face in her neck.

Chapter Twenty-Eight

"Couldn't you secure more comfortable accommodations?" Aoibhe threw back the hood of her cloak as she surveyed the simple room in which Ibarra was living.

The garret was in a partially renovated building that stood on the bank of the Arno, across from the Uffizi. Saw horses and tarps littered the ground floor, and most of the ceilings and walls were in various stages of repair. Dust and grime coated many of the surfaces, as well as the staircase.

Ibarra squatted under the roof. He'd tidied the room somewhat and moved in some furniture. The garret's only entry was a leaded-glass skylight; the door had been boarded shut from the outside, making it a very suitable place for a vampyre to hide.

"We could meet at your home instead." Ibarra gave her a wolfish grin.

"And have the Prince cut off my head? No, thank you." She lifted her crimson skirts high above her ankles as she crossed the dirty floor. "You should have quit the city by now. It's only a matter of time before the Prince finds you."

"I'm not leaving until I have my revenge." He pulled her into his arms and kissed her soundly. "Now, what news?"

"A policeman stumbled onto Teatro. Gregor was quite worried, but the Prince has emerged from his precious villa and ordered him to have the police take care of it."

"Interesting."

"There's more." She kissed him and withdrew, taunting him.

"Tell me."

Aoibhe twirled, the folds of her red velvet dress peeking from beneath her black cloak.

"This particular policeman has an interesting history. He's been investigating a robbery at the Uffizi, and he's taken an interest in the Prince's pet."

Ibarra scoffed. "The pet seems very popular. Does it bleed gold and silver?"

Aoibhe laughed, tossing her long, red curls. "No, but once again, there's more. It seems this officer is looking for William York."

Ibarra's dark brows lifted. "The Prince? How is that possible?"

"It seems he's been involved in the human world, and somehow the policeman has learned his name. Apparently, he's a suspect."

"The Prince would never be so careless."

"Ah, but it's well known he has a weakness for art. Perhaps he stole from the Gallery."

"That wouldn't be enough to give a policeman his name."

"No." Aoibhe rubbed at her chin. "That is rather puzzling."

"And interesting." Ibarra pulled her close once again, his dark eyes dancing. "Finally, something to our advantage."

"In what way?"

"In the way in which human beings have always been useful, as a tool for our agenda."

She pushed him away. "The coup failed. The Curia isn't coming, and the Princess of Umbria withdrew her troops from our borders. If we are patient, the Prince's time will elapse, and he'll weaken. Then we can strike."

"Aoibhe, I'm not waiting for the Prince to gain his thousand years."

"I won't be party to another coup," she snapped. "I nearly lost my head in the last one."

"There won't be a coup."

Her brown eyes narrowed. "Then how do you suggest we seize the throne?"

"We allow our enemies to dispose of the Prince, and then we take control."

"What makes you think we'd survive a war with Venice? Or Umbria?"

"Ah, that is the beauty of my plan. We don't provoke a war. We simply motivate our enemies to assassinate the Prince."

She flounced across the room. "That was Lorenzo's strategy. See how successful it was."

Ibarra straightened his spine. "I am more cunning than Lorenzo."

"The Prince was made by the Roman. He has his protection. No one will move against him now."

"Now, perhaps not." Ibarra smiled. "But with the appropriate tinder…" He gestured upward. "An explosion."

Aoibhe gazed at him suspiciously. "What are you planning?"

Ibarra's eyes gleamed. "A bonfire of vanities."

Chapter Twenty-Nine

William was always serious, always focused. But after the unexpected conversation while he washed her hair, Raven observed a new cast to his movements as he carried her to bed.

His naked body was taut with determination and resolve. He spread himself atop her on the large bed, his forearms bracketing her shoulders.

She looked up into the gray eyes of a panther, assessing and unblinking. The muscles in his chest were hard and unyielding as they grazed against her breasts.

Raven found his silence unnerving. She bit at her lip, waiting for him to speak. But he remained silent.

Without breaking eye contact, his hand found her cheek. His cool fingers danced down the curve of her neck, making her body shiver.

Then he touched her breasts.

William's movements were unhurried, a contrast to the hunger in his eyes.

He continued to stare as his hand cupped her full breast, his thumb passing over her nipple, feather light. He repeated the motion several times before moving to the other breast.

Raven sighed as he teased, her excitement heightened by the way his eyes remained fixed on hers. He watched her, reading her, anticipating every reaction.

Her skin bloomed with heat, despite the coolness of his touch.

His palm slid down her curves from breasts to hips, smoothing over her abdomen and drifting down, down to the apex of her thighs.

William shifted his weight, withdrawing his hips so he could kneel between her legs. But still, his glittering eyes remained focused on hers.

He placed his hands on her thighs and pressed, separating her legs. His hand slipped to where she desired him most, his touch prompting her to slide closer to him.

He traced, he tempted, he teased.

Raven closed her eyes as his fingertips skated between her legs. With a growl, he cupped the back of her head.

"Look at me," he commanded.

She opened her eyes, but before she could speak, he claimed her mouth.

William's kiss was firm. It made promises and exacted them in return. All the while, his fingers danced between her legs.

Raven panted.

He gazed down into her eyes as he maintained his pace, his touch slow and even.

Raven gasped as she felt the orgasm build and finally seize her.

William continued his ministrations until Raven jerked backward.

"Too sensitive," she murmured.

He kissed her, his tongue sliding against hers as he shifted atop her once again.

He pulled her knees so they pressed into his sides. The tip of him brushed against her entrance.

Raven gripped his shoulders as he filled her.

Once he was seated inside her, William refrained from moving. Instead, he caressed her face and traced the fullness of her lips, made damp by his mouth.

An exhale escaped him, the gentle waft of breath against Raven's skin a studied contrast to his glittery, impatient eyes.

She lifted her hips, and he initiated a slow, deep rhythm.

Raven moved with him, clinging to his shoulders as his powerful thrusts pushed her toward the headboard.

She kissed him, their tongues matching the movements of their lower bodies.

William trailed down to her breasts, grazing a nipple with his teeth before pulling it into his cool mouth. He began a strong, sucking motion, alternating with gentle licks that had Raven teetering on the edge between pleasure and pain.

Her fingers slid down his spine and along the firm curves of his backside. She clutched him, urging him into her again and again.

William would not speed. His pace was sure but slow, and breathtakingly deep.

"I want to drink you." His expression grew dangerous.

She managed a nod as he surged forward and withdrew, again and again.

He shifted the angle, and Raven groaned, scratching at his lower back.

"It seems I've taken a tiger to bed." He grinned wickedly.

Raven scratched harder, trying to force him to increase his pace. Her nails barely made an impression on his pale, impervious skin.

"Why hurry?" He gripped the hip above her uninjured leg, adjusting the angle so he could enter her more deeply. "We have hours to enjoy one another."

She moaned at the suggestion. Surely she would explode into flames before a few more minutes elapsed.

He kissed her nose. "Relax."

His mouth tasted her breasts. "Savor the sensations."

"I need to come." She arched her back and lifted her breasts.

"You deserve more." He nipped across her chest. Then, with his mouth fastened on a nipple, he increased his pace.

Raven gripped his backside, pulling him into her.

He lifted his mouth to her neck, his tongue tasting the skin. He rolled the flesh in his mouth before using the edge of his teeth.

Raven murmured something that collapsed into a moan as William began to suck her neck.

Two more thrusts and she was climaxing, holding her breath as she gave herself over to pleasure.

William growled and bit her neck, his teeth penetrating her artery. He drew blood into his mouth in pace with her heartbeat, his lips fastened to her neck. All the while, he continued thrusting, as her body seized and contracted around him.

A third orgasm chased the second, and Raven drew an uneven breath as her body remained tightened.

William swallowed and lessened the suction at her neck, waiting for her to relax in the wane of her climax. When she began to soften, he withdrew his teeth.

She inhaled, arms flopping to the mattress.

The tip of his tongue made lazy circles against her wound. He fluttered his lips up and down her neck, as if he couldn't bear to part from it.

"You didn't," she whispered, feeling lightheaded from the sudden blood loss.

"Not yet." He slid down her body, making sure his chin scratched a line between her breasts and down to her belly button.

He pulled her legs open, his mouth hovering above the place where she still trembled. "I am in a mood to savor."

He lowered his lips to the tender flesh.

Chapter Thirty

"*It isn't your case.*"

The voice of Batelli's superior rang in his ears as he hurried across the Piazza della Signoria.

"*Forget about the club.*"

It was easy enough to discover the true owner of Teatro, the club he'd been forbidden to search. A Swiss corporation owned it. And although he couldn't find out very much about the corporation, he took the fact that it was Swiss to be confirmation Teatro was somehow connected to William York.

When it came to the elusive Mr. York, all investigative roads led to Switzerland—all except for Raven Wood, who had mysteriously disappeared from Florence after a dead body turned up in her building.

The police investigating the murder had given the corpse to the FBI because the victim was American. The FBI had transferred it to Rome for an autopsy. They'd promised to share their findings with the Florentine police.

Batelli had read the police file, invoking a favor from a friend who had access to the documents. Raven Wood was a person of interest in the death, but so was her sister, who had also gone missing.

It seemed the murder investigation, like that of the robbery of the Uffizi, had stalled.

Batelli had forensic evidence, but he'd kept its existence out of the newspapers. He had a piece of parchment that presumably bore the handwriting of one of the thieves. The forensics team from Interpol had identified the writer as male, but they were puzzled by his style of handwriting. He used a very old, very out-of-date hand — one more in keeping with medieval manuscripts than contemporary European modes of writing. The letters seemed to have been penned with a quill.

The parchment, like the financial trail that led from a mysterious donation to the Uffizi back to a numbered Swiss bank account, was a piece of a much larger puzzle. Teatro was another piece.

For this reason, Batelli was eager to investigate the club. He'd learned of its existence from an anonymous source, but his supervisor had ordered him to abandon the investigation and he'd flatly refused to allow him to search the premises.

Batelli lit a cigarette as he stood several feet away from the Loggia dei Lanzi.

He knew better than to challenge his superiors. He was already a joke around the world — the detective who had no leads and no prospects relating to the greatest art heist in Uffizi history. It was a matter of pride as well as justice that he continue the investigation, even though his superiors had already assigned him to another case.

He'd made copies of his file on the robbery, including the information on the parchment and the Swiss bank account. He'd transcribed his rough, handwritten notes, including his remarks on Raven Wood and William York, and her sister's murdered fiancé. Although it was completely against protocol, he'd made arrangements to have the file delivered to a reporter at *La Nazione*, the local newspaper, should something malicious befall him.

Batelli was no fool. Although Agent Savola's death had been attributed to Russian organized crime, Batelli's gut told him the death was linked to the robbery. It was only right that he take precautions.

But he would not abandon the case.

He had allies helping him look for Raven Wood and her sister, while he resolved to find a way inside Teatro.

A short look around, he told himself.

That's all he needed.

Chapter Thirty-One

Raven dug her cane into the gravel, making a haphazard pattern. She was in William's garden, braving the August sun near an enormous and elaborate fountain that featured the god Neptune.

The garden was neatly arranged with flowers, hedges, and orange trees. Large terracotta pots held various plants, while roses bloomed in between the hedges.

The fountain was located at the end of a terraced walkway that lay between two large flower beds like the center aisle of a church. The air was perfumed with citrus and roses.

Two sketches lay abandoned near Raven's feet. She'd taken charcoal to paper and sketched William's face, dearer to her than her own. When she'd finished and the Muse had still hovered over her, she'd drawn Borek.

She did not draw her sister.

If she closed her eyes, she could conjure up happy days, when her father was alive and they were living in Portsmouth. She remembered his laughter, his calloused hand holding hers, the deep timbre of his voice.

"Daddy," she whispered, the tears threatening.

How disappointed he would be with her. How she'd failed him in looking after Cara.

The merest sigh of a breeze touched her face, drawing a long strand of dark hair across her eyes. A single word echoed in her heart, spoken in her father's deep voice, *No.*

You can't do everything. You can't be perfect. You just have to be yourself, and be the best self you can be.

Such was the simple wisdom of her father, or what she could remember of it.

The breeze sighed again, and Raven was seized with the impression her father would have understood.

Father Kavanaugh, for all his blind faith, would not hurt Cara. He'd read scripture to comfort her in her grief. He'd pray for her and send her home with Dan's body. If he were willing to risk his life and the ire of the Roman in order to save Raven herself, he would ensure the Curia didn't mistreat Cara.

Raven believed this. But a week had passed with no news from Father Kavanaugh or Cara. Raven had called, texted, and sent an email. There had been no response.

Raven blinked up at the sun, realizing she should have worn sunglasses or a hat. She felt as if she'd been living in a cave, as if she hadn't seen the sun in months, rather than days. She wanted the warmth to bake into her pale skin and into her heart. But it was beginning to get too hot.

William had promised he would find out what was happening with Cara, but in the days that followed their return to Florence, he'd had very little to report. Last night he'd learned the Curia had manufactured a story about Dan and Cara being the victims of a mugging. They'd both suffered head injuries, which was why, they'd said, Cara had no memory of the assault.

Raven hoped that in time Cara would find healing, although she realized Dan's loss would form a scar that would never disappear.

"Here is a lark, blessing my garden."

She turned and found William a short distance away, standing under a trellis covered in vines, shaded from the sun.

She smiled. "I wasn't expecting you until after sunset."

"The city is quiet, and my brethren are resting." He gazed at her solemnly. "I have news of your sister."

Raven felt her heart skip a beat. "Where is she?"

"On her way to America. Your priest was ordered to accompany her and the corpse. He's also spreading the fairy tale about what happened."

"Is she all right?"

William pressed his lips together. "She is grieving. But I was told by one of our sources that she is healthy."

"Will she talk to me?"

"I believe so, but you should give her a few more days. Wait until she's settled in America and we're able to determine the Curia's influence on her."

Raven turned her head. "I don't want to wait."

"I understand, but so long as your priest is with her, any information you give to her will be given to him."

Raven changed the subject. "When are we leaving for the Accademia?"

"I'm afraid our plans must be postponed. I must meet with the Consilium tonight."

Raven used her cane to dig in the gravel, trying to hide her disappointment.

"I am sorry." He sounded contrite.

"It's all right. As long as you come back."

"Why so downcast?"

She made an exasperated noise. "I can't speak to my sister. I can't leave the villa. What can I do?"

William moved to the very edge of the shade. "There's been too much unrest, too many whispers. By now I'm sure it's clear you are my greatest weakness."

Raven regarded him, a centuries-old vampyre with untold powers and the wisdom of ages. "No one who looked at you would ever think you weak."

"No one who looked at me when you were absent, perhaps. But we are attached, you and I. It must be plain to those around us, despite how hard I've tried to hide it."

Raven dug in the gravel again.

"I have made an error," William said at length.

Now Raven looked at him. "What do you mean?"

"You are unhappy."

"I'm not used to staying in one spot all the time. I like to go out."

William passed a hand over his mouth. "*A lark who is caged is never as beautiful as a lark who is free.* I said that to you once. Now I've caged you."

"There must be some way for me to leave the villa and still be safe. You're the Prince of a secure kingdom. You have the support of the Roman."

He lowered his voice. "I have many fears as well."

Raven lifted her hands in exasperation. "Share them. Let's be afraid together. But don't shut me out, and please, please don't keep me in a cage."

William looked around quickly before venturing into the sun.

His movement was so quick, Raven gasped when she saw him standing beside her.

Tenderly, he touched her cheek. "My greatest fear is that I can't protect you."

She grabbed his wrist. "I'm afraid I'll lose you. Or the Curia will come and take you away."

"I am fighting so that won't happen."

"Then let me fight at your side, William, not inside your villa. When I told you I was afraid of being destroyed by love, you told me my fears were shared. Your fears are shared, too. I'm terrified of losing you or having someone take away my memories of you." A cry of anguish escaped from her chest. "I love you, knowing it may destroy me. Love me as I am—disabled, mortal, and breakable—for as long as you can."

"I do," he whispered. "I will."

"Then take me with you."

William's expression grew conflicted.

She frowned. "I don't mean to Consilium meetings. I don't ever want to go to one of those again. But I'd like to go to the Opificio. The Pitti Palace. I used to volunteer at the orphanage. Can I do that again?"

William looked at her gravely. "Is it important to you?"

"Very much. I like working with children. I have to do something useful for society and not just sit around being waited on all the time."

"You can contribute to society by being who you are."

"That isn't enough."

"I disagree. But you also contribute by preserving great works of art."

Frustrated, she shook her head.

"If you wish to volunteer, I'll assign someone to go with you," William offered. "We lost the other security guards."

Raven remembered Maximilian attacking Marco and Luka. They'd died trying to protect her. "Thank you."

"Tonight, when I meet with the Consilium, will you stay here?"

"Of course." She gathered up her art supplies. "I know the sun is making you uncomfortable. Let's stand in the shade."

William took her by the elbow and helped her to her feet. He escorted her back to the trellis.

He took the supplies from her hand, along with her cane, and put them on a nearby table. He gathered her hands in his and placed them over his heart.

Raven was distracted momentarily by the strange silence underneath her palms. And then, his heart thumped.

"I—" William frowned. "I have thought many times of the price I would pay for love. But I should have been thinking of the price you'd have to pay."

"I knew when I lost my father my life would never be sweetness and light," Raven said. "Mostly, I'm sad for my sister. Having to stay here by myself for hours on end makes it worse because I can't stop worrying about everything."

William's eyebrows drew together. "I should have realized. I am sorry. I should have dealt with Maximilian when I had the chance."

"No one knows the future. I certainly don't blame you for what he did to Dan."

William wrapped himself around her.

Raven's grip on him tightened as she drew comfort from his nearness. "This is what we have to hold on to."

Chapter Thirty-Two

"Daniel was a good man."

Father Kavanaugh looked down into the blue eyes of Raven and Cara's mother, Linda. He nodded but made no movement to shake her hand or embrace her.

"Why didn't Raven come with you?"

Father started at her question. His hand went into his pocket and closed on the relic he carried. "Raven is recovering from the attack. She isn't well enough to travel."

Linda gave him a pained look. "Do you think she will come home?"

"I can't answer that."

"But you are close to her," Linda pressed. "She trusts you. Maybe you could talk to her about coming home? She could stay with us. We have plenty of room."

"Mrs. Shannon, I can't repair your relationship with your daughter. Only you and Raven can do that."

"But my family is in shambles." Linda placed her hand on his arm. "We need your help."

On instinct, Father pulled his arm away. "Your family was in shambles a long time ago, Mrs. Shannon."

"What's that supposed to mean?" Linda raised her voice.

Father noticed that the few remaining mourners, including Linda's new husband, had turned their attention in his direction.

His hand went to his forehead, and he rubbed at the creases. "Forgive me. I'm sorry for your loss."

He tried to walk away but she stepped in front of him. "I demand to know what you meant."

His eyes moved to hers. "I'm talking about what happened to Raven and Cara when they were children."

Linda reddened. "Raven is unbalanced. She doesn't know what she's talking about."

"Why would you dismiss her claims before I told you what she said?"

Linda mumbled a vague response.

The priest's expression grew severe. "Your ex-husband's recent arrest in California for child molestation corroborates Raven's account of what happened to Cara."

Mrs. Shannon began to protest vehemently, but he lifted his hand. "You can lie to yourself, and you can lie to everyone else, including your children. But you cannot lie to me. You knew."

Something in her eyes shifted.

She adjusted her very expensive handbag. "I have no idea what you're talking about."

He leaned closer. "You know exactly what I'm talking about. You knew what was going on, and you did nothing. So Jane, your twelve-year-old daughter, took matters into her own hands. And she paid for it with her leg."

"You don't know what he was like!" she shouted. "You don't understand."

"Then tell me." His voice grew quiet once again. "I'm listening."

The woman hesitated, something working behind her eyes.

She glanced around and saw the remaining mourners watching the exchange.

"Thank you for performing the service, Father. Please tell Raven I hope she feels better soon." Linda spun on her heel, and marched away.

Father Kavanaugh watched her departing form. He watched her take the arm of her husband and walk toward the long black limousine that waited nearby.

He lifted his eyes heavenward.

He'd tried to help Raven and her family for many years. Cracking Linda's denial for the first time should have felt like a victory. But he felt far from victorious.

She needed healing and love as much as her daughters. And he'd been harsh with her.

"Forgive me," he whispered.

His thoughts strayed to Raven, and he reflected on her character and intelligence, her bravery and compassion.

Standing in the cemetery, with the hot Miami sun streaming down on him, the Jesuit felt something move in his heart.

He knew what Raven encountered at the hands of the fiend who claimed to own her. He would not turn a blind eye. He wouldn't abandon her to her fate as a vampyre's pet, even if that meant the sin of disobedience and expulsion from the Curia.

The infinite worth of one soul far outweighed any responsibility he had to the Curia or to the Jesuits. He knew in his heart that God agreed.

"Help me," he prayed. "Show me what to do."

As if in a whisper, a germ of an idea took root in his mind.

Chapter Thirty-Three

Late one evening the following week, William and Raven exited the Mercedes under the cover of darkness and entered the Accademia Gallery.

"How did you manage this?" Raven peered past the security guard into an empty hall.

William smiled, his gray eyes gleaming. "The Gallery is available for private tours after hours. At a price."

He led her downstairs to a private garden that opened out from the Gallery's book shop. The garden was lit with candles and small lamps. A table shrouded in linen stood with a champagne bucket atop it.

Raven covered her mouth in surprise. "This is so beautiful. I don't think I've ever been out here."

William's hand spanned her lower back as he whispered, "Your beauty puts the garden to shame."

Raven lowered her head and fussed with her gown. It was black and overlaid with crimson roses, almost reaching her knees. The dress dipped low in the front, drawing attention to her generous cleavage, and bared most of her back, as well as her arms.

Her cheeks flushed under William's unabashed appraisal.

For his part, William had shocked her by donning a white shirt, rather than his usual black, with a black suit. He'd shunned a tie and unbuttoned the top two buttons of his shirt, exposing his chest to great effect.

"This dress is short." She pulled at the hem, vainly attempting to lengthen it.

William retreated a few feet in order to gaze at her. "I have observed you in much, much less."

"In bed, yes."

"Not just in bed." He smiled. "In the shower, in my library, on the terrace, in my garden—"

"Point taken," she interrupted, the flush heightening in her cheeks.

He stood in front of her and looped his arms around her waist. "I wanted to see you happy."

"Thank you."

He squeezed her backside. "My pleasure."

He offered her his arm, and she took it. They explored the garden briefly before William led Raven to a low stone bench so she could rest her leg.

She patted the space next to her. "Do you mind if I ask you a few questions about the Renaissance?"

William joined her on the bench. "Not at all."

"What was Beatrice like?"

William looked off into space. "She was beautiful. She was regal. She had many admirers, but Dante was probably the most obsessive."

"You didn't like him?"

William made what could politely be called a disgusted face. "He was proud, arrogant, and wily. He used many contrivances to get her attention. And he was already married."

Raven looked at the garden, at the glass windows that divided the interior of the gallery from the outside space. "Dante made her immortal. Because of his love, people have been reading about her for centuries."

"I could make you immortal." William's gray eyes lasered into hers.

"Art is the only thing that lasts."

"I disagree. Let me change you."

She looked away. "We've talked about this."

William shuddered a sigh. "Yes, we have. I thought perhaps you'd change your mind."

Raven hastily changed the subject. "It's sad that more people can't enjoy your Botticelli illustrations of Dante and Beatrice."

William bristled. "They have copies. That must be enough."

He rested his hand on her shoulder before moving to the table. He lifted a bottle from the ice bucket.

Raven recognized the label. *Dom Pérignon*.

She'd never tasted it before.

She watched in anticipation as William removed the cork.

"What are we celebrating?" Raven took the proffered glass, once it was filled.

"You. To your happiness." He lifted his glass and tapped it against hers.

"To our happiness, William."

She tasted the champagne—cool and dry, with the smallest bubbles. It was crisp and fresh and absolutely nothing like anything she'd tasted before.

They sipped in silence for a few moments. William watched her over the rim of his glass.

When she'd finished her champagne, he placed her glass along with his on the table.

He lifted her hand to his lips. "Unlike the rest of the humans who pine after vampyres, you don't dream of being immortal. Tell me what you dream about."

"I dream of living with you in peace. I'd like to travel with you, someday."

"Where?"

"I'd like you to show me York. I'd like to visit my sister and make sure she's all right."

"Other dreams? Things you would like to accomplish?"

"I want to continue volunteering at the orphanage. I'm grateful I was able to go back this week.

"I enjoy my work at the Uffizi. We will be starting work on one of Artemesia Gentileschi's paintings in September. I'd like to continue being part of that team."

"I shall do everything in my power to ensure you are safe enough to do that."

Raven smiled, for the thought made her happy. "I'd like to continue working on your collection as well, especially the Michelangelo."

"Everything I own is at your disposal." He kissed her fingertips, one by one. "Peace will come to my city, and I shall be able to take you abroad."

"You would take me to see my sister?"

"I was in America over a century ago. I should probably pay another visit."

"Thank you." She drew him down to sit next to her and leaned her head against his shoulder. "What are your dreams?"

He placed his arm around her.

"To spend as much time inside you as possible." He gave her a meaningful look before taking her mouth.

Chapter Thirty-Four

Ispettor Batelli smoked a lonely cigarette around the corner from the underground club. He'd spent the last few days working on the new case he'd been assigned, while continuing his surveillance of the club after hours.

He was tired, he was frustrated, but he was determined.

Tonight was the night. He was going to find a way inside the building.

He'd already noticed the comings and goings of men and women of various ages. He'd marked the bouncer who stood in the alley outside the only visible entrance to the entire building.

He had to admit, the bouncers were exceptional. They were large, they were intimidating, and they never, ever took a break. Batelli wondered about the size of their bladders.

He extinguished his cigarette and moved into position, standing across the street. From this shadowed vantage point, he could see the bouncer and the door, but hopefully, the bouncer couldn't see him.

Batelli had only been in his new position ten minutes when the door to the club swung outward.

"Never return," an ominous voice warned.

A man of medium height held two larger men by the scruff of their necks. With a strength that belied his slim stature, the man threw them past the bouncer and toward the opposite wall.

They crashed into the wall and fell to the ground, motionless.

"Banned for life," the man ordered, speaking to the bouncer. "They insulted Lady Aoibhe."

Batelli's ears pricked up at the unfamiliar name.

With a nod, the man retreated into the club, closing the door behind him.

The bouncer walked over to the two men, who appeared conscious but dazed.

He lifted them, one on each side of his large body, and dragged them out of the alley and down the street.

Batelli wasted no time in sprinting toward the club's door. He tried prying it open, but to no avail.

He looked around for a security panel or keypad, but could find nothing.

He glanced over his shoulder. The alley was still empty.

But time was short.

He curled his fingers around the edge of the door, groping for some kind of latch.

"What do we have here?"

Batelli jerked away from the door.

A hooded figure stood at the closed end of the alley, having materialized out of the darkness.

Batelli took a step back. He'd checked the alley only a moment before. It had been empty.

The figure cocked its head to one side. "And you are?"

"Lorenzo," Batelli lied. "I'm just meeting a friend."

"I knew someone named Lorenzo. He didn't have any friends." The figure paused. "And neither do you."

Without warning, the figure flew toward Batelli and grabbed him, before scaling the side of Teatro and climbing to the roof.

Chapter Thirty-Five

J ust before sunrise, Patrick Wong and Gina Molinari wandered into the Piazza Signoria, near the Loggia dei Lanzi.

It had been one of those restless, hot summer nights. They'd had a late dinner and gone to a bar with friends. One drink turned into several, and they'd moved to a dance club. Then they'd proceeded to another bar.

They hadn't stayed out this late in a very long time. Even though they were exhausted and intoxicated, they decided to take a detour to the *piazza* and walk around a little.

The *piazza* was empty — a rare occurrence — as if the beautiful space had been reserved simply for the pair of lovers.

They wandered over to the Loggia and began to kiss, their bodies backing against one of the stone pillars. A carved lion stared down at them.

Patrick smiled at his beloved, his fingers playing with her hair.

She hugged him, and he reciprocated, his eyes closing.

When they opened, he found himself gazing up at the statue of Menelaus and Patroclus, which stood at the center of the Loggia. It was not a particularly romantic scene.

Patrick stared drunkenly at Menelaus' helmet. Then he lifted his eyes to look above it.

Suspended from the ceiling was a long, iron chain. At the end of the chain was a hook, which had been embedded in the abdomen of a naked body.

Patrick pulled away from Gina and stumbled up the stairs. He rubbed his eyes, fearing he was hallucinating.

But no, at the end of the iron chain that hung from the top of the Loggia was suspended a dead man—limbs outstretched, head back. He was naked and covered in blood.

Gina screamed.

Patrick stumbled to her side. He leaned against a pillar and retched, the contents of his stomach splashing on the ground.

He retched again.

Gina supported him at the waist, murmuring worriedly in his ear.

When he'd finished, he wiped his mouth with his shirtsleeve and stared out at the *piazza*.

It was empty.

He took Gina's hand and led her away from the Loggia, to the center of the *piazza*. He retrieved his cell phone and shakily dialed the police.

"I found a body," he stammered, staring up at the corpse that hung from the Loggia.

Chapter Thirty-Six

A knocking sound woke Raven from a very sound sleep. William, who lay naked beside her, rose from the bed and wrapped himself in an antiquated dressing gown.

She rolled to her side, unwilling to open her eyes.

She heard the door open.

"What is it?" William's tone was curt.

"Forgive the interruption, my Lord." Ambrogio was almost stuttering. "There's been an incident."

"What kind of incident?"

Raven opened her eyes to see William move into the hallway, closing the door on his conversation.

She heard murmurs from the hall but couldn't make out the words, until William swore, loudly.

He re-entered the bedroom and strode to one of the closets, removing a set of clothes.

Raven sat up. "What is it?"

"Ispettor Batelli's body is hanging from a meat hook in the Loggia dei Lanzi." William tossed his dressing gown to the floor and began to pull on his trousers.

"What?"

"Photographs of the scene have been made public. The Curia will have learned of it by now."

"Are you in danger?"

William turned his head.

His expression softened. "No, my lark. But I must act immediately."

He continued dressing as she blinked away sleep. "Why would someone kill Batelli?"

William buttoned his shirt. "It's the posing of the body that is more telling. He was positioned in a public place, just as the sun was rising. Whoever did it knew our attempts at covering up the kill would be hampered by the sun."

"You don't think the Curia did this?"

"It's possible. But it's more likely this was a vampyre, looking to attack me personally."

"How?"

"By exposing my connection to the illustrations and those cursed Emersons. By exposing my connection to you." He moved to her side and kissed her deeply. "Be careful. Be alert. I'd prefer you didn't leave the villa today, but if you do, please have Ambrogio inform me. Be sure to take the security guards with you."

He disappeared through the door.

Chapter Thirty-Seven

"What the fuck?" Gabriel Emerson clasped his head with both hands as he stared in shock at the image on his laptop.

He was seated at the kitchen table in his house in Harvard Square, keeping Julia company. Clare had an ear infection and had spent most of the evening crying. Julia held the child in her arms, pacing the kitchen floor in an attempt to soothe her.

It had been a long night.

"Language," Julia chided him, frowning at him over the baby's head.

He ignored her rebuke, scrolling through a few pages on his computer.

"What is it?" She walked toward him, but he closed the laptop with a snap.

"Don't look."

Her eyebrows crinkled. "Why not?"

Gabriel ran his fingers through his tousled hair. "Do you remember the *carabinieri* officer who was assigned to investigate the Uffizi robbery?"

"Yes, what about him?"

"He's dead."

"Dead?" Julia's hand went to Clare's head, as if by covering her she could protect her.

"Murdered." Gabriel gestured to his laptop. "There are photographs of the body, all over the internet."

"They shouldn't post pictures like that. Have they no respect for his family?"

Gabriel cursed again, his hands in his hair.

"The poor man." Julia snuggled Clare into her shoulder. "I wonder if he had children."

"This is also bad for us." Gabriel's blue eyes blazed. "The inspector's body was posed near the Uffizi. Someone is making a statement."

"You mean the robbery is connected to the murder?"

"It's possible. Actually, it's more than possible. It's likely. He was the lead investigator. Those illustrations are worth a lot of money. Perhaps he was close to finding them."

"What about the strange man who came to see you in Umbria? Do you think he's involved?" Julia held Clare even more tightly, bouncing her lightly as she whimpered.

Gabriel stood, pushing his chair aside. "I'm going to call Vitali. It's morning there, and I'm sure he will have heard the news."

"Gabriel…" Julia faltered, her gaze moving from her child to her husband. "That man threatened you. Are we in danger?"

"I'll know more once I speak to Vitali, but it's too much of a coincidence. I'm not taking any chances, not with you and Clare."

"What are we going to do?"

"After I speak with Vitali, we're going to pack our bags and head to Logan Airport. We're going to be on the next flight out. Once we're out of Boston, we can decide where to go next."

He placed his arms around his family and kissed his wife's temple. "We'll be traveling west."

Chapter Thirty-Eight

The great council chamber was empty, save for the Prince and his head of security.

Gregor approached the throne and bowed, keeping his head lowered.

The Prince huffed impatiently. "Out with it."

"I'm sorry, my Lord. News of the policeman's death has been widely reported. Because the body was found as the sun was rising, witnesses were able to take photographs."

"I am well aware of the security services' failure. Have you anything new to report?"

"The human intelligence network was able to secure the body, but not before a preliminary autopsy was conducted."

The Prince banged his fist against the armrest. "How could they be so careless?"

Gregor felt for his neck. "It's a high profile case, my Lord. The autopsy was conducted immediately."

"You are head of security. Have you made any progress in finding the killer?"

Gregor cleared his throat. "The security services have been speaking to the brethren. No one admits killing him, but the policeman was seen near Teatro before his death. A hooded figure was caught on videotape. He appears to have abducted the policeman."

The Prince leaned forward on his throne. "You have a suspect. Good. Are you sure the figure is male?"

"Yes, my Lord. For various reasons, we used footage of Lady Aoibhe as a comparison. In size and in proportion, the figure was male. If I may be allowed to speculate, the figure put me in mind of Ibarra."

"Have you spoken with Aoibhe?"

"No, my Lord. Many witnesses can attest to her presence at Teatro before and after the abduction. Since then, we have been unable to locate her."

The Prince's eyes alighted on the empty chair in which Aoibhe sat during Consilium meetings. "If Ibarra is still in the city, he must be found, and quickly."

"Yes, my Lord. I have been hunting him personally, but he is elusive." Gregor shuffled his feet.

The Prince's eagle eyes noticed Gregor's movement. "I take it you have more to report?"

"Yes, my Lord. *La Nazione* has published an article detailing the dead policeman's investigation of the Uffizi robbery. The reporter claims to have access to the inspector's private papers. He is demanding that the *carabinieri* and Interpol take up the investigation, and that they pursue the prime suspect."

"And who is the prime suspect?"

"William York."

The Prince pinned his assistant to the spot with his glare. "How was this allowed to happen?"

Gregor looked up at the ruler in acute distress. "Our intelligence network had no knowledge of a connection between the policeman and the reporter. It seems materials were transferred from one to the other with the instruction that they should be made public should something untimely occur."

William's hands curved into fists. "We are just learning of this now? After the entire world has read about it?"

Gregor winced. "Yes, my Lord. The article also reports that the files have been transferred to Interpol. Even if we were to deal with the reporter, the information will have been seen by numerous people."

"Where do we stand?"

"Someone from the medical team leaked details of the autopsy to the press. It's being reported that the human's body was drained of blood prior to death and that there were bite marks on his neck."

The Prince lifted a gold chalice from a nearby table and threw it across the council chamber. It struck the back wall, which was hewn from stone, and shattered on impact.

"Tell me the newspapers aren't mentioning vampyres."

Gregor swallowed noisily. "I cannot tell you that, my Lord. However, they are also mentioning Satanists."

"If only the Satanists would claim responsibility," the Prince muttered. "I expect the Curia is already on its way."

"In this respect, I can offer good news, my Lord. Word from Rome is that the Curia are merely observing, too wary of the Roman to act against his ally."

"That is something positive." The Prince straightened. "Order the human intelligence network to manufacture evidence supporting an alternative scenario, one that would implicate someone other than a vampyre. Satan-worshippers are convenient enough.

"Deal with the reporter, and identify a new suspect related to the Uffizi robbery—someone from the security staff."

"With what evidence, my Lord?"

"With whatever evidence can be created in a short period of time," the Prince growled. "The human intelligence network is supposed to be intelligent. Tell them to use their heads."

"Yes, my Lord."

The Prince fixed his head of security with a severe look. "The security service needs to find Ibarra and bring him to me. I shall go in pursuit of Aoibhe.

"See that we have troops posted at our borders in case of an incursion, and contact our spies in Rome. I want to know if we can expect any reaction from the Curia.

"Send word to the Roman as a courtesy, thanking him for our alliance and reassuring him that I am in control of the principality and all security risks will be dealt with expeditiously." He paused. "And Gregor, take care to improve your service."

"Absolutely, my Lord."

Gregor bowed and raced from the council chamber as if the hounds of hell were chasing him.

Chapter Thirty-Nine

Raven was in the hallway looking for William when she heard voices from behind the closed doors of his library. Without bothering to knock, she entered the room.

Lucia and Ambrogio stood at the far end of the library, in front of William's desk.

William beckoned to her as he concluded his instructions. "To Geneva. But only in dire circumstances."

"Yes, my Lord." The servants replied in unison.

"You are dismissed."

The two humans bowed and left the library, nodding at Raven as they exited.

She leaned on her cane as she crossed to his desk. "What's in Geneva?"

"The Trivium."

"What's that?"

"My bank." William came out from behind his desk. He took her hands in his. "If you need to flee Florence, go to Via San Zanobi, number thirty-three. Ask for Sarah. She will provide you with safe passage out of the city."

"You've told me this before." She searched his eyes. "Has something changed?"

"A newspaper has printed the story of Batelli's death. They mentioned my name and yours."

Raven was horrified. "Why?"

"Batelli was investigating us in connection with the robbery of the Uffizi."

"But that's a lie! I was interviewed, but I was never an official suspect."

"The newspaper is reporting what Batelli recorded in his personal papers."

Raven pressed a hand to her forehead. "The director of the Uffizi will see this. So will Professor Urbano. I could lose my job on the next restoration project."

William took hold of her arms. "I am not going to allow that to happen. Even now, my intelligence network is putting out disinformation. In a few days, the pendulum will swing in our direction."

Raven leaned against the desk. "I want to continue to live in my world. My job at the Uffizi is really important to me."

He wrapped his hand around her neck. "Understood. Just give me a few days."

"Someone is trying to take the principality away from you. There's the Curia on one side and whatever vampyre interloper on the other."

He removed his hand and took a step back. "That's true, but we have the support of the Roman. We have allies in Venice and Umbria. The tide will turn."

She grabbed his hand. "Are you sure?"

"Yes. If I'm wrong, I have already made a way for you to escape the city."

She gripped his hand tightly. "I won't leave without you."

"You won't have to." William looked down at their hands. "I have an idea who the traitor is, and I am going to find him. I just need a little time."

"What about the Curia?"

"The Curia doesn't want a war with the Roman. They'll make noises, I'm sure, but they'll be slow to act.

"I must show the Curia and the world that Florence is firmly in my control. It will take a couple of days." He lifted his eyes to meet hers. "Can you give me that?"

"I'm not leaving you, William." She leaned against him. "But if the city falls, and we need to flee, will you do it?"

"Ask me when the time comes," he whispered, pressing her head against his chest.

Chapter Forty

The Prince of Florence stood on a rooftop in the city center, biding his time.

He knew Ibarra was either still inside the city or close by, watching the aftermath of his public violence with glee. Aoibhe knew where he was, if she wasn't with him.

With practiced ease, the Prince had tracked Aoibhe over the course of the evening, following her to an abandoned building that stood a few doors down from a church. The site wasn't close enough to completely deter other vampyres, but it was close enough to give them pause. No doubt she'd chosen the location accordingly.

He would not be deterred.

Aoibhe was ready to feed and had led a pretty young man into an apartment on the top floor. She liked to play with her food, which was why the Prince was waiting.

He'd taken care to tamp down his wrath. Aoibhe had been an ally and had fought at his side. She'd given her blood to aid Raven's sister. But she'd always been ambitious. She'd bedded down with Ibarra in hopes that he could help her overthrow the city.

The Prince didn't care who she fornicated with or why. He would not forgive her treason.

When he was confident the time was ripe, he climbed down from the roof and swung his feet through the glass window, shattering it.

Cries came from a nearby bed.

Aoibhe was astride her lover, her red hair streaming down her naked back. Her head turned toward the Prince, her expression one of horror.

"What the hell?" The youth grabbed Aoibhe by the hips, attempting to move her.

Aoibhe slapped him. "Shut your mouth, if you want to live."

She climbed off him and stood next to the bed.

"What is the meaning of this?" Her hands went to her hips.

"Tread lightly, Aoibhe," the Prince whispered. "You aren't the offended party."

Aoibhe lowered her arms and smiled artfully. "Your presence is always welcome, my Lord. I'm simply surprised."

"Get dressed." He pulled a pile of green velvet from a nearby chair and threw it at her.

"Hey, what's going on?" her lover demanded.

"Silence your pet, or I shall." The Prince kept his angry eyes focused on Aoibhe.

"You need to leave." Aoibhe dismissed the man before pulling the dress over her head.

"Why doesn't he leave?" the man pouted, rolling onto his side.

Aoibhe flew on top of the youth and took hold of his throat. She squeezed until the man fell unconscious.

Then, as if nothing untoward had occurred, she slid to the side of the bed and stood, arranging her green velvet dress to best effect.

"Pardon, my Lord." She slipped her feet into a pair of slippers. "How can I serve you?"

The Prince's upper lip curled in distaste. "Where is Ibarra?"

"I don't know." Aoibhe pushed her hair behind her shoulders. "He's probably in Basque country."

In a move fast as lightning, the Prince retrieved a dagger from his belt and sped past Aoibhe.

She shrieked and clutched her scalp as a sudden pain shot through her. "What are you doing?"

The Prince was already on the other side of the room. In one hand he held a large clump of red hair. In the other, he held the weapon.

He threw the curls to the floor and sheathed his dagger. "Next time, it will be your head. I repeat, where is Ibarra?"

Aoibhe touched her hair and another clump fell. The Prince had sawed the long locks that hung over her left shoulder precisely in half.

She stared down at the curls, as if she couldn't comprehend what had happened.

"Aoibhe!" he snapped. "Where is Ibarra?"

"I don't know." She lifted her head slowly, as if in shock. "I haven't seen him in a couple of days."

"You admit you've seen him."

"Yes," she whispered. Her slender, pale throat moved as she measured his reaction.

"Did you know he was going to hang a policeman at the Loggia dei Lanzi?"

Her eyes met his. "No. He wants his revenge against you, but I thought he'd be caught before this. Gregor and the security team came close to capturing him more than once."

"He could have been caught if you'd told me where he was."

Aoibhe scowled. "And have you execute me? I'm not suicidal."

"Show me where you saw him."

Her left hand went to her shorn locks. "And be executed as soon as you find him? No."

"You betrayed me, Aoibhe." His voice was glacial. "You are already dead."

"Then find Ibarra yourself." She crossed her arms over her chest, her dark eyes defiant.

The Prince's mouth pressed into a hard line. "You aren't in a position to negotiate."

"Our relationship has been one large negotiation. I didn't know Ibarra was going to kill a policeman and string him up. He's gone mad."

"I'm waiting."

"You want Ibarra. I want my head. I lead you to him, you rid the city of a mad man, and I escape the sword. We both get what we want."

"Mercy is too great a price."

"It's an exchange—his death for my life. I'll agree to leave the city when he's dead." Aoibhe's hand went to her hair again.

The Prince noticed the slightest tremor in her hand.

"Lead me to him."

"I want your word."

He growled his response, but she stood there, stubbornly.

Impatient with the delay, the Prince relented. "Very well. Lead me to Ibarra, and I won't be the one to execute you."

"I won't be taken in by your sophistry. Promise me my life."

At this, the Prince bared his teeth and snarled.

Obediently, Aoibhe lifted her skirts and stepped over the hair, heading for the door.

"You've given me your word," she said in a small voice.

The Prince glared at her coldly. "How many promises to me have you kept?"

Chapter Forty-One

The following morning, Raven rose early, dressing in a pretty yellow sundress and low sandals.

William hadn't returned after their conversation the previous day.

Over breakfast, Lucia informed her that his lordship was busy, but planned to return before sunset.

After breakfast, Raven retired to the library, where she spread out her paper and charcoal and began sketching the view above her, through the enormous, domed glass ceiling. It was a bright, sunny day, and the sky was a vibrant blue. Only the smallest wisp of cloud sailed overhead.

Her fingers were black from the charcoal an hour later when her cell phone rang.

Father Kavanaugh.

She declined the call.

A few seconds later, he called again.

She declined the call.

He called again.

With a huff, she tossed her charcoal aside, wiped her hands on a cloth, and answered the phone. "Yes?"

"Raven, where are you?" Father's tone was anything but casual.

"I'm in Florence."

"Where in Florence?"

"I'm not going to tell you that. Where are you? Where's Cara?"

"You need to leave Florence at once. It's very dangerous. There are—"

"I'm fine," she interrupted. "Tell me about Cara."

The priest paused, and Raven heard something muffled in the background.

"I'm back in Italy. Cara is in Miami with your mother."

"How could you?" Raven reproached him. "You just deliver her to our mother, after everything?"

"Cara needed a place to stay until she's ready to return to the house she shared with her fiancé." Father cleared his throat. "Raven, you have to leave Florence. Things are falling apart, and I won't be able to protect you."

"I don't need your protection."

"Don't hang up!" Father shouted.

Again, Raven could hear something muffled in the background, as if the priest was in a moving car.

"I heard what you said. I'm not leaving the city. Call me when you want to talk about Cara." Raven tapped her screen to end the call.

Father called again.

She declined.

He called again, and she let it ring.

She picked up her charcoal and returned to her drawing. Art had always provided a solace for her, as well as an occupation. She was glad to forget her strife with Father Kavanaugh and her anxiety over her sister, and lose herself in her sketch.

Fifteen minutes later, a loud, shrieking alarm sounded.

Raven covered her ears. She couldn't tell if it was a fire alarm or a burglar alarm, but the sound was deafening.

She picked up her cane and had begun to walk toward the door when Lucia stormed in, bolting it behind her.

"There's been a security breach. Someone has come over the fence." Lucia took her arm and hurried her toward one of the bookshelves. "You need to evacuate."

"Evacuate?" Raven looked around the room. "Can't we call the police?"

"This is the protocol. His lordship will be notified, but he's unreachable at the moment." Lucia opened a drawer and withdrew a flashlight, a cell phone, and a piece of paper, all of which she thrust into Raven's hands. She touched a volume on the bookshelf, and the entire bookcase swung inward.

Lucia escorted Raven to the secret entrance. "Go down the staircase. Turn right. Go to the end of the corridor. Enter the number written on that piece of paper in the keypad next to the door. It will open to reveal a passage that runs beneath the city. Make sure you close the door behind you."

"Wait." Raven planted her feet. "What about you? What about Ambrogio?"

"We're following his lordship's orders."

"Forget about that! You need to come with me."

Lucia stared at her impassively. "His lordship's orders are always obeyed. Once you enter the passage, you'll find a network of tunnels. His lordship will find you, but you must go now. The intruders are armed."

Lucia pushed her through the door as the sound of heavy, booted footsteps echoed from outside the library.

Someone began rattling the door handle.

"Hurry." Lucia pushed her again and retreated, closing the secret door.

Raven was left standing in total darkness.

She fumbled with the flashlight, and a beam of light shone down the spiral staircase.

The stairs were familiar, but Raven couldn't remember when she'd seen them. Perhaps the night William had taken her to see her stepfather.

Her stomach rolled.

She limped awkwardly down the stairs, breathing shallowly against the damp air. It smelled musty and ancient.

A long corridor lay at the foot of the staircase, punctuated by a series of wooden doors.

Raven heard noises from above—loud footfalls and raised voices.

She quickened her pace, walking with as much speed as she could muster toward the door at the far end of the corridor.

She heard more footfalls above. Something began to thud loudly and repeatedly.

As she approached the door at the end of the corridor, she saw a numbered keypad.

She put her cane aside, fumbling for the piece of paper Lucia had thrust at her. She shone the flashlight on it so she could see the numbers.

Someone shouted above her, and she heard the clatter of things being thrown to the library floor.

With shaking fingers, she punched in the code. The keypad beeped at her and…

Nothing.

She tried the door and was surprised to find it opened easily.

Blocking out the sounds from the library upstairs, she grabbed her cane and passed through the door. She closed it quickly and leaned against it, taking a deep breath.

Something slithered across her foot. Without thinking of the consequences, she screamed.

Chapter Forty-Two

"We could blow the door." The commander of the Curia's special forces unit banged his fist against the secret door he'd uncovered. "But the local police are probably on their way. We don't have much time."

Father Kavanaugh stood next to him in the Prince's library, holding Raven's cell phone. "She left her phone. I have no way of tracking her now."

"We came prepared to storm Palazzo Riccardi." Commander Sullivan's tone was testy, his New York accent more pronounced. "You didn't provide schematics for this building."

"Our sources told us there was a secondary residence, but no one believed it could be this one. There are relics here."

The commander shrugged. "You're the Padre."

"Nothing at the seminary prepared me for this," Father muttered.

"We agreed to a simple extraction, Padre, off book. I can give you until an hour before sunset and then me and my guys are packing up and getting out, with or without the girl."

Father stared at the soldier incredulously. "We can't leave her."

"I'm not getting hemmed in here after dark with only nine guys."

Father tugged at his beard. "What do you suggest?"

"We traced the SIM card in her cell phone. She was in this room until we came over the wall. Behind the door there could be a safe room or access to a tunnel. We can enter the tunnel system outside and do a sweep. But we aren't armed for a large-scale engagement."

"Do you have time to locate the relics?"

"Negative. We need to vacate before hostiles get the drop on us."

The priest glanced around the room. It was in chaos. Papers and books had been flung on the floor as the soldiers searched for a hidden exit. They'd succeeded in antagonizing the Prince without securing Raven.

He'd failed his mission and was probably about to be ousted from the Curia, if not defrocked.

But he wasn't going to give up.

"Let's find the tunnels," he told the commander, who ordered his team to retreat.

Father took one last look around before pocketing Raven's cell phone.

Chapter Forty-Three

Aoibhe touched her shorn locks, comparing them with the longer strands of her hair. She'd been stripped of her position in the Consilium and barred from her usual seat of honor near the throne. She'd been forced to stand by the wall, guarded by two soldiers, while the Prince attended to the business of state.

Ibarra hadn't informed her of his plan to kill a policeman and hang his body for the world to see.

She had to admit, it was a devious and ingenious way to destabilize the principality. She should have gone into hiding to see how it played out.

Now she was the Prince's prisoner and assured of death, since she'd been unable to lead him to Ibarra.

She cursed him. If she ever set eyes on Ibarra again, she'd destroy him herself.

Her poor hair.

A vampyre's nails and hair grew terribly slowly. It had taken decades for her to grow the long, lustrous locks that were her crowning glory. Now her hair was horribly asymmetrical. She wanted to weep.

"My Lord?" A hesitant voice came from the door to the council chamber.

The Prince gestured to Theodore, one of his servants from Palazzo Riccardi, to come forward. "What is it?"

"An urgent message from the villa, my Lord." As he approached the throne, Theodore glanced at Aoibhe.

"Come closer," the Prince beckoned.

The servant moved close enough to whisper. "The villa has been breached. I'm told your pet was able to escape into the tunnels."

William gripped Theodore by the shirt. "When?"

"Within the hour. It took time for the message to be relayed because the intruders held Lucia and Ambrogio hostage."

"What news of my pet?"

"None, my Lord." Theodore blinked rapidly. "She must still be in the tunnels."

"Find out from Ambrogio if there's any way for her location to be determined. Report back immediately."

Theodore nodded, and the Prince released him. "What is the state of the villa?"

"The servants are trying to repair the damage done by the intruders." Theodore cleared his throat. "Ambrogio reports that one of the men wore a clerical collar and spoke of intelligence sources."

A strange kind of silence filled the council chamber as both the Prince and Aoibhe absorbed the servant's ominous revelation.

"Tell Ambrogio to ready himself in case we need to initiate the Geneva protocol. And fetch Gregor," the Prince added, pressing a fist over his mouth.

The servant bowed a second time and scurried away.

"What's the Geneva protocol?" Aoibhe asked, her expression curious.

"None of your concern," the Prince snapped.

Wisely, Aoibhe clamped her mouth shut.

A few minutes later, Gregor appeared, looking a good deal more harried than usual. "My Lord?"

"We have a security breach. Armed men, one with a clerical collar." The Prince glared at his head of security. "Perhaps you were going to inform me of this?"

"Pardon, my Lord." Gregor bowed very low. "I was just informed. But I can tell you that the priest is a member of the Curia, a man called Kavanaugh. The team appear to be one of the Curia's special forces units."

Aoibhe gasped.

The Prince cursed. "How many are they?"

"A unit of ten, plus the priest, my Lord."

"Where are they now?"

"They were seen entering the tunnel system near the Piazzale Michelangelo."

"Wake the army and place them on the highest alert. Send the General to me immediately. Send a message to Rome, informing the king that the Curia has made an illegal incursion. Ask for his support.

"Tell Commander Borek to put together a team of his own and have them report to me here." The Prince stood, his black velvet robe billowing behind him as he strode down the stairs from his throne.

"Yes, my Lord. Shall I inform the commander of his mission?"

The Prince stopped. "We're hunting Curia. Tell them to arm accordingly."

If Gregor could have gone pale, he would have. He bowed quickly and raced out of the council chamber, all decorum cast aside.

"You can't be serious." Aoibhe stood, her expression drawn and anxious.

The Prince glared. "At the moment, there are only eleven of them. They must be destroyed before others join them. Even if the Roman sends soldiers immediately using modern transport, they won't arrive before sunset. We have no choice but to engage the invaders now."

"We can't fight the Curia and win."

"But we can die trying." He gave her a challenging look. "You have a chance to extend your life, Aoibhe. Join me or die on the spot."

Aoibhe withdrew a step. "You would commit suicide? For what? A city? A pet?"

The Prince's eyes glittered. "I've grown tired of your insolence. Choose."

She watched him for a long moment. She nodded.

The Prince turned on his heel and approached the door, with Aoibhe trailing after him.

Chapter Forty-Four

Raven screamed and nearly dropped the flashlight.

The thing that had crawled over her foot retreated, its own feet making a scratching noise against the hard dirt floor.

She shone the light ahead in the tunnel and saw a large rat trotting away. It turned and stared back at her.

She shivered.

The tunnel was damp, and the scent of earth and decay filled her nostrils.

She kept her flashlight pointed toward the ground in front of her as she leaned on her cane, her eyes darting warily to and fro.

When she'd gone a thousand feet, she pulled out the cell phone. It was different from her own, but simply arranged. There were only a few applications visible on the screen.

Unfortunately, she couldn't get a signal.

It took patience and a few minutes to check out the different applications, but eventually she discovered a compass. She found north, which meant she could walk in the direction of the city center. She doubted the tunnels were dug in straight lines. That, coupled with her disability, made the journey from the Piazzale Michelangelo to the city center seem interminable.

Raven put the phone away, since it was impossible to hold it, the flashlight, and her cane all at once.

She continued walking through the tunnel, pausing from time to time in an effort to hear whether someone was coming. All she could hear was the occasional scurry of rats or the distant sound of dripping water.

A few times she passed other tunnels that branched off. On each occasion she stopped to check her compass, continuing to travel north.

She'd been on foot for almost an hour when she felt the hairs lift on the back of her neck. A sudden gust of wind swirled past her.

Something yanked the flashlight out of her hand and switched it off. She heard it thud to the ground.

A low laugh sounded nearby.

She was bathed in absolute darkness, completely disoriented. Something cool grabbed her wrist, toying with the bracelet William had given her.

"Here is the Prince's pet. Where is your master?"

She pulled her arm away, shrinking from the direction of the voice. "He's right behind me."

The voice sounded amused. "I doubt that. It seems the Prince has left his precious pet all alone. How careless of him."

"Who are you?"

The voice laughed again.

Raven's heart began to pound. She held her hand out, attempting to locate the wall so she could inch along it. "Show yourself."

The voice moved closer. "Reveal the spider to the fly? This is far more entertaining."

"If you're weak." Raven's hand found the wall and she began moving, tightening her grip on her cane.

"Weak?"

"If you're a vampyre, you can see in the dark. I thought such a powerful species wouldn't need an advantage."

The voice growled.

Raven lifted her cane, wielding it as a weapon.

Out of the darkness, the flashlight switched on, shining in Raven's direction.

"I know what I look like," she complained, squinting against the bright light. "Who are you?"

The light swung away, and Raven saw the figure of a male vampyre with thick, dark hair and glittering, dark eyes.

He smiled, arms stretched wide. "I am the resurrection of the dead."

Chapter Forty-Five

At the sight of his lieutenant, the Roman tossed the man he'd been feeding from aside, unhurriedly arranging his imperial robes to cover his lower body.

The naked man fell to the floor and was quickly removed from the throne room by a pair of Praetorian guards.

The Roman wiped blood from his mouth with the back of his hand. "Am I never to have pleasure without interruption?"

He turned his back on his lieutenant and ascended the steps to the throne. He arranged his robes leisurely, licking his lips.

"I beg pardon, your excellency, but you gave permission for me to enter." Cato walked briskly toward the throne.

"*Cave*," the Roman growled.

Cato prostrated himself before his ruler.

"Why are you here?" The Roman's voice resumed its normal tone.

"There are disturbing reports from Florence." Cato's voice was muffled, as he spoke against the mosaic tile floor.

"Get up."

Cato struggled to stand, his toga catching beneath one of his feet. "A policeman was found dead, naked, and drained of his blood in a *piazza* in the city center."

"And?"

Cato frowned. "Panic has ensued, your excellency. Photographs of the body have been sent around the world. There are discussions about the existence of vampyres in Florence and the suggestion that the policeman was murdered by one."

The Roman's gaze fell on one of the frescoes. He studied it intently, but offered no comment.

"Your excellency, although we haven't received any formal communication from the Curia, our spies have revealed that a small group of black robes has entered Florence."

"A small group of black robes won't fell the city. My son is stronger than that."

"If the human population is in chaos and the suggestion that vampyres exist begins to take root, the Curia will act in greater numbers."

The Roman turned peering eyes to his lieutenant. "Has the Prince requested our assistance?"

"Yes, a message has just arrived." Cato lifted his eyes. "Florence is unstable. Clearly, one of the Prince's subjects is attempting to unseat him. He survived a Venetian assassination attempt only to crush a coup a short time ago. Now there is the public display of a dead policeman."

"Unstable," the Roman repeated, closing his eyes.

"The Curia knows you support Florence. That is the only reason they have not marched on the city."

The Roman remained silent.

Cato frowned. He moved a bit closer to the throne. "There are precious few old ones left in Italy. There's Simonetta of Umbria, but she's content where she is and would never challenge you. The Prince of Florence might."

The Roman's eyes opened. "What are we speaking about?"

Cato's eyebrows drew together. "Your son, excellency, the Prince of Florence."

The Roman closed his eyes again. "Ah, yes. My beloved son."

Cato coughed theatrically. But the Roman did not open his eyes.

"If I may speak freely, excellency, I believe the Prince's visit was a ruse."

"To what end?"

"It's clear he has some strange attachment to his pet. Why else would he risk the ire of the Curia and come to you for support? He sounds like Faustus of Sardinia."

Now the Roman's eyes opened. "You believe Florence's conflict with the Curia is caused by the pet?"

"The Curia wants it. The Prince wants it. The Prince won the last contest of wills by invoking your alliance. But an exsanguinated policeman in full view of the human population is certain to attract Vatican attention, even if the pet were not an issue."

"If Florence is not under attack, I have no need to defend it."

Cato paused, conflicted as to whether or not he should press the matter. It was not in his interest as an ambitious lieutenant to encourage the Roman to go to war. But the king was capricious and likely to blame him for any missteps.

"Shall I send word to Florence that we will not send troops?"

"Tell my son he has my confidence that he can best a few black robes." The Roman focused on the fresco to his right, the image of a young and beautiful man dressed in Dominican robes being changed by an older, dark-haired man. "Order him to surrender the pet to the Curia and put an end to this petty squabble.

"I am hungry and require another feeding." He bared his fangs. "Send in another, something young and fresh."

Cato watched his ruler's expression carefully, surprised by the non sequitur. "I shall procure something for you immediately."

"You are dismissed." The Roman closed his eyes once again.

Cato bowed, his smile growing wider as he quit the throne room.

Chapter Forty-Six

The vampyre smiled, arms stretched wide. "I am the resurrection of the dead."

Raven frowned. "And a plagiarist. I've heard that line before."

He studied her for a moment. His smile widened. "You are a wit."

"And you are?" She lifted her eyebrows.

"I am Ibarra of the Euskaldunak." He bowed theatrically. "Late head of security for the principality of Florence and former Consilium member."

"Former? What happened?" Raven stalled.

"Your master executed me."

Raven made a show of inspecting his body, which seemed very fit. "You don't look executed."

"How is it you came to be wandering these tunnels all alone?" he snapped.

"I'm not alone. I told you, the Prince is with me."

"I don't see him. Perhaps he's at his villa, resting." Ibarra moved a step closer. "You aren't under mind control, that much is certain. Feeding from you will be all the more pleasurable."

Raven cringed. She had her cane in hand, but even if she struck him, she could never outrun him. She wondered if she could outsmart him.

"If you're going to feed from me, can we at least move somewhere more comfortable? It's damp down here, and I'm wearing sandals."

Ibarra laughed, and the sound echoed. "So the Prince's pet doesn't mind someone else feasting on her. Perhaps the reason you're in this tunnel all alone is because the Prince tired of you?"

Raven's heart pounded. If Ibarra thought William no longer wanted her, he'd probably kill her.

She pretended to be insulted, sticking her nose in the air. "Of course he hasn't tired of me. He fed from me a short time ago." She touched the bite mark on her neck.

Ibarra stood in front of her and pressed two cold fingers to her throat.

His dark eyes met hers. "It's a pity he fed from you so recently. I intend to use you hard before letting him know I have you. I can't have you dying on me."

His hand smoothed down her neck and trailed across her collarbone, which was exposed in her sundress.

Raven's hand tightened on her cane. She knew if she attacked him now, he would likely knock her unconscious or worse.

Surely William was aware of the security breach at the villa by now. He would come looking for her. Her best chance for survival without serious injury was to accompany Ibarra willingly.

She placed a hand on her hip. "Can I have the flashlight? I can't see very well."

Ibarra switched the flashlight off. A crash sounded, as if he'd thrown it against the wall.

"I can't see!" Raven protested.

"I suppose you'll have to stay with me." Ibarra grabbed her elbow. He began pulling her forward.

Raven continued to use her cane, exaggerating her disability so as to slow their pace to a crawl.

"Faster," Ibarra hissed, almost pulling her off her feet. "I'd like to make it to new quarters before sunset."

"I'm going as fast as I can."

Ibarra tugged her cane out of her hand and threw it away, then lifted her into his arms.

"Much more comfortable." His nose brushed her neck. "You smell delicious."

"I have to go to the bathroom."

Ibarra lifted his head. "What?"

"I have to use the toilet. Can we move this along?" Raven squinted against the darkness, trying to see. But it was no use.

"Humans are disgusting," Ibarra muttered.

"Vampyres are parasites," she retorted.

Ibarra ignored her remark and started jogging through the tunnel.

Raven kept her eyes closed.

She was forced to place her arm behind his neck, simply to hang on. Ibarra moved at a high rate of speed, jostling her from time to time.

He seemed to enjoy it, however.

They ran for some time, and all the while, Raven's mind raced from scenario to scenario, trying to think of a means of escape. If he took her to a house that had a bathroom, perhaps she could crawl out the window. It was at that moment she remembered the cell phone in her pocket.

She hoped Ibarra wouldn't find it.

Her vampyre captor made a number of turns, so many that Raven had no idea in what direction they were headed.

Abruptly, he stopped. His body went still.

"What is it?" She opened her eyes.

"Listen," he whispered.

Raven couldn't hear anything. "What's happening?"

Ibarra placed her on her feet and shoved her against the wall, putting his body in front of hers. "Be quiet," he ordered.

Raven pressed herself against the damp earth, shrinking away from him.

He simply moved closer, his back flush with her front.

Raven didn't like the experience of being pressed against damp dirt by Ibarra, but she surmised he was trying to cover her, and perhaps mask her scent as well.

She strained her ears for the slightest sound.

In the distance, she could hear a low hum.

The hum grew louder as it approached, morphing into the frenzied cacophony of multiple footsteps.

A gust of wind swirled past, accompanied by the pounding of feet, as if a herd of animals was stampeding toward them. Raven cringed as the terrible noise approached, along with the sounds of curses and shoving.

She held her breath, worrying she would draw the creatures' attention.

Then Ibarra's body was gone.

"What is it? What's happening?" he asked.

"Curia. In the tunnels," a panicked voice responded.

"Curia? Are you sure?" Ibarra sounded incredulous.

"They felled four of us. They're right behind me!"

There were sounds of a struggle and the noise of footfalls moving away.

Ibarra inhaled, slowly and deeply.

"I can't scent them. We need to run." His voice was tight.

He hefted Raven over his shoulder and took off. She fisted the fabric of his shirt with both hands, trying to hang on.

Chapter Forty-Seven

Father Kavanaugh waited at the entrance to the tunnel for the special forces unit to secure it. The commander in charge had given him a communications link so he could speak with the team. He was not invited to join them.

He had no intention of retreating. He was armed with holy water and relics and willing to lay down his life for the woman he thought of as a daughter. Even so, he followed orders, pacing the entrance while the soldiers attempted to track Raven.

He'd been waiting about twenty minutes when he heard footsteps.

He exited the entrance and wisely stood in sunlight, partially hidden by an obliging tree.

Sullivan and his men ran out of the tunnel. The commander spotted the priest and signaled to him to follow them.

"We ran into a nest. We took down four, and the others retreated, but our mission is compromised. We need to evacuate now." Sullivan's tone was abrupt.

Father struggled to keep up with him. "Any sign of her?"

"Negative. We didn't get very far." The commander gestured to his men to increase their pace.

They jogged about a mile to where two black Suburbans had been parked and climbed in. The engines roared to life, and they screeched away from the curb.

Father's cell phone vibrated.

He glanced at the screen. The Director of Intelligence of the Curia had sent him a text.

Update your position and status immediately.

Father was not in the habit of cursing, but a curse word or two entered his consciousness. (Also, he was not in the habit of texting.)

He ignored the message and returned his phone to his pocket.

Sullivan, who was seated in the front passenger seat, turned around to look at him. "Is that the old man?"

Father nodded.

"In a few minutes, everyone will know we're here." The commander jerked his chin at the driver. "Step on it."

The priest's phone vibrated again as the Suburbans formed a military convoy and sped away from the villa.

Other Curia agents are inside the city.
Advise of your position and status immediately.

Now Father cursed aloud.

"Padre?" Sullivan addressed him.

"There are other Curia agents inside the city. I have to make contact."

The commander swore.

Father Kavanaugh touched the screen on his phone and pressed the device to his ear.

The intelligence director answered on the first ring. "I know you're in Florence, and I know who you're with. Advise me of your position."

"During our incursion, we discovered that the Prince's residence housed some powerful relics."

There was a short pause on the other end of the line. "Are you sure?"

"Yes. We traced the pet to a villa, and local intelligence confirmed it's the primary residence. The unit I'm with can corroborate the presence of relics."

"Where are you?"

"Near the Church of San Miniato, heading to the highway. We're on our way out."

The director's voice was loud enough to fill the vehicle. "You are to proceed to the Jesuit safe house near the Duomo, immediately."

The commander ripped the phone out of the priest's hand.

"Sir, this is Sullivan. We did a sweep of an underground tunnel and encountered a nest. Several hostiles escaped before they could be neutralized. We need to evacuate."

"This is a direct order. There are over a hundred agents inside the city. Three centuries of soldiers are en route from Rome. You are to report to the safe house and take your orders from General Vale."

"Yes, sir. I didn't know the General was here."

"As always, there is a point to my orders, which is why I approved your mission."

Father Kavanaugh sputtered at the revelation.

"Yes, Jesuit," the director patronized. "I knew exactly what you were planning, and I gave Sullivan and his team permission to accept your proposal because I wanted them inside the city." The director paused. "Providentially, the Roman has withdrawn his support until the Prince surrenders the girl. That is all."

The commander disconnected the call and tossed the cell phone back to the priest.

"Make a U-turn," Sullivan ordered the driver. "We're going downtown."

The commander flicked on his communication link. "Rover two, change of plans. We're pulling a U-turn and heading downtown. Over."

"Copy that," the driver of the second vehicle replied.

Father Kavanaugh crossed himself, and his hand went to the relic he carried in his pocket. "War?"

The commander kept his eyes fixed on the road. "They don't send General Vale to tea parties."

Chapter Forty-Eight

Ibarra sprinted as fast as he could while Raven bounced on his shoulder, her skirts flying.

She clutched at his shirt, a myriad of thoughts rattling in her mind. She hoped the vampyres had mistaken hunters for the Curia. But that seemed like a remote possibility.

Her thoughts moved to William. If the Curia had entered Florence, they must have done so ignoring the Roman's support. She wondered how many Curia soldiers were inside the city. She wondered if war had begun.

They'd been running for ten minutes when Ibarra slowed. He turned in a circle, his body tense, as if he were combing the silent tunnels for sound.

"They aren't following us." His body relaxed somewhat. "Whoever they are."

"Do you think it's the Curia?"

Ibarra's body jerked. "You know about them?"

"I'm the Prince's pet, remember? I hear things."

Ibarra swore in Basque. "If the Curia are here, the devil take us all."

Raven ruminated on that for a moment.

Then, without warning, she found herself flying through the air.

Something reached out to catch her.

Still surrounded by darkness, she was confused. Cursing and scuffling could be heard close by.

Raven was placed on her feet, and the person who'd caught her withdrew.

"You should have stayed in Rome." An Irish-accented voice spoke. "You're the most unlucky human I've ever met."

"Aoibhe." Raven's voice was shaky.

The vampyre sniffed in response.

"William?" Raven groped for him in the darkness.

A familiar hand stroked her face. "Are you injured?"

She grabbed his hand. "There are Curia soldiers in the tunnel. A group of vampyres ran past us, saying they'd been attacked."

"Is that true?" The Prince seemed to turn away from her.

"True." Ibarra groaned, his voice coming from the ground.

"How many?"

"I didn't stay to count them," Ibarra retorted.

"Captain Borek, take your men and continue into the tunnel. If you encounter Curia soldiers, engage them. Send one of your men back to report your position," the Prince commanded.

"Yes, sir," Borek replied.

Raven heard footsteps pass, echoing in the tunnel.

"Aoibhe, escort the traitor to the council chamber. If either of you tries to escape, I'll rip your heads off." The Prince's calm tone belied the threat in his words.

He pulled Raven against his chest and flew with her through the tunnel.

Chapter Forty-Nine

"You touched what is mine." The Prince was quiet, but loud enough to be heard in the great council chamber.

Ibarra stood before the throne, flanked by ten soldiers.

At the Prince's behest, Raven sat in a chair to his right, watching the politics of reality unfold.

The Basque spat on the ground. "You executed me."

"It seems you found your head." The Prince's gaze flickered to Aoibhe. "Or rather, someone found it for you.

"Ibarra of the Euskaldunak, did you kill a policeman and suspend his body in the Loggia dei Lanzi?"

"Yes."

"Did Aoibhe assist you?"

Ibarra grimaced. "I acted alone."

"You lie. You have committed treason against the principality of Florence, and you have violated our treaty with the Curia. For your punishment, you are to be held until you can be delivered to them. Unlike mine, their execution will no doubt be successful."

Ibarra took a step forward, but was restrained by a soldier. "Execute me now. Death at your hand would at least be honorable."

The Prince looked incredulous. "After betraying the principality that protected you for so many years, you beg for an honorable death?"

"I beg for nothing. I was loyal." Ibarra pushed the soldier aside. "It was Lorenzo and Niccolò who betrayed you and made me a scapegoat."

"You failed in your duties as head of security and were executed accordingly. Now, because Aoibhe returned your head, I must have you executed *again*." The Prince laid heavy emphasis on the last word. "You brought the Curia here with your anarchic act. You will endure their wrath. And Aoibhe of Hibernia, who betrayed the principality in assisting you, will join you."

The Prince nodded at the soldiers amidst Aoibhe's loud and vocal protests. "We had an agreement! You gave me your word!"

The Prince's voice was thunderous. "You betrayed me by allying yourself with a traitor."

A solider took hold of Ibarra's arm, and Ibarra pushed him aside. "You know what they will do to us. You'd deliver us to our enemies to be tortured?"

"Killing a policeman and hanging him in a public square attracted the attention of the Curia. You live by the sword, you must be prepared to die by the sword." The Prince's gray eyes glittered.

"I captured the Venetian who tried to end your life. I served Florence with honor!"

"Save your curriculum vitae for the Curia inquisition."

Ibarra snarled and ran toward Raven, teeth bared.

In a movement so swift it was a blur, the Prince blocked Ibarra's path. He swung his right arm and struck Ibarra in the chest.

Ibarra went flying backward, several feet in the air, until he came crashing to the stone floor near the entrance to the chamber. He lay on the floor, unmoving.

"The next one who attempts to touch my pet will be destroyed." The Prince turned his threatening gaze on Aoibhe, who appeared ready to strike. "I am an old one, son of the Roman himself. I have strength and abilities you can only imagine. Oppose me at your peril."

Silence filled the council chamber at the Prince's revelation; the soldiers gazed at him in shock.

He adjusted his robe and regained his throne. "Take the traitors to the holding cells and await further instructions."

"This is a mistake!" Aoibhe shouted. "If the Curia is here, you need my help!"

"Get her out of my sight."

"I've served you for years! This is my payment? You're going to turn me over to the black robes?"

Two soldiers approached, and a struggle ensued. She felled them both and disarmed a third, wielding his sword.

"I've waited years for my chance at the throne!" She shook with anger. "Fight me yourself, you coward."

The Prince lifted a dagger from his belt and hurled it through the air. It struck Aoibhe's hand.

She howled and dropped her sword.

"Take them away." The Prince looked at the traitors in disgust. "Keep close watch on both of them."

Four soldiers pinned Aoibhe's arms to her sides, even as black blood welled up around the dagger sticking out of her hand.

Another soldier helped the Basque to his feet and led him, limping, to the door.

Raven twisted her hands in her lap, visibly shaken. Her green eyes were active, watching the soldiers' retreating backs before coming to rest on the Prince's face.

He placed his cool hand over hers. "Are you all right?"

She managed a quick nod.

"I am sorry it took me so long to get to your side." William's expression was blank, as if he were concealing something. "When you were in the tunnels, did he touch you?"

"No," Raven croaked.

She cleared her throat before continuing. "He threatened me, but we were interrupted by the vampyres fleeing the Curia."

"You should not have been placed at risk. I never expected they would attack the villa."

"Father Kavanaugh called me on my cell phone right before the trespassers came onto your property. He must have been tracing the SIM card."

"Is the device with you now?"

"No. Lucia gave me another." She withdrew the phone from her pocket.

"If your priest was behind the incursion, it was probably a small group of soldiers intent on liberating you."

"He doesn't understand I've been liberated already," Raven remarked. "He refuses to listen to me and to what I want."

William squeezed her hand. "Although the experience is not one I would have wished for, it's a preferable scenario to an invasion. Since the priest failed, he and his men will probably retreat. I will make arrangements to hand Aoibhe and Ibarra over officially."

Raven shivered, far from comforted by his analysis.

A guard entered the council chamber and strode up the aisle. "A member of the security team requests an audience, my Lord."

"Show him or her in." The Prince released Raven's hand.

The guard bowed and returned to the door, opening it and escorting a young vampyre into the chamber. The two figures marched up the aisle.

The young vampyre was dressed casually in a white shirt and jeans. He looked to be no more than twenty.

The Prince waved him closer.

"Pardon, my Lord." The young one bowed jerkily. "I am Emiliano, from the security team. I just delivered a message to Lord Gregor, and he sent me to you."

"I know who you are. What is the message?"

"Our s-spies in Rome—" the young vampyre stuttered. "Our spies in Rome sent an urgent message warning us that Curia soldiers are on their way."

"Is this report in reference to the eleven men who have already entered the city?"

"No, my Lord. This is a report of a massive movement of troops from Rome."

The Prince sat forward. "Are the sources reliable?"

"We checked with more than one. There are civilian reports as well."

The Prince's hand curled into a fist. "How many?"

"At least three centuries."

"*Sard.*"

Emiliano ducked his head, wringing his hands in front of him.

"How long before they arrive?"

"We are tracking their movements, but we expect them in less than three hours."

"Send word to the Princess of Umbria, warning her of the incursion. Ask that she send Umbrian troops to the border in support of our alliance."

"Yes, my Lord."

"Send a message to Venice, ordering them to send supporting troops as soon as possible. And send a message to Ambrogio at my residence, ordering him to initiate the Geneva protocol. Find Gregor. I need to speak with him. Now."

Emiliano bowed once again and ran at top speed to the door, far in advance of the soldier who was supposed to be escorting him. Both vampyres disappeared into the corridor.

"Soldiers?" Raven whispered.

The Prince nodded tersely. "Your priest must have been attempting to rescue you before the invasion."

"Does this mean war?"

The Prince looked grim. "The Curia wouldn't send three hundred soldiers from Rome unless they were intent on war."

"What will we do?"

"We have the support of the Roman. I'll send an urgent message asking for reinforcements. Hopefully, the Umbrians and the Venetians will send soldiers as well."

Raven met his gaze and offered a sympathetic look, but the paleness of her complexion belied her calm.

"If the Curia fear the Roman, why would they provoke him?"

"I don't know." William was pensive. "Perhaps this is a show of force in order to motivate the signing of a new treaty. Vampyres are supposed to keep their existence hidden. Ibarra flouted the treaty."

He touched her hand, and she gripped him tightly.

"Pardon, my Lord." Gregor announced his arrival, bowing just as he entered the chamber.

"Gregor, I've just spoken with Emiliano. I want you to send an urgent message to the Roman, asking him to send reinforcements immediately."

"Yes, my Lord." Gregor eyed Raven as he approached the throne. "But I have news you should hear."

"Proceed."

"This news would be better spoken in your private ear."

"You may speak freely."

Gregor swallowed noisily, giving one last fleeting glance to Raven. "The Roman replied to our initial request for support." He held out a piece of paper.

The Prince snatched it from his hand. He read the message quickly. "Was there no other answer?"

"No, my Lord. As you can see, Lieutenant Cato sent the message electronically so it would be received quickly."

"Was the sender confirmed?"

"Yes, it arrived as a secure communication."

The Prince tossed the paper back. "Clearly, Rome has not heard about the movement of troops. Inform the king we will shortly be under siege and need his immediate intervention."

Gregor retrieved the paper from the floor. "And the other matter?" His eyes moved to Raven.

"Send the message as I commanded, and send it now!" William snarled, his anger getting the better of him.

Without thought, Raven reached out and placed her hand on his arm.

"Yes, my Lord." Gregor flew down the aisle and out of the chamber.

Once the door closed behind the head of security, Raven turned to William. "What did the Roman say?"

The Prince paced in agitation in front of the throne. "It wasn't the Roman; it was Cato. I can't be certain the Roman even saw my initial communication."

Raven stood on uneasy feet, blocking William's pacing. "What did Cato say?"

"He said I was to hand you over to the Curia and put an end to the conflict."

Raven gasped. "Is that why the Curia are sending troops? Because of me?"

"No. Why would your priest come for you with ten soldiers when he could have come with three hundred?" William shook his head. "Something has changed since your priest left Rome."

He closed his eyes and lifted his chin, his body going still.

Raven watched him, wondering what he was doing.

At length, he opened his eyes. A look of cold resignation shone from the gray depths.

"The Curia is gambling that if they march on Florence, the Roman won't intervene. Perhaps they are colluding with Cato. Perhaps the

Roman has been led to believe the Curia is willing to wage a war in order to rescue you."

"If I went to Father willingly, would it avert a war?"

"No, for I would be obliged to come after you."

Raven encircled his waist with her arms. "We could escape. We could leave the city now before the soldiers come."

"Now is not the time to flee, not when I have a chance to save the city. The Curia are angry about the policeman. I can hand over Aoibhe and Ibarra to placate them.

"Hopefully, my message will make it past Cato to the Roman himself. We can try to hold off the troops until they arrive."

"Is that possible?" Raven whispered.

"Possible, yes. Likely, no." William bowed his head toward hers.

Chapter Fifty

"My orders are clear, and they come from the Superior General himself: destroy the Prince of Florence." General Vale addressed a group of Curia agents who had gathered in the Jesuit safe house.

"For some reason, the Prince is resistant to relics and perhaps able to walk on holy ground. We don't know if he has other anomalous abilities."

Murmurs lifted from the group.

"Our primary objective is to destroy the Prince before he is able to create an army of anomalies like him. To that end, my second in command is transporting troops here as we speak." The General walked over to an aerial view of Florence that he'd projected onto a screen.

A priest in black stood. "The Prince is an old one. How do we know he hasn't created an army already?"

"We have multiple agents inside the city, some of whom are in this room. None of them have observed Florentine soldiers with any special powers. In the conflict between Venice and Florence, the Florentines demonstrated no exceptional abilities."

"What about the Roman?" The priest persisted. "I heard the Roman is the Prince's maker, and that he has vowed to protect him."

"The Roman's threat has been neutralized."

Loud murmurs and whispers filled the room until the General called the group to attention.

Father Kavanaugh surveyed the room from his vantage point near the door. Some of the agents were male, some female. Some were dressed in the robes of an order, some wore plainclothes. And then there was the special forces unit, which lined the back wall like tall, silent trees.

Father stood apart from the others, his hand in his pocket. What had begun as a simple rescue mission had evolved into a war, something he'd hoped they could have avoided.

Despite the Curia's powers, some of the agents in the room would die. There would be destruction and mayhem. Those vampyres that escaped the Curia would flee to other cities, possibly disturbing the current balance in Europe. As always when the supernatural world went into upheaval, human lives would be lost.

Raven's life could be lost.

Father felt the weight of his actions. Although he was sure his cause was just, he questioned the methods of his superiors.

There had to be another way.

Chapter Fifty-One

Aoibhe wasn't stupid.

She couldn't remember much about her life before she became a vampyre. But she remembered being poor and beautiful. She remembered her beauty catching the eye of a rich English lord, who'd raped her and sent her back to her family in shame.

She remembered the boy she'd loved — who she'd known since childhood — telling her he couldn't love her anymore.

As a vampyre, she'd always been ambitious. She knew the Prince of Florence was too powerful to challenge, so she'd seduced him. She'd hoped, over time, she'd be able to convince him to raise her to consort so they could rule Florence together, until he met an untimely death at her hand (should she catch him at a weak moment) or until he approached his thousand years and madness ensued.

Then he'd met the pet.

Aoibhe had been present the night he killed three men because they'd touched it. She'd seen the way he looked at the pet — as if he cared about it, and for more than just sex and blood.

Now the pet sat next to the throne playing the role of consort, and she was on her way to the Curia.

Aoibhe had survived by relying on her wits both before and after her transformation. She wasn't about to abandon them now. She wasn't about to be handed over to the black robes like a lamb to the slaughter.

As she marched toward the principality's dungeon, she tried to make eye contact with Ibarra.

It was no use. He was too far behind her, and several soldiers stood in between.

No matter.

Aoibhe eyed the dagger still embedded in her hand as an idea formed in her mind.

When they approached the point at which the tunnel split into several different passages, one of which led down to the dungeons, she pitched forward.

"Ah!" she cried, feigning pain as she fell.

The soldiers around her stopped, while the soldiers guarding Ibarra continued marching.

One of the soldiers extended his hand to her.

She manufactured a moan, waiting until Ibarra drew closer.

She pulled the dagger out of her hand and rose to her knees, sticking the weapon into the soldier's belly. She wrenched it from left to right, almost ripping him in half.

The soldier fell to his knees, grasping his innards with both hands as they spilled from the wound.

With the soldiers thus distracted, Ibarra disarmed one of the guards and beheaded him, then thrust his sword in another soldier's side.

Without waiting for Aoibhe, he fled through one of the tunnels that led under the city. Several soldiers followed.

Aoibhe was already gone. Having stolen a sword from the vampyre she'd gutted, she fled into a passage that led to the overworld.

Chapter Fifty-Two

William sat on his throne, his face in his hands.

Only one other time had he felt so alone, so abandoned, and that was the day his teacher died. He found it strange that his current trouble left him similarly bereft.

Simonetta had ignored his request for help, although she had refused the Curia permission to enter Umbria.

But the Curia didn't need to travel through Umbria to arrive in Tuscany; they could travel the length of the Lazio region in which Rome was situated, and pass directly into Tuscany.

Similarly, the Venetians had ignored Florence's request, despite being under the Prince's control. Neither Umbria nor Venice was willing to engage in open armed conflict with Curia forces — not without the backing of the Roman.

The Prince tugged at his hair.

Aoibhe and Ibarra had escaped. Captain Borek and the remaining members of his detachment had split into two groups in order to follow them. But the traitors were cunning and knew the city well. They were probably hiding until sunset, when they could make their way north.

The Roman had responded directly to the Prince's message, informing him that he'd withdrawn all support. William's failure to surrender his pet to the Curia had been viewed as a betrayal. The Prince of Florence had been officially disowned and publicly condemned, which meant every principality in the kingdom of Italy would side with the Roman against him.

William knew first hand of the Roman's possessive caprice. Faced with the dilemma of surrendering Raven to the Curia or disobeying his father, he'd chosen disobedience. He'd done so knowing his decision carried risk, but he hadn't expected the consequences to be so great. The Roman had stripped him of his position and had communicated the same to the Curia. Such a move was equivalent to handing the Curia the keys to the principality and offering license to turn Florence into Prague.

The former Prince of Florence sat on his throne in the great council chamber, sorrowing for his beloved city.

A gentle hand rested on his, light as an angel's touch. "There must be something we can do."

William lifted his head to look at Raven. "The Curia will level us. I'm considered a traitor now. Even if we were to flee, the Roman would hunt me."

"Would he hunt us in the United States? In South America?"

"I don't think I would make it out of Italy. The Curia will hunt me too."

"There has to be a way."

He shook his head. "My only hope is to see you escape to freedom."

"I'm not leaving you." Her expression grew fierce.

He looked at her sadly. "I disobeyed the Roman and refused to hand you over to the Curia. But they are going to take you anyway."

"I'd rather die with you!"

"If you survive, a part of me will survive also." He took her wrist, marveling at the slim arm that lay below the gold bracelet he'd given her. "Don't let your death be added to my sins."

"Father is still inside the city. If I can get a message to him, maybe we can negotiate a truce."

"It's too late." He released her.

She leaned against the throne, taking the weight off her injured leg. "I have to try."

"I will lead my troops into battle. My mind would rest easier if I knew you were safe. Go to Sarah."

"Listen to me, William." She bent at the waist, her green eyes sparking with anger. "I'm not giving up. I'm not going to let you give up either. War with the Curia is suicide. You'll die in battle, and I'll die at your side because I won't leave you.

"You say there's no way for us to escape Italy without being hunted by the Roman. So our only option is to try to make peace with the Curia and prevent a genocide."

William laughed bitterly. "They don't want peace."

"Father does."

"He wants peace and he comes to my city with soldiers?"

"I'm sorry about the citizens who were killed. But Father must have some influence if he was able to command a group of soldiers. I want to talk to him. I want to try."

William stood quickly. He touched her hair, her eyebrows, and her cheeks. "At least he can keep you safe. If you remain with me, you could be killed, or turned, or made someone's pet."

"I'm not interested in making a deal with the Curia to save my own ass. It's both of us or nothing."

William's forehead crinkled. "They are marching three hundred soldiers here to destroy me. They will never spare my life. And even if they did, there's the Roman to contend with. I am as good as dead, *Cassita*. Save yourself."

Her cheeks reddened with anger. "I am not giving up, William Malet. Don't you dare give up."

William's gray eyes searched hers for a long time.

Almost imperceptibly, he nodded.

She wrapped her arms around him.

"It seems fitting," he murmured, pressing a kiss to her hair.

"What is fitting?"

"That you should be my only hope." He held her tightly, as if by his hold he could ensure their safety.

He tipped her chin up and kissed her, cupping her face with both hands.

William shouted for his guards and asked one of them to retrieve Gregor. When Gregor arrived, the Prince and Raven accompanied him to one of the communications rooms hidden in Palazzo Riccardi.

"Curia troops are on their way." Father's voice could be heard through the speakerphone.

"Yes, we know that." Raven exchanged a look with William.

"The Roman won't protect him. We know he was ordered to surrender you, and he refused."

"War means death—death for the Curia and death for the Florentines. You don't want the lives of all those people on your conscience. Help me stop it," Raven pleaded.

Father paused. "War is not in our interests. But my superiors will not rest until the Prince is captured and destroyed. I will not rest until you are safe."

"You offer nothing," William said, shaking his head at Raven.

"Wait." Father cleared his throat. "My superiors want regime change. Our intelligence indicates the Roman wants the same. Surrender the city and Raven, and we will have peace."

"Once again you offer nothing," William growled. "My people and I would rather die fighting than turn the city over to the Curia."

"There are agents inside the city. Even now, they have been assembled. War could break out at any moment. I am the only one standing between you and certain death."

William's expression hardened. "This conversation is over."

"Wait! Let me speak to you directly."

William's gaze moved to Raven. "Your folly, priest, is that you think you can divide and conquer. You speak to both of us or neither."

"Release her from your thrall, and we can have an open conversation."

"I can hear you, Father." Raven threw her hands up in frustration. "I can hear, and I can speak for myself. I'm not in anyone's thrall, and you need to listen to me. I'm trying to help you save countless lives."

"Very well." The priest drew a deep breath. "I may have a solution that would benefit both of us."

The Prince scowled. "I thought lying was a sin."

"Tell us," Raven interjected. "What's your solution?"

The priest mumbled part of the Hail Mary.

"What do you propose?" the Prince pressed, his eyes fixed on Raven.

"As I said, my superiors want regime change and so does the Roman. It's coming, and there's nothing that can be done to stop it.

"But the Curia offers exorcisms on rare occasions, to return a vampyre to his former state. I believe I can persuade my superiors to exorcise you in exchange for the city."

"No." Raven gripped William's arm, an expression of horror on her face. "That means you'll kill him."

"An exorcism is not an execution." Father's tone was insistent. "We can free you, William. We can return you to what you once were."

"You know as well as I that that is the same as an execution," the Prince scoffed.

"You'll be human once again, free of the darkness. Free of the control of the evil one. You will have a normal life."

"This body should have died in the thirteenth century. What makes you think it could survive such a ritual?"

"God."

"God?" Raven laughed. "You ask us to place our trust in God?"

"Without him, we have nothing," the priest replied stubbornly.

"Have any of your members performed an exorcism on an old one?" William's expression changed.

Raven tugged at his arm. "You can't be considering this."

William lifted a finger, waiting for the priest's response.

"I have no knowledge of an exorcism of an old one," the priest admitted. "But the principle is the same."

"It's too risky," Raven concluded. "What if we were to agree to leave the city?"

"*Cassita*," William gently reproved her.

"You would be able to leave after the exorcism," the priest promised. "But Raven, your memories would have to be adjusted. And William would need to return to Rome with me, to be debriefed."

"Would that be before or after the black robes kill me?" William asked.

Father ignored his barb. "Raven, you say you aren't in his thrall. You say he loves you. But can't you see he's the one putting you in danger? Once the war starts, you could be killed. I'm the only one who can protect you."

"We want to be together." Raven gripped William's hand.

William lowered his voice. "It's too dangerous. If they're offering you safe passage, you should take it."

"No," she whispered. "I'm not leaving without you."

"If I abandon my city, I'm a coward."

"There's no reason to see this as abandonment," the priest interrupted. "You would be surrendering the city in order to avoid bloodshed. In exchange, we guarantee Raven's safety and your life. You become human once again, and we will no longer be enemies."

"*No*," Raven mouthed to William. "*It's too risky.*"

"What's to prevent you from turning me over to the Roman once you've finished?" William asked.

The priest raised his voice, as if he were in earnest. "You seem to forget who we are. Our goal is to save human life, not destroy it. We wouldn't hand you over to the Roman or to any other vampyre, if you were human.

"If you agree to these terms, you too will save life — the lives of your citizens and the lives of my men. And Raven will be protected. I swear to you, I will keep her safe. And I will not let my brethren destroy you."

The Prince rubbed his chin in agitation. "If I were to accept those terms, I'd want them written in a treaty that would be signed and circulated. I don't want you marching on Florence after I'm deposed."

"No," Raven objected. "You can't put your trust in an exorcism. It's like placing your life in the hands of a magic trick. What makes you think it will work?"

"There will be no treachery," the priest said, ignoring her characterization. "I will have the terms drawn up, and you may march a detachment of your soldiers to a neutral location. We'll sign the treaty and end the war before the troops arrive."

"Allow me time to consider your terms. You shall have my answer in half an hour." William ended the call.

His eyes moved to his head of security. "Give us a moment."

Gregor bowed and left the room.

"William, Father said himself they've never performed an exorcism on an old one."

"It offers us a chance, with the added value of saving my city."

"What if they kill you?" Raven's body began to tremble.

"Then I'll be dead. But you will be safe and so will the city."

"It's too high a cost." She grabbed his arm.

William hung his head. He covered his eyes with his hand.

At length, he opened his eyes. "You were the one who taught me to hope, *Cassita*. The priest is offering me hope, hope that we can both survive this. I have to consider it."

Chapter Fifty-Three

General Vale stared at the Prince of Florence, his face impassive. The two leaders stood on opposite sides of a wide, wooden table, on which rested a few sheets of printed paper.

The General had already signed the treaty, on order of the Superior General.

The Prince held the pen in his hand. "If this treaty is violated, my troops have orders to strike."

"Noted," the General replied gruffly.

"You may have ousted me, but you still have the Roman to contend with. I've sent him a copy of the treaty. He will see it upheld."

"You're escaping with your life, which is far better than you deserve."

"The opportunity to kill has not been taken away from you entirely," the Prince growled. "I've revealed the identities of the vampyres responsible for the death of the policeman."

"General," Father Kavanaugh interjected. He stepped forward, facing the Prince. "Peace is in all of our interests. The General knows this."

The Prince lowered his voice, addressing the priest. "And I have your word?"

"On my soul."

The Prince stared at the priest. The other inhabitants of the room, which included the special forces unit and a detachment of Florentines, began to grow uneasy.

The Prince glanced at Raven. Then he pressed pen to paper and signed.

"I acknowledge your surrender." The General inclined his head in the Prince's direction. "Your soldiers may return to their barracks." The Prince saluted the Florentine captain and shook his hand. "Thank you for your service. Report to Lord Gregor for further instructions. Remind him to notify the Roman if even the smallest part of this treaty is broken."

The captain bowed low, his hand on his sword. He and his detachment marched toward the door and exited.

"Commander," the General ordered.

Commander Sullivan marched forward, holding a pair of manacles.

"What are you doing?" Raven surged toward William and the commander.

"It's all right." William's tone was calm as he held out his wrists.

"No, it isn't." Raven turned on the commander. "He surrendered. You can't chain him!"

The commander sidestepped her, keeping his eyes trained on the Prince as he shackled his wrists and another soldier shackled his ankles.

One of the soldiers blocked Raven from touching William.

"Father?" She tried to grab the priest, but he was already moving, throwing a rosary over the Prince's neck.

A hush fell over the assembled group as the rosary had absolutely no effect on him.

Father Kavanaugh began reciting prayers in Latin and holding a cross out in front of him.

"William!" Raven pushed past the soldier, but another caught her around the waist. "You're humiliating him. He surrendered. Stop!"

"It's for our safety." The priest gave what was intended to be a comforting look.

"To the Duomo," the General ordered, leading the commander and three other soldiers as they escorted the Prince out of the room.

Father took Raven's hand and they followed close behind.

Chapter Fifty-Four

"Please let him go," Raven begged, as she followed Father Kavanaugh through one of the underground passages that led from the Jesuit safe house directly to the Duomo.

"We made an agreement. In exchange for his surrender, his life would be spared." Father began removing the gold bracelet from Raven's wrist.

She snatched it back. "That's mine!"

"You don't need it any more. You are no longer under his control."

She replaced the bracelet on her wrist. "It was never about control. It's about love. Why are we going to the Duomo?"

Father gave her an odd look. "It's the safest place to exorcise the demon."

He assisted her as they ascended the staircase that led into the Duomo and passed through a set of doors into the sacred space.

Raven lowered her voice. "You're going to let us go after the ritual, right?"

"We will require a few things from him first."

She looked at the priest in horror. "He's already surrendered. What more could you want?"

Father Kavanaugh averted his gaze to look toward an assembly of fifty black robes lining the aisle that led to the high altar of the Duomo. Each man was armed with a sword.

Raven watched William pass through them, a lamb being led to the altar in chains.

She grabbed Father's arm. "You're going to turn him into one of your soldiers? You're going to make him kill his own people?"

"If that is what my superiors wish, yes."

Raven cursed, loud and long.

"Enough." Father's expression grew severe. "We are in a house of God. You speak with respect or you will leave."

"You deceived us," Raven hissed. "You promised him freedom. Now you're planning to make him a slave."

The priest removed Raven's hand from his arm. "We don't keep slaves. But the Prince knows secrets about the Roman. He must share what he knows. And yes, I hope that after he tastes freedom, he will want to help us provide that freedom to others."

Raven pulled at her hair, frantically trying to keep her fury at bay. It was too late—William had already signed the treaty. But perhaps there was still time to warn him.

The beauty of the great cathedral opened up before her as she walked with the priest over the elaborately decorated floors toward the altar.

Raven ignored the artwork and Brunelleschi's incredible dome that stretched over them. She was fixated only on William as no less than ten black robes dragged him across the floor.

He submitted to their actions wordlessly, his heavy chains crashing and clanking.

"William," she lifted her voice.

The Prince turned his head but couldn't see her because she was too far behind.

She approached more quickly, but Father blocked her progress. "It isn't safe."

"I don't care." Raven sidestepped the priest, limping as fast as she could toward William.

One of the black robes caught her arm.

"William!" Raven shouted, struggling against the soldier who held her. "They lied to us. They're going to turn you into a killing machine. Save yourself."

The black robes lifted their voices in disapproval. One of them moved to Father Kavanaugh's side, whispering furiously in his ear.

The Prince was finally able to make eye contact with her. His eyebrows knitted together at the sight of her being restrained by a black robe.

"Don't touch her," he spoke through gritted teeth. His eyes moved to Father Kavanaugh's. "You promised to protect her."

"All the promises are lies," she cried, continuing to struggle. "I don't want to be protected by him. I want you."

William's expression grew pained. "*Je t'aim*," he whispered.

A tear streaked down Raven's face. "I love you. Please don't let this happen."

Her response was almost drowned out by the sound of boots on the floor. The black robe restraining her pulled her away, almost violently, and pushed her against a pillar.

A procession of eleven priests led by a man in the vestments of a cardinal marched past her toward the altar.

The cardinal turned to face Raven and Father Kavanaugh. "Keep her quiet or take her away."

The priest hesitated, his gaze moving between William and Raven, who was crying.

"Father Kavanaugh," the cardinal snapped.

Shaken from his musings, Father bowed. He stood next to Raven, giving her a conflicted look. "I've never seen that before."

"Seen what?"

"A demon professing his love in a house of God."

Father's ruminations were interrupted by the cardinal, who held up a large crucifix, addressing the black robes who flanked the prostrate Prince. "Bring him here."

The cardinal pointed to a spot on the floor, and no less than ten black robes did his bidding.

William was placed face down in front of the altar, shackled. Eleven priests, robed in white, arranged themselves around him in a semi-circle.

He turned his head to the left, shifting until he could see Raven's face.

"*Sarah*," he mouthed, his gray eyes intense.

Raven nodded.

"What's he saying?" Father spoke in her ear.

"He's saying he's sorry," she lied, wiping away tears.

The cardinal made the sign of the cross and took holy water, sprinkling it over William, over himself, and over everyone standing nearby.

William hissed as the water made contact with his body, but the water didn't burn him.

The cardinal knelt and began to recite the Litany of the Saints, in Italian. Everyone except Raven and William participated in the responses.

Then Raven noticed William's lips moving.

"*Brother Thomas, pray for me. Pray for my woman, whom I love.*" Raven wasn't sure she'd read William's lips correctly, but she knew the name of his teacher. It made sense he'd beg his teacher for help.

"*Brother Thomas, they betrayed us. Please help William.*" Raven's own lips began to move as desperate supplication bubbled up from her heart.

She didn't question her words, or censure herself for addressing a dead man. She was desperate. Adding her voice to William's only seemed right.

William's body convulsed. The chains wrenched and clanged against the floor.

The cardinal raised his voice so he could be heard.

William's lips continued to move, "*Have mercy on me.*"

"It isn't possible," Father Kavanaugh muttered. He'd stopped participating in the responses, focusing his attention on the fallen Prince.

"What isn't possible?" Raven's gaze swung from William to the priest.

William's voice lifted still higher, speaking in Latin, "*Lord, I am not worthy to receive you, but only say the word and I shall be healed.*"

"What isn't possible?" Raven pinched Father's arm.

The priest's blue eyes moved to hers, and he tugged at his white beard. "*A house divided against itself cannot stand.*"

"I told you he was different from the others." Raven swiped at her tears. "Let him go before it's too late."

"I can't do that." Father wore a look of uncertainty as he re-joined the other priests in their responses.

Once the litany was finished, the cardinal turned to William and addressed a few words to the demon, asking for its name.

William groaned, and his body curled in on itself. He seemed wracked with pain and began to cry out.

Raven moved toward him with speed she didn't know she possessed. She stumbled and crawled, the skirt of her yellow sundress dragging across the stone floor.

He turned his head to look at her.

"William, I'm sorry. I'm so, so sorry."

"I—" He closed his eyes and made an agonized noise as his body convulsed.

The cathedral echoed with his cries as the large assembly of priests and black robes fell silent.

"I'm here," Raven's voice cracked. "I'm not leaving you, William. I'm right here."

He struggled to make eye contact. "I pledge myself to you."

His shackles clanked as he moved his hands in her direction, his fingers questing hers.

"I pledge myself to you, too. Forever." Raven reached across the floor, but before she could touch him two black robes grabbed her and pulled her away.

Out of nothing, a breath of air materialized and swirled around the Prince. In the whisper of the breeze, a voice said its name, *Despair*.

William's eyes were shut, his body seizing.

"No!" Raven cried, even as she was dragged across the floor. "William, no!"

Father Kavanaugh pushed the black robes aside and freed Raven. But he wouldn't let her return to William's side.

"The demon is there," Father explained. "Stay back."

He stood in front of her protectively.

"He doesn't have a demon." Raven tried to move around the priest, but the black robes stood on either side, poised to intervene.

The cardinal placed his hand on William's head and recited another prayer before reading a text from one of the Gospels.

William's body continued to seize. The color of his skin changed and deepened, and sweat appeared on his brow. The mysterious breeze swirled above him, a private whirlwind, the voice growing louder and more ominous. "Despair."

The temperature in the room seemed to drop.

Raven rubbed her bare arms against the cold. Panic filled her, along with a feeling of defeat. The situation was hopeless. They were torturing William, and she couldn't free him.

She felt short of breath, as if the figures guarding her were pressing closer. All her striving, all her words, had come to naught. The person she loved most in the world suffered in front of her, and she could do nothing.

The cardinal prayed, making the sign of the cross over himself and over William. He took the stole he was wearing from his shoulders and placed it on William's back.

Then, in a loud voice that rang out in the great cathedral, the cardinal addressed the demon Despair and commanded it to come out.

The breeze swirled into a whirlwind, spinning and gusting furiously. The voice shrieked and cursed.

All of a sudden, the whirlwind ascended toward the dome and vanished.

William remained perfectly still, prostrate before the altar, face down.

The cardinal touched William's head, making the sign of the cross as he continued his prayers. He addressed the demon once again, commanding it to leave.

A strange white mist appeared over the Prince's body, like a fog descending in night air. The mist shimmered and vibrated, then it too vanished.

"It's finished," the cardinal announced.

As the feeling of dread lifted from Raven's body, like a heavy coat being removed, her legs buckled. Father caught her before she fell to the floor.

The cardinal prayed a final prayer. Kneeling beside William's body, he placed his hand on his head. "You have been healed. Arise."

William didn't move.

The cardinal bowed very low, examining William's face.

The cardinal lifted his head immediately. "Medic!"

SYLVAIN REYNARD

One of the black robes ran to his side and fell on his knees. He rolled William to his back, the shackles and chains crashing against the floor.

William's head lolled, his eyes closed.

The medic lowered his ear to William's chest. "No heartbeat."

He began doing chest compressions.

"What's wrong?" Raven pushed against Father's arms, finding her feet once again.

"Sometimes the demon tries to destroy its host as it leaves." Father joined the others standing around William. He added his voice to their prayers.

Raven stumbled toward them, startled that the black robes moved aside for her.

She watched as the medic continued performing cardiopulmonary resuscitation, moving from time to time to exhale air into William's mouth.

"Call an ambulance," the medic grunted.

The cardinal sat back on his heels. "Are you sure?"

"Now!" The medic snapped.

One of the black robes pulled out a cell phone and walked some feet away, dialing a number.

"You said an exorcism wasn't an execution." Raven turned accusing eyes on Father Kavanaugh. "You said he'd be alive!"

She struck him with her fists even as the medic continued to work a few feet away. The great Duomo echoed with her anguished cries and the sound of urgent prayers.

Chapter Fifty-Five

"*Apparently, she wasn't possessed. We had to sedate her, but the sedative will wear off in a few hours.*"

"*After that?*"

"*We will leave it to you to adjust her memories. The body is at the morgue. We're waiting for it to be released.*"

Raven sat in a small bedroom, staring at a crucifix on the wall.

Since she awoke, she'd been waiting for her mind to clear. Slowly, very slowly, her memories returned, along with scraps of conversation she must have overheard.

She remembered being taken by the black robes to the Jesuit safe house. She remembered Father Kavanaugh telling her William was dead. He'd been rushed to the hospital, but was dead on arrival.

She'd attacked the priest in a fury, screaming that he was a murderer. Black robes had restrained her while another plunged a needle into her vein.

She didn't remember anything after that.

She'd awoken in a narrow bed, disoriented and feeling strangely subdued. The sedative had numbed her. She couldn't cry or feel anger, even as her heart wept blood.

Raven sat quietly, waiting for her equilibrium to return, and took stock of her surroundings—a narrow bed, a chair, and a desk. A short bookcase that held a few books, all theological, stood next to the desk. A crucifix hung on the wall next to a brass rendering of the symbol of the Society of Jesus. A small window revealed the night sky and the barest sliver of moonlight.

She stretched her legs and stood, leaning against the bed. The sedative must have numbed her leg because she didn't feel any discomfort.

She walked slowly to the door. It was locked.

Father Kavanaugh was no longer the benevolent man she'd thought he was. While he and the others truly seemed shocked that William had died, they couldn't have been ignorant of the possibility. They'd shackled him and placed him in an incredibly stressful situation. Perhaps it was the power of suggestion, along with the stress, that killed him.

Raven didn't believe in demons. She didn't have a scientific explanation for the strange whirlwind or the disembodied voice, but she knew William had not been possessed.

She'd begged Father over and over again to free William. He could have intervened. He could have put a stop to the entire bizarre ritual. But he hadn't. He and all the other black robes had simply stood and watched William die.

Murderers.

Father Kavanaugh and the Curia were now her enemies. They'd been duplicitous in their negotiations for peace and treacherous in their actions. The fact that the priest, who she'd trusted with William's life, had betrayed them cut her deeply.

Listlessly, she returned to the bed and sat down. The window was too small to crawl out of, and she appeared to be on the second floor.

Perhaps an opportunity to escape would present itself before the Curia attempted to wipe away her memories.

She hugged her pillow, noticing that her gold bracelet was gone. The Curia must have taken it from her. The Curia had taken everything away from her.

She closed her eyes, trying with all her might to catalogue every moment, every word she'd exchanged with William, hoping some of the memories could be hidden from the Curia amongst the memories of her childhood and its own betrayals.

Raven awoke with a start.

The room was dark except for the moonlight that spilled onto the floor from the small window.

She'd been dreaming. She and William were walking in his garden, hand and hand, in bright sunlight. She'd broken down when she saw him, hardly able to say the words that expressed how relieved she was that he wasn't dead.

He'd smiled at her gravely and opened his mouth to explain.

Something moved, making the sound of a broom sweeping across a floor.

The room was empty, save for the furniture. As she sat up in bed, she saw something.

She slid her legs over the side of the bed and unsteadily crossed to the door, bending to retrieve a piece of paper.

She held it up in the moonlight.

Open the door and walk to the end of the hall. Take the staircase to the ground floor. Someone will be waiting for you.
—Sarah

Raven read the handwritten message twice before the words penetrated her foggy mind.

The paper was too solid in her hand to be a figment of imagination. She wondered if someone was manipulating her or if the letter had truly been written by the Sarah William had wanted her to find.

As far as she knew, she and William and Sarah were the only ones who knew about the address on Via San Zanobi. Perhaps the mysterious Sarah had learned of her whereabouts and come to her.

It didn't matter to Raven if the author of the note could be trusted or not. She wanted to escape and was willing to risk it.

She tried the doorknob and was surprised to find that it turned easily. She opened the door and stuck her head into the hall. It was empty.

As quietly as she could, she exited her room and hobbled to the end of the hall. She opened the door to the stairwell and closed it quietly behind her. The staircase was narrow, and she leaned on the railing as she cautiously descended, her ears straining for the slightest sound.

When she reached the bottom, she came face to face with a teenage boy. He placed a finger against his lips.

He took her hand in his, which was stunningly warm, and led her outside into the alley.

They moved to the street as fast as Raven could manage and walked hand in hand about a quarter of a block. In the distance, she could see Brunelleschi's dome.

She winced at the realization.

The teenager opened the passenger door of a small Fiat and helped her into the seat. He walked around the car and started it. They pulled away from the curb and sped down the street, the headlights penetrating the darkness.

"Who are you?" she asked in Italian.

"A messenger." He gave her a small smile before returning his concentration to the road.

It was only a short drive to Via San Zanobi. Raven saw the sign as they made a right turn onto the street.

The boy parked in front of number thirty-three. He leaned his head toward the building. "Press the buzzer, and give them the password."

"Thank you." Raven reached into the pockets of her sundress. "I'm sorry I don't have any money."

"I have been well paid." He flashed her a smile. "Go. They will realize you are gone at any moment."

Raven thanked him once again and exited the vehicle.

The teenager waited as she crossed the street and pressed the buzzer. As soon as she spoke the password, he pulled away, his taillights disappearing around the corner.

The lock on the door buzzed and Raven opened it, stepping into a lightless corridor.

Chapter Fifty-Six

The corridor opened up into a lit courtyard that housed a garden. Doors lined the walls around the courtyard.

A woman stood next to an open door, beckoning.

Raven limped toward her.

The woman appeared to be in her fifties and had shoulder-length brown hair and brown eyes. She seemed unsurprised by Raven's disability and moved to her side, offering a shoulder to lean on.

She ushered Raven through the open door and into an apartment, bolting the door behind them.

The apartment was spacious, with an open-concept kitchen and dining area that had sliding glass doors leading out to another garden.

The woman led Raven through the kitchen to a sitting room.

Raven was grateful to take the weight off her leg and sank onto a low couch. "How did you find me?"

"It's best if you don't ask too many questions," the woman replied in English, sitting in a chair opposite. "I have been paid to help you escape the city. I couldn't do that with you being held captive."

"William hired you?"

"We don't have much time." The woman ignored her question. "If you wish to escape, you must leave within the hour."

"So soon?"

"The police would like to speak to you in connection with the murdered inspector who was found in the Loggia dei Lanzi. I was also told you wish to escape other interested parties."

Raven fidgeted with her fingernails. "You could say that."

"Because of the nature of the threats against you, my services were engaged to provide you with a new identity and a new life."

Raven's heart skipped a beat. "Is that really necessary?"

The woman frowned. "You can refuse my assistance, of course. But according to the risk assessment I was provided, you are in danger. Whether you leave Florence or not, the life you have lived up until this point is over.

"I'm offering you a new identity, a new job, and a new life. If you accept this new life, you can never return to Italy. You cannot see or speak with anyone from your old life, including your family."

Raven inhaled sharply. "What about my sister?"

"If your sister learns that you are alive, your enemies will learn that too. And they will come for you."

"I can't even say goodbye?"

"I'm afraid not." The woman gave her a sympathetic look. "If you choose to do this, we end your old life. Your family will believe you're dead."

Raven fell silent.

The woman looked at her watch. "It's your decision, but you must choose quickly. Your presence puts me and many others at risk."

Raven's mind moved slowly from scenario to scenario. She knew she was still feeling the after-effects of the sedative, so her ability to feel strong emotions was somewhat depressed. Even so, she found it difficult to choose an action that would cause more pain to Cara.

"It isn't my place to persuade you," the woman interjected. "But you should know that your current identity poses a risk to your family."

Raven lifted her eyes to meet the woman's. "Someone wants to kill me?"

"Someone wants revenge that will probably end with your death," the woman corrected her.

"Who?"

The woman smoothed the wrinkles in her skirt. "There are at least two creatures of the underworld who bear a lot of anger toward someone who was close to you. Let's leave it at that."

Raven caught her meaning immediately. "I could return to the Jesuit house and escape the creatures, but Father Kavanaugh will take away my memories."

"You should also consider your family. Unless someone is willing to protect you and your family for the rest of your life, all of you are vulnerable."

Understanding washed over her. Raven nodded.

"Time's up." Sarah stood. "If you're prepared to do this, we must get ready now."

Raven closed her eyes. She thought of her sister. She thought of her mother. She thought of her sister once again.

So much pain. So much death. Even if the Curia decided to send her back to Florida, the Roman might send someone to hunt her, just for spite. Without her memories of William and his world, she wouldn't know how to protect herself. And she wouldn't entrust her safety and the safety of her sister to the Curia.

"I'm ready."

The woman led Raven down the hall and into a back room.

Less than an hour later, Raven climbed into a black Mercedes M Class. Her long black hair had been cut to her shoulders and dyed a dark red; her green eyes had been covered with blue contact lenses.

The male driver placed her luggage and her new wheelchair in the back of the vehicle while the mysterious woman handed her a very expensive handbag. "Your passport for your escape from Italy is inside. You're Portuguese, from Braga."

"I don't speak Portuguese."

"It doesn't matter. You're staying within the European Union, so no one will check your passport at the border. You will be given your new identity before you reach your final destination." The woman handed her a piece of paper. "Memorize this number. If you see someone from your old life, telephone this number and ask for Matthew. If you are threatened or your identity is compromised, travel to Geneva and report to the Trivium Bank."

"A bank? What can they do?"

"Wear this at all times." The woman looped a gold necklace over Raven's head and pointed to the two items suspended from it. "The vial contains a small but powerful relic. Don't take it off.

"The gold charm has a number stamped on it. Present the number at the Trivium Bank, and they will assist you."

A few minutes later two young women entered the vehicle. One sat in the front and one in the back next to Raven.

"What's going on?" she asked Sarah, who still stood next to Raven's open door.

"It's safer to travel in a group than to travel alone. Don't engage in conversation with them. Your driver has instructions about what to do in case of emergency." The woman extended her hand and Raven shook it. "Good luck."

"Thank you."

The emotion of the moment caught Raven unaware. She blinked back tears.

Sarah closed the door, and the driver started the car.

They exited the hidden garage at the back of the building and drove through the streets of Florence until they reached the highway, heading north.

Chapter Fifty-Seven

In the space between three worlds, two beings argued over a man's soul.

"There's nothing for you here," the dark angel said, his voice like the scraping of fingernails against a chalkboard. "This soul belongs below."

"It is not for you to determine the place a soul belongs after death," the saint rebuked.

"This soul is ours." The dark angel reached out his hand.

The saint blocked the demon, standing over the soul that lay prostrate between them.

The dark angel roared. "His soul is damned!"

"He repented at the end."

"Repented?" The dark angel sneered. "He fully embraced the deadly sins. He abandoned hope and allowed Despair to own him!"

"The demon did not own him. The transformation was incomplete because he prayed for help."

"That's sophistry. Your brother priests dispatched his soul to hell."

"Yet here we stand."

The demon craned his neck to look around the saint and view the soul. The man's chest lifted and fell, slow and steady, with human breath.

The saint smiled at the sight.

If the dark angel could have pushed the saint aside, he would have. He examined the soul more closely, leaning over him.

"You cheated," he hissed. "The man was dead."

"It is not for me to give life. But I have prayed for him for many years, that grace would take root in his soul." The saint pointed down. "Go back from whence you came. There is nothing for you here."

As soon as the command left the saint's lips, the dark angel vanished, snarling and cursing as he departed.

The saint bent down and made the sign of the cross on his student's forehead. He prayed in Latin, as was his custom, beseeching mercy and grace and thanking God for the man's deliverance.

When he had finished, the student—who had been half-asleep during the encounter—fell into a peaceful slumber.

Chapter Fifty-Eight

The shock hadn't worn off.

Raven sat at an outdoor table at Café Mozart in the old town square of Prague, drinking coffee on a Saturday morning, still feeling numb.

She'd been a resident of Prague for two months.

She'd traveled from Florence to Austria with the young women and their driver. Once they'd entered Innsbruck, the driver had dropped off the other women at an opulent residence. Then he and Raven had switched vehicles at what appeared to be a safe house. They'd been met by a woman who changed Raven's hair from red to a sandy brown with blond streaks, and cut the already-shortened strands into a bob. Raven switched the blue contact lenses for brown and exchanged her Portuguese passport for a Canadian one.

The driver had then taken her to Prague, to an apartment building behind the National Theatre, near the Vitava River. She'd been given the keys to a furnished one-bedroom apartment, an envelope filled with various currencies, and a set of instructions relating to her backstory and the job that had been secured for her at St. Vitus Cathedral.

Raven was now Cassandra MacDonald, who had a B.A. in English from Queen's University in Kingston, Ontario, and was interested in history.

Her job at the cathedral wasn't in art restoration. Presumably, showing her ability in that area would be too conspicuous. Instead, she had a position in an office, writing and editing materials in English.

The cathedral was incredibly majestic, as was St. Wenceslas Chapel, which was housed inside the cathedral and featured priceless frescoes of the passion of Christ and the life of St. Wenceslas.

The chapel was home to several relics. But Raven continued to wear the relic Sarah had given her. She touched it absently as she stared at the astronomical clock on the tower opposite, waiting for it to strike and display figures of the twelve apostles.

Her pain over the loss of William was acute, but she had been able to push it aside as she tried to adjust to her new life. And that was how she knew she was still in shock.

She told herself the shock would wear off. When she wasn't distracted by so many new things, she would be able to grieve properly. For now, she had difficulty fathoming the fact that William was gone. Forever.

Losing him was like breaking her leg. It took time for her to accept that she would never run or dance again, apart from the wondrous days after William had healed her. It would take time to accept that the Curia had murdered him, and she would never again be held in his arms.

She sipped her coffee, noticing a man skirting the crowd that had gathered to watch the clock's display. The man was dressed all in black, his hair pale in the sun.

She placed her coffee cup on the table with shaking fingers. The figure looked so like William.

She left cash for the coffee and the untouched pastry and grabbed the brace she'd been using instead of a cane.

The figure was still visible, walking away from the crowd.

She moved as quickly as she could into the square, following him. She didn't dare shout his name.

The clock's bell began to ring and the man stopped.

Raven hastened her pace, ignoring the pain that shot up her injured leg.

The man turned around.

Raven shaded her hand against the sun in order to make out his features.

He was very handsome; it was true. But he wasn't William.

She stopped in the square and watched as the man in black was joined by a group of friends.

As the clock finished striking, she wondered how she could know that William was dead and still be convinced she'd seen him in a square in Prague.

That evening, Raven lay awake, watching the light and shadows play across the ceiling and walls of her bedroom.

"You were the shadow on my wall," she whispered, a sharp pain piercing her chest.

The shadows didn't reply.

Chapter Fifty-Nine

A week later, Raven was returning to her apartment late at night. She'd indulged in an evening at the opera, losing herself in the magic of Verdi. Her building was only a short walk from the National Theatre, where the opera was performed. She took her time walking home, her heart and mind filled with music.

As she turned onto her quiet street, she felt a prickle at the back of her neck.

She looked over her shoulder. The street was empty.

She hastened her steps, leaning hard on the brace. Her mind began to play tricks on her, as memories of walking home after Gina's party flashed before her eyes.

She ignored the pain in her leg as she moved as fast as she could. A sudden gust of wind blew past.

Some distance away a figure stood in the shadows of the building across the street.

Raven reached her front door, fumbling in her pocket for her keys.

"Stop," a voice commanded in Italian.

Raven pretended she didn't understand, as she'd been cautioned by Sarah.

"You are in danger." The voice came closer.

Raven found her key and put it in the lock, struggling to open the door.

"Wait!" The voice switched to English. "You're wearing a relic. You know I can't harm you."

"I don't know what you're talking about," Raven replied in English.

"I come to pay a debt. The Prince would have executed me. You stayed his hand."

Raven turned to see the figure move out of the shadows and into the light shining from one of the windows next door.

She opened the door and held it, preparing to flee inside. "What do you want?"

Borek lifted his hands, showing he was unarmed. "It's dangerous for me to be here. The presence of the Cu—our enemies—in Prague is small, but exists nonetheless. It's only a matter of time before they realize I'm here."

Raven scowled. "You've put me in danger. Now they'll hunt me."

"They're hunting you already."

"What do you mean?"

Borek surveyed the area quickly. He lifted his noise and sniffed.

"A body was found matching your description, but it was cremated before anyone could examine it. Aoibhe and our enemies are curious."

Raven leaned against the front door. "Aoibhe? I thought she fled with Ibarra."

"The black robes put in place a puppet prince. Aoibhe returned two weeks ago. She killed Gregor and seized the principality. Now she wants revenge."

"Won't the black robes depose her?"

"They have found another enemy nearer home."

"What about Ibarra?"

Borek shrugged. "He never returned."

"The Roman betrayed us," Raven couldn't keep the bitterness out of her voice. "He promised William his support but withdrew it."

"Cato has too much influence. An old one's madness has finally caught up with our king."

"You think he's mad?"

Borek nodded. "When we were in Rome, I heard a few things from the guards. Cato had all the old ones in the principality slain because they were a threat to him. He mediates everything, controlling the information the Roman receives. But the Roman is paranoid and uses the guards as spies. Even so, his memory is unreliable. He'll give an order and when a guard carries it out, he'll punish the guard for acting without approval. The palace is in a constant state of terror.

"The Prince was the only credible threat to Cato. So he manipulated the Roman into having the Curia destroy him."

Raven rubbed at her eyes. "How did you find me?"

"Aoibhe sent me to track you, but we thought you were in Geneva. When I didn't find you, I continued the hunt on my own. Budapest and Prague were obvious choices. Both cities have been cleared of vampyres for years, so our enemies feel little need to police them. I was hesitant to return here because of my history. I went to Budapest first."

"You're here to kill me."

Borek didn't blink. "That is my mission."

"You've failed. I'm wearing a relic and I won't take it off." Raven entered the building and prepared to shut the door.

"Wait!" Borek stretched out his hand, still maintaining his distance. "If I can find you, so can she. You have to leave. Tonight."

"So you can track me to my new destination? I don't think so."

"Aoibhe may have sent others. She may have sent Ibarra and he's far more powerful than me."

Raven examined Borek's face. "At any time, I can call my priest and tell him where I am. He'll send agents to rescue me."

"I wouldn't be too sure of that." Borek gave her a knowing look.

"What do you mean?"

"The black robes may come, but it won't be to rescue you. Aoibhe told me there was a report your priest had quit the black robes and returned to America."

"I doubt that. He only just arrived in Rome."

"Perhaps he acquired a conscience." Borek's tone was sarcastic. "Clearly I'm wasting my time here." He turned to go.

"Wait," Raven called. "If I could, I'd start a war between the Curia and the Roman and watch them destroy each other. They murdered my William." Her voice broke. "I hate them all."

"Finally, something we agree on." Borek faced her once again.

"Will you help me?"

"Help you do what?"

"Start a war."

Borek laughed. "That's madness. You'd never get near Rome; Aoibhe has too many spies."

"Help me. We have common enemies."

Borek paused, almost as if he were tempted. "I'm not committing suicide for a human's revenge."

He stood very tall and placed his hand on the hilt of his sword. "I've paid my debt. May fortune smile on you."

"What will you tell Aoibhe?" Raven asked, trying to keep the anxiety out of her voice.

"Nothing. She's a tyrant. I won't live under her yoke.

"Much as I had reason to dislike the Prince, he gave his life to save Florence when the Roman betrayed us. The Prince died for all of us." The expression on Borek's face shifted, as if the realization haunted him. "The entire principality is in his debt. It pleases me to honor his sacrifice. And yours.

"Farewell, Lady Raven." With a ceremonial bow, Borek melted into the shadows.

Chapter Sixty

When Raven entered her apartment, she didn't bother calling the number she'd memorized. Instead, she reached for the guidebook Sarah had given her, which provided her with instructions and advice, along with a list of safe houses scattered around the world. Raven didn't know how wide Sarah's network was or who precisely it was for, but she knew all its resources were at her disposal, ostensibly because William had paid Sarah for a comprehensive relocation plan.

Raven made note of the guidebook's instructions on how to escape by train and packed a small carry-on bag. She took the SIM card out of her cell phone, as instructed, and flushed it down the toilet, replacing it with a new, unused SIM card. She left behind most of her clothes but took her passport and all the cash she'd been hiding in a container in her freezer. Once the sun had risen above the horizon, she took a taxi to the central train station.

Using cash, she booked a ticket on the first train to Moscow and sat in one of the busy waiting areas in the station, staying alert to her surroundings.

When it was time, she boarded the train. But just as the train was getting ready to leave the station, she exited, limping as quickly as she could to the train that stood just across the platform. She climbed aboard and found a seat in a crowded second-class compartment, intent on pretending to be a hapless Anglophone tourist who had no idea how to use an automated ticket machine. When the conductor arrived, she played her part and paid for a ticket in cash.

As she endured the four-hour train ride to Vienna, she thought about her encounter with Borek. She thought about Father Kavanaugh quitting the Curia and returning to Florida. She wondered if his actions were a sign that he regretted what happened to William. Mostly, however, Raven meditated on her anger with the Curia and plotted revenge.

The shock of losing William was finally wearing off, and she was no longer content to accept her current fate with passivity.

The Curia had killed William by accident, allegedly. She didn't remember everything that had transpired after the ambulance came to take William away. But she remembered the shock on everyone's faces, including Father Kavanaugh's. She remembered Father whispering to her that it shouldn't have happened.

But they'd killed him. No matter their intentions, William was dead.

As she watched the scenery flash by her window, she thought about revenge. Her unguarded words to Borek played over and over in her mind. She wondered if she could travel to Rome and start a war.

Borek was right. It was far more likely that Aoibhe's spies would find her first. Then she'd be dragged back to Florence to face God knew what.

If she wanted to start a war, she needed allies and a plan. She needed relics and weapons. It would cost a great deal of money to fund such an undertaking.

That's when she remembered the bank. Sarah had told her to present the number stamped on the charm around her neck at the Trivium Bank in Geneva. She was pretty sure the Trivium was the bank William had mentioned.

If she could travel to Geneva, perhaps she could withdraw enough money to finance her revenge. Perhaps Borek would help her if she paid him enough.

Aoibhe had known to look for her in Geneva. That had been some time ago, however — before Borek visited Budapest and Prague. Hopefully any other spies she'd sent would have quit Geneva and begun looking for her elsewhere.

To Geneva she would go.

Chapter Sixty-One

Raven arrived in Vienna, and after a short layover and a last-minute change from one train to another, she was bound for Geneva.

The trip from Vienna to Geneva was long. She spent the night on the train and arrived at the station just before seven o'clock the next morning. She secured a taxi and asked the driver to take her to the Trivium Bank. He gave her a strange look but pulled away immediately.

She slipped the necklace Sarah had given her over her head and looked at the number stamped on the charm. The numbers were very small.

She took a photo of the charm with her camera and then looped the necklace back over her head.

Using the photo application on her phone, she enlarged the image so the numbers were visible. She withdrew a piece of paper and a pen from her carry-on and quickly copied the digits.

Some time later, the taxi driver pulled up in front of an impressive building that sat behind a high wall. The bank was located on Rue des Alpes, near Lake Geneva.

"I can't pull in." The driver pointed to the enormous iron gates and the security guards posted on either side.

Raven thanked the driver and paid him, exiting the taxi.

She approached the gates, but the guards stopped her immediately.

"*Bonjour*," she greeted them nervously. She handed one of them the piece of paper.

The guard indicated that she should wait, and he entered the guardhouse, leaving her with his companion. She watched as the first guard lifted a telephone and began speaking to someone.

In short order he returned, and one of his associates appeared on the other side of the iron gates.

The gates opened, and the associate, who was armed, addressed her in Italian. "This way, please."

Raven shuffled behind him, following him to a large, metal door that led into the central stone building. The door swung open, and she followed the guard inside.

"Good morning." An attractive woman wearing a white lab coat greeted Raven, once again speaking Italian. "Before we can admit you, we need to conduct a DNA test."

Raven's mouth dropped open. "DNA? Is that necessary? I gave you the number."

"We need to know you are the person associated with the number." The woman's tone was firm.

"What about my passport?"

The woman's forehead wrinkled, as if Raven was asking a very silly question.

"Will you take blood?" Raven asked, beginning to feel squeamish.

"Just a mouth swab." The woman pointed to a small office and ushered Raven inside.

Raven sighed. She'd come this far. Presumably, she was safe inside the bank. At least for the present.

The woman snapped on a pair of latex gloves and opened a small kit while Raven sat in an armchair.

She was very tired. She hadn't slept much on the train, fearful as she was of someone accosting her.

"Open," the woman instructed.

Raven opened her mouth, and the woman scraped the inside of her cheek, placing the sample in a plastic tube. She sealed it, placed tape over the top of it and wrote something on the label.

"How long will it take?" Raven asked.

"Not long. Wait here." The woman took off her gloves and placed them in a waste can. She took the tube and the kit and disappeared down the hall.

Raven leaned back in her chair and closed her eyes, just for a moment.

A throat cleared above her.

"Madame?"

Raven startled awake. "What is it? Who are you?"

She looked up into the face of an older man with neatly trimmed salt-and-pepper hair, who was wearing small, wire-rimmed spectacles and a very expensive-looking suit and tie.

He extended his hand. "Good morning, madame. Welcome to Trivium. I am Henri Marchand, the director."

Raven shook his hand, still in a daze from having been fast asleep only a moment before.

"I'm sorry it took so long for me to greet you. Because it's Sunday, I was not in the building when you arrived. And we had to confirm your identity. This way, please." He waved his arm toward the corridor.

"What were you testing my DNA for?" Raven struggled to her feet.

"We were matching it against the sample your husband provided some time ago." The director lifted her bag to his shoulder and paused as she got her bearings.

She leaned on her brace. "My husband?"

"You and he are our most important clients, and I do apologize for the invasive measures. But they are necessary, as I am sure you can appreciate." He waited for her to enter the hall and followed her.

"I should mention immediately that the artwork your husband had transferred from your home has arrived. Everything is in excellent condition. We have an art conservation specialist on staff, and he matched the items with the inventory sent by your husband. It appears the entire collection has arrived safely."

Henri smiled down at her. "Of course, with your expertise in art restoration, you will probably want to assess the condition of the collection yourself. Would you like to see it now?"

Raven stopped. She closed her eyes, more confused than she'd been in a long time. "When you say *my husband*, you mean William?"

"Of course, madame."

"And when you say art collection, do you mean the pieces from Florence?"

"Yes, madame. As I said, everything appears in excellent condition, but of course we defer to your expertise."

"You spoke to William?" she whispered.

The director pushed his glasses up his nose. "We have always spoken through his staff, which is why your presence here is a great honor. We've been expecting you."

They continued walking down the hall.

"When did the art begin to arrive?"

"Two months ago. The last piece arrived yesterday. The shipment was divided up and sent via different routes for security reasons. Can I offer you breakfast or some sort of refreshment before we visit the collection?"

Raven stopped, the wheels of her mind turning over this new revelation. William had been murdered over two months ago, which meant Ambrogio and Lucia must have begun transferring the art collection to Geneva around that time.

Raven wondered if the Geneva protocol she'd heard William mention before his death included the evacuation of his artwork.

"Monsieur Marchand, I've been traveling for twenty-four hours. I need a shower and a change of clothes. Could some of your guards escort me to a hotel and escort me back?"

"Forgive me, madame. I'll take you to the private apartments that have been prepared for you and your husband." He led her down a side corridor to an elevator and promptly placed his hand flat on a fingerprint reader.

The reader glowed green, and the elevator opened.

He gestured for Raven to precede him into the elevator.

"William has an apartment here?"

"Indeed." The director removed his spectacles and positioned his eye for a retinal scan. The scan glowed green and a keypad appeared below it. He pressed a series of numbers.

"But William never used the apartment?"

"No, madame. You are its first occupant."

"How safe is the bank?"

Monsieur stood tall with pride. "Extremely safe, madame, and from all kinds of threats. Should you need to leave the bank, we can provide you with safe transport anywhere in the world."

"I don't believe it," she muttered.

The director frowned but didn't reply.

When the elevator doors opened, Raven found herself in front of a pair of tall, gilded doors. Once again, the director submitted scans of his palm and retina and used an additional code. The sound of something loud and metallic echoed in the vestibule. The director placed his hand on the doorknob and opened it.

Inside, Raven found an opulent sitting room, featuring blue carpet and gilded walls. The furniture was also gilded and upholstered in blue velvet. It was a room for a king.

"This is Simone." The director motioned in the direction of a woman wearing a black uniform. "She will provide you with what you need."

Henri transferred Raven's bag from his shoulder to Simone. "If there's anything I can do, please let me know. I can show you the inventory at your convenience. If you'd prefer to view it tomorrow, we can do so."

Raven shook her head. "No, I'd like to see it today. Perhaps in a couple of hours."

"Very good." He smiled and retreated, closing the door behind him.

Raven heard the sound of a heavy lock snapping into place.

"This is the strangest bank I've ever visited." She turned to take in her surroundings.

Given the thoroughness of Sarah and her network, Raven wasn't surprised that William had taken other detailed measures to preserve his art collection and her safety. Clearly, the bank staff had no idea he was dead. She wasn't about to tell them, for they might withdraw their protection.

She wondered what the staff knew about William and the world of vampyres. She wondered if the bank simply viewed him as a wealthy, eccentric client, or if they understood he had been the Prince of Florence.

"I can show you the other rooms, madame," Simone's voice intruded on Raven's musings. "Shall I draw a bath?"

"Yes, please."

"Shall I unpack for you?"

"No, that isn't necessary."

"Very good, madame." Simone escorted her through a side door and into a large bedroom decorated in a similar fashion to the sitting room, except the velvet was red. A large canopied bed stood in the center of the room.

The room reminded Raven of the bedroom she'd shared with William in his villa.

Simone placed Raven's bag on the bed and walked to one of the side walls, pushing a button to reveal a concealed door, which swung inward to a spacious marble bathroom.

"Your clothes have already been cleaned, pressed, and unpacked." Simone moved to another wall and pressed another button. This time double doors opened.

"My clothes?" Raven tried very hard to hide her shock.

"Your husband's things are over here." Simone crossed to the other side of the room and opened the matching closet.

Raven stared after her.

Rows and rows of black shirts, trousers, and jackets hung neatly in the large closet. Rows and rows of black shoes rested below on a series of racks. It looked exactly like William's closet in his bedroom in Florence.

"If there is anything you would like pressed or freshened up, please let me know. It can be done immediately." Simone gave Raven a little smile and disappeared into the bathroom. The sound of running water echoed through the apartment.

Raven walked to William's clothes and grabbed the first shirt she touched, tugging it carelessly from its hanger and pressing it against her nose. There was still a trace of his scent. She waded into the closet, disappearing into the shirts and inhaling deeply. Tears filled her eyes. She clapped a hand over her mouth to stifle a sob.

By the time Simone returned, she was seated on the bed, one of William's shirts lying next to her. She'd tucked several of his hand-kerchiefs into her bag.

They were small things, but they were all she had left of him.

Chapter Sixty-Two

"I trust breakfast was to your satisfaction?" Monsieur Marchand smiled as he escorted Raven into an elevator in a remote area at the very rear of the bank.

"Yes, thank you. You've been very kind." Raven toyed with the tie to her green wrap dress. She felt funny dressing up, but it was comforting to wear one of her favorite outfits. William had always praised it.

"The artwork is stored in a series of subterranean vaults. The vaults are controlled for light, temperature, and humidity. We used the Uffizi's specifications, but everything can be adjusted."

"And the inventory?" Raven followed the director out of the elevator once they'd reached the lowest level.

"I've prepared a paper copy for you." The director repeated the security measures before entering a narrow, white-walled hall.

He performed the palm and retinal scan at the first door on his right.

When they entered the room, dim lighting shone from overhead. A desk and chair stood nearby, along with a leather folio.

"This is the inventory." The director handed it to her. "It's alphabetized by artist, and each work has a corresponding location. I can assist you in viewing the vaults. Or perhaps you'd rather proceed item by item?"

Raven leafed through the inventory to the letter B.

Botticelli—Illustrations of Dante's Divine Comedy. Vault A9C.

"I'd like to see these first." She pointed to the entry.

"Very good."

Within a few minutes, they were inside one of the temperature-controlled vaults, and Monsieur Marchand was lifting a wooden box from a labeled shelf. He placed it on a nearby desk and gestured to Raven to take a seat behind it.

She put on a pair of white gloves he'd provided and carefully opened the box. There, in a series of folios, were the illustrations that had caused so much trouble; illustrations William had acquired from Botticelli centuries earlier, and that had somehow been stolen from him by Lorenzo, the lieutenant who'd betrayed him.

Raven leafed through the folios until she found the drawing of Dante and Beatrice in the sphere of Mercury. She removed it carefully.

It was so beautiful. So fragile.

"Assessing their condition may take time." Raven spoke without lifting her head, hiding her emotions.

"Of course, madame. There is an intercom to your right. Please contact me if I may be of assistance." The director left her in privacy.

She replaced the illustration in the box, closed it firmly, and removed her gloves. Leafing through the inventory, she discovered the prized Michelangelo on the list, along with Botticelli's alternative version of *Primavera*. William had even arranged to have some of her own sketches transferred. It was a bittersweet revelation.

A tear streaked down her cheek.

She continued reading the inventory, so engrossed that some time later she barely heard the door open and close.

Raven twisted away from the door, clutching the inventory to her chest.

"I need more time," she faltered.

"More time?" a familiar voice asked.

"Yes." Raven held the inventory more tightly.

"*Cassita*," the voice whispered.

Chapter Sixty-Three

Next to the door stood a man dressed in black.

His hair was fair and tinged with gray at the temples. Laugh lines radiated from his eyes. A scar marred his chin.

His eyes were familiar—a light and beautiful gray—and so was his voice.

"*Cassita*." He smiled, like the shining of the sun, and held out his arms.

The pages of the inventory fluttered to the floor. Raven shrieked and put the desk between them. "How did you get in here?"

"It's me," he said, his smile vanishing. "It's William."

"William is dead."

"Look at me. I am not dead." The man began unbuttoning his dress shirt.

"Stop!" she cried. "What are you doing?"

He exposed his chest. "My heart beats normally now. Come, feel."

"No, thank you." Raven narrowed her eyes, examining his face, chest, and hands. He looked like William, it was true, but William at about age forty rather than the twenty-something vampyre she'd known him as.

"You changed your hair." One side of his mouth tipped up. "And your eye color."

She didn't respond.

He rubbed his thumb across his lower lip. "This reminds me of the day I had to prove to you I was a vampyre."

He lifted his hand and stared at it. "I've been transformed. My heart beats, and red blood flows through my veins. I can't be driving daggers into this body without doing damage."

Raven ignored his display and kept her gaze focused on his eyes. "How do you know about that?"

"I think you know the answer." He studied the floor, as if he were measuring the distance between them.

Raven flattened herself against the wall, her eyes moving to the brace she'd abandoned next to the desk. It was her only weapon.

The man's gaze moved to hers, and his expression took on a new intensity. "Do you remember the first time I came to your apartment? When I gave you the relic from my teacher?"

Raven's eyes widened, for as far as she knew, she and William had never discussed the events of that night with anyone.

"I called you Jane by mistake, because I'd seen the name in your passport. We talked about mercy and justice. I ordered you to leave the city." He chuckled. "Of course, you didn't listen. I'm glad. If you'd fled the city, I'd never have known you. I'd never have known hope, dancing in my arms."

Raven covered her mouth with her hand.

The man's brow crinkled. "I brought your stepfather from California and presented him to you as a macabre birthday present. But you instructed me to send him to the police instead. You asked me to set up a fund to help the children he'd abused. Did Monsieur Marchand tell you that he and his staff manage the fund? It was set up in your name, your name and Cara's."

Raven shook her head, too surprised to speak.

The man took a step forward. "I'm sorry it took me so long to find you. When I woke up, I had lost my memory. I thought it was 1274, and that my teacher had just died. I only came to myself a few days ago. But I'm here now. I love you, Raven. I swear by all that is holy I will never leave your side again, so long as I live." His expression grew tortured.

"William?" she whispered, hoping against hope.

"I swear on my teacher."

She rushed over to him, throwing her hands about his neck.

William's arms were strong as they wound around her, crushing her to his chest. "Did they hurt you?"

"Sarah was able to get me away from the Curia before they could adjust my memories." She spoke as her tears rained down on his chest.

"You're crying."

"Of course I'm crying. You're alive."

Beneath her ear his heart pounded, strong and steady. She pulled back in wonder. "Your heart is beating."

"It tends to do that now."

"Don't you dare! Don't you dare make a joke. I saw what they did to you." Her voice broke. "I watched you die."

William's own eyes began to water. "I am sorry you had to see that. I'm sorry it took me so long to return."

Raven brushed the tears from his eyes, and William grasped her hand, staring at the evidence of his emotion.

"Those are the first tears I've cried since 1274."

Raven placed her palm inside his opened shirt, against his chest. The rhythm of his heartbeat continued without any of the strange pauses it had favored while he was a vampyre.

She shook her head. "You're human?"

"Yes. I've aged, as you can see. The scar I earned in a fall from a horse when I was sixteen has returned." He gestured to his chin.

Reverently, Raven traced his scar. She placed her hands against his face, studying it intently. "You're older than I am now."

He chuckled. "I was always older than you."

"You know what I mean. You were in your twenties when you were changed. You look older than that now."

"Is that a problem?" he asked quickly.

"Of course not. I just don't understand what happened."

"I can't explain why I've aged. This was the face I saw in the mirror after I awoke. But as for the transformation, *Cassita*, it's nothing short of a miracle. I don't know if you'll believe me. But first…"

Tentatively, he grazed her cheek. When she didn't pull away, he brought their mouths together. His warm lips poured over hers, a contrast to the coolness of his previous form.

He kissed her intensely, but with patience, tasting and savoring her lips and the inside of her mouth. When they parted, he pressed her ear to his heart and kissed her hair, over and over again.

"I didn't expect you to be here. I thought Sarah's people evacuated you to Prague."

"They did, but Borek paid me a visit."

William pulled back. "Borek? Were you wearing a relic?"

"Yes." She pointed to her necklace. "Borek said he came to warn me—that Aoibhe sent him to hunt me. He looked for me here and in Budapest, then decided to visit Prague. That's where he found me."

"You believe him?"

"I don't know. He warned me Aoibhe could have sent others and that I should flee. He also told me she had seized control of Florence. He didn't want to live under her rule."

"I can imagine. So Aoibhe gained the throne she always wanted. My poor Florence." William wore a faraway look on his face. "We should go upstairs."

They exited the vault and retraced the path to the elevator. The doors opened to reveal Monsieur Marchand, who was holding a large, flat wooden box. "I have the items you requested, sir."

"Excellent." William took the box from him. "We wish to retire to the apartment, undisturbed."

"Of course." The director accompanied them upstairs and to the other elevator before taking his leave.

William punched a code into the elevator keypad, and the doors opened.

"You don't have to have your palm read? Or your eyeball scanned?" Raven gazed at him skeptically as they entered the elevator.

"No."

"Why not?"

He pressed his lips to her temple. "Because I own the bank, and I didn't want to give them vampyre biometrics."

"Do they know you're a vampyre?"

"That I *was* a vampire? No."

"You own the whole bank?"

"Yes. I founded it in the fourteenth century, because I didn't trust the Medici with my money. Over time, I have notified the bank staff of my death and the name of my heir. Funny how all of them were named William." He winked.

"But the artwork, our clothes—how did you arrange everything to be moved?"

William's features grew grim. "Long before I met you, I put in place an evacuation plan for the things I treasured most in case of a human war, fire, or some other threat. When it looked as if the Curia would march on Florence, I ordered my staff to send everything here. I wanted the art collection preserved for you."

The elevator doors opened, revealing the entrance to the apartment. Once again, William entered a number on a keypad, and the doors swung open.

Raven headed for the bedroom, and William followed.

She sat on the bed and put her brace aside. Then she removed her colored contact lenses, discarding them onto a side table.

"Much better." William took her hands in his. "The brave young woman with the great, green eyes. I knew the night I first saw you that you were one of the greatest goods of the world and I should do whatever it took to save you. See how blessed I am because of you?"

Raven tugged at his hand, and he sat next to her.

"What's in the box Monsieur Marchand gave you?"

"The relics of my teacher." William kissed her fingertips, one by one. "They were transferred with everything else. I can't bear to be separated from them."

"Monsieur keeps referring to you as my husband."

"Along with the art transfer, I left instructions for the bank to welcome my beautiful wife. I wanted you to have a refuge." William fumbled in the pocket of his trousers.

He withdrew his hand. Nestled in his palm were two plain gold bands.

"It was not the best of circumstances in which to make a vow, but do you recall the words we exchanged in the Duomo?"

Raven's gaze lifted from the rings to his eyes. "Yes."

"I pledged myself to you before God. You did the same." He lifted the smaller ring, and his face held a question.

She held out her left hand, and he slipped the ring over her finger.

"No hesitation." His expression grew thoughtful.

"I made up my mind a long time ago." She plucked the larger ring from his palm and slipped it over his finger. "I would have married you before, if you'd asked."

A deep sigh of relief escaped from his chest.

She placed her arm around his waist. "Did you doubt me?"

"No, I'm just grateful for this second life. I swear I will do all I can to love and protect you."

"I swear the same." She kissed him.

William made a hungry noise in the back of his throat and pulled her atop him. His hands caressed her back before sliding down to the fullness of her bottom and gripping it sensuously.

Raven pushed his shirt open and peppered his chest with kisses. She latched onto the side of his neck and drew the flesh into her mouth.

William groaned.

"This will be different," she whispered, bringing her face within inches of his.

"Yes." His gray eyes clouded.

"I promise I'll be gentle." She winked with a grin.

He kissed her nose.

"Thank you. Do you—" William's unspoken question hung in the air.

She squeezed his shoulders. "Ask."

"Will you miss it? The way it was, the way *I* was before?"

She cocked her head to one side. "Are you William?"

"Yes."

"Do you love me?"

He squeezed her tightly. "Without question."

"Then there's nothing to miss. I was devastated when you died. I wondered if the pain would ever lessen. I'm not going to waste time coming up with silly pseudo-problems to keep us apart."

She placed her hand against his face, marveling at the stubble that scratched her palm. "For some reason, the universe gave you back to me. I'm not going to question it, and I'm not going to criticize it. They could have brought you back broken or burned, and I would have taken you gladly and thanked God for you.

"This is our chance at happiness, and we shouldn't waste a moment second-guessing it. Love me, William, as you have always loved me. And it will be everything."

William switched their positions, carefully tending to her injured leg.

"I always liked this dress." His hands worked between them, unwrapping her.

Raven pushed his shirt off his shoulders and unfastened his belt.

"Magnificent," he murmured, gazing appreciatively at her body as he divested himself of the rest of his clothes.

He took his time removing her under things, his hands gliding across her skin.

"You haven't been eating." William appeared dismayed as he explored her curves, curves that were uncharacteristically modest.

"It's difficult to enjoy food when you're in sorrow."

"I'm sorry." He pressed his lips to each rib, kissing them repentantly.

Raven looped an arm around his neck, drawing him to her so their mouths could meet. She slid her hands down his spine, reveling in the warm smoothness of him and the small imperfections she encountered for the first time.

William tasted her breasts, nipping and sucking as his hips aligned with hers.

He was warm, so warm. And the heat between their bodies grew as they made contact.

"I need you." Raven's green eyes burned into his.

His thumb found her cheek, and he brushed it tenderly. Then, with his other hand at her hip, he entered her.

Raven shut her eyes. It was a fullness she had never expected to feel again. But he was there, above her, inside her, surrounding her with love and warmth.

William groaned, bracing his arms next to her shoulders.

She opened her eyes just as he thrust against a most delightful place.

"I don't think I can—" William gritted his teeth, unable to complete his sentence.

"It's okay. I'm close." Her hands trailed down to his backside, urging him forward as she lifted her hips in time with his thrusts.

She moaned softly with his movements. And then, she felt it. The beginning of a glorious completion, like a note that hung in the air for several beats. The pleasure coursed through her body, igniting every nerve.

William grunted his frustration and began to thrust erratically.

As her orgasm crested and waned, Raven's body relaxed.

"Did you?" he whispered roughly, his pace quickening.

"Oh, yes." She grinned.

"Good." With a loud cry, William thrust deeply, pouring himself into her.

His arms gave out, and he collapsed, burying his face in her neck.

"Usually you bite me during and not after," Raven remarked.

William nipped at her skin.

She laughed, and he joined her, the happy sound echoing through the opulent apartment.

"I didn't think I'd ever laugh again," she confessed, running her fingers through his mussed hair, paying homage to the gray bits at his temples.

"I didn't either." He shifted to his side, his hand on her abdomen. His eyes were grave.

Raven read the question on his face. But she took her time choosing her words.

"I think, perhaps, there were three different Williams."

"Three?"

"The William you were when you were young, the William you were as a vampyre, and the William you are now. But something has remained constant. Some part of you remained the same. That core, that soul, is who I love.

"Not the money, or the power, or even the beautiful art collection they're hiding downstairs. I would have traded all those things to have you with me for one more day." She hugged him close. "Now I have you, I'm never letting go."

He kissed her forehead. "Skillfully put."

"I speak the truth, Mr. Malet."

"Thank you, Mrs. Malet." He cleared his throat, and his gaze wandered to her breasts. "Let's try the never letting go part one more time."

✿ ✿

Two hours later, the couple had showered and finished lunch.

"Why didn't you go to Prague first?" Raven asked, sitting on William's lap.

"I needed money, and I needed to arrange safe transport for both of us. So I came here."

"How safe is the bank?"

He traced a pattern on her thigh. "As a fortress, it's modest. But the relics of my teacher are strong enough to make the bank as safe as our villa against vampyres. If Borek followed you from Prague, and I surmise he did, we are safe from him and his kind—unless the Roman learns I'm here."

"Could he attack a building that houses relics?"

"No, but he's powerful enough to find a way around it or perhaps even to join forces with the Curia."

"Borek thinks the Roman is going mad."

William gave her a long look. "I think Borek is right. I didn't see it clearly before, but I think madness has seized part of the Roman's mind. In his twisted thinking, he believes I betrayed him for you. He was always jealous of my affections. Perhaps he took perverse pleasure in handing me over to our enemies."

Raven muttered a curse. "Do the Curia know you're alive?"

William scratched his newly shaven chin. "I don't know. Obviously, they don't have my body. But I don't know if reports of my current state have reached them. For both our sakes, I've been praying they remain ignorant."

"If you aren't a vampyre, why would they want you?"

William grimaced. "They want both of us, Raven. Your priest wants your memories adjusted so you won't be a security risk. The Curia wants me to inform on the Roman and other powerful vampyres. But they'd interrogate me first, trying to understand what made me different from the others."

"Do you know the answer?"

"I think so. But I only realized it after I died." He gave her a half smile. "It's a strange story, and a bit of a long one."

"I want to hear it." Raven adjusted herself into a more comfortable position on his lap, resting her head on his shoulder. "I should probably mention that Borek said Father Kavanaugh quit the Curia and returned home."

"That would be the honorable thing to do."

"You haven't forgiven him, have you?"

William studied her. "I don't believe he intended to kill my human nature. I think they wanted to destroy the vampyre."

"That's still killing."

William tightened his arms around her. "The last thing I remember before everything went dark was the sound of you screaming. I felt my soul leave my body, and I hovered over everyone. I saw you and Father Kavanaugh. I—"

William's story was interrupted by the ringing of a telephone. He frowned. "I told them we were not to be disturbed."

The telephone rang again.

"Excuse me." He helped Raven to her feet and strode over to the bed, lifting the handset of the telephone. "Yes?"

Raven followed, catching Monsieur Marchand's last words, "—military-style convoy, with diplomatic plates."

"Where?" asked William, his eyes meeting Raven's.

"Just outside the city, sir."

"And the intelligence report?"

"We have been unable to identify the convoy, sir. If they're headed here, they'll arrive in thirty minutes."

"Right. We're leaving at once. Prepare for our departure." William hung up the phone.

Raven grabbed his hand. "Curia?"

"We don't know, but I don't want to take the chance. Pack whatever you can't live without."

Raven twined her fingers with his. "You. You are what I can't live without."

He lifted her hand to his mouth and kissed it.

Within twenty minutes, Raven and William had changed their appearances and were carrying Swiss diplomatic passports.

A decoy Mercedes had already left the Trivium through the back gates, heading for Geneva Airport.

Raven and William rode in a black Range Rover with diplomatic plates, accompanied by a driver and an armed guard, heading south to the French border.

Another twenty minutes and they had crossed into France, entering Saint-Julien-en-Genevois, where a private jet waited for them.

Raven held her breath as the plane taxied on the airfield. Anxiously, she surveyed their surroundings and the snow-capped mountains in the distance.

Next to her, William exhaled loudly and drew a deep breath.

"It's going to be all right," she whispered, her gaze sweeping the landscape. "It has to be."

The plane took off, and when they'd finally reached their cruising altitude, William began to relax.

Raven gave him an encouraging smile. "You still haven't told me what happened to you."

"I will," he cleared his throat. "But I think we need to discuss our next steps first."

He turned in his seat to face her. "I want to live the rest of my days with you, in safety. If you want to stay in Europe, we can. But I believe it will be safer for us to go far, far away. At least for the near future."

"Where would we go?"

"I own property around the world. My recommendation is that we place as much distance between us and the Curia as possible. I own a secret island in French Polynesia, near Bora Bora. We can travel to the island in about a day and a half."

"What about the pilots? Can they fly that far?"

"They're being well paid. They will take us wherever we want to go."

Raven's mouth widened into a smile. "You want to take me to Tahiti?"

"Thereabouts."

"Okay."

He chuckled. "You don't want to think about it?"

Raven turned and looked out the window. She examined the landscape beneath them and the snowy Alps that climbed to the clouds.

When she spoke, her tone was wistful. "I miss my sister. I hope someday I'll be able to tell her I'm alive. But I don't want to do anything that will make her a target for the Curia or anyone else. I agree we need to disappear." Raven half-smiled. "Tahiti is warm. You can join me in the sunshine now."

"It doesn't have to be forever." William's face grew serious. "But the island is the safest place I can think of for now."

"What's the island called?"

William grinned sheepishly. "I always referred to it as *the island*. You'll have to pick a name for it."

He sat back in his seat and rested his head against the headrest. "Now it's time for me to explain what happened…"

Chapter Sixty-Four

"After I felt my soul leave my body, everything went dark. My first thought was that I'd failed you. I'd failed the city and my people. I'd failed my teacher." William's voice grew thick.

At Raven's signal, the flight attendant retrieved two bottles of water from the mini bar and opened them, pouring the water over ice.

William drank the water gratefully. "Do you remember the story of Guido da Montefeltro?"

"Yes, I think we talked about this once. Dante tells Guido's story in the *Inferno*. Guido claimed that St. Francis of Assisi came for his soul when he died but lost it to a demon."

"Yes." William studied her.

"You aren't telling me that St. Francis came for your soul?"

"No." His gaze dropped to the carpet of the plane. "But I saw my teacher.

"I thought I was dead, but I could hear voices. I could hear my teacher arguing with someone, arguing about my soul. And then, all of a sudden, my teacher said, 'He is not dead.' And I realized I was still alive." William's eyes lifted.

"You saw him?"

"I'd know him anywhere. I recognized his voice, his face. He was there. He spoke to me." William stopped, momentarily overcome.

"I was given mercy—a second chance. When I opened my eyes, I was alone, lying on a table.

"I realize now I was in the hospital in Florence. But at that moment, I had no idea where I was. My memory of being a vampyre was completely gone. I couldn't even remember listening to my teacher a moment earlier. All I could remember was his death and being in mourning in Fossanova. That's where I thought I was.

"I was half-naked, so I wrapped a sheet around my body, determined to return to the monastery. I stumbled outside and collapsed in the street.

"I'm not sure how long I was there, but someone found me." William hesitated.

"Who?"

"A Dominican. My mind was so scrambled, I couldn't speak Italian or English. I could only speak Latin and Anglo-Norman. The brother thought I was mad and tried to take me back to the hospital, but I kept telling him I was a Dominican and my teacher had just died. I think he brought me to the Dominican House just to placate me."

"But what about the Curia? Aren't the Dominicans part of them?"

"Some of them are. But these brothers seemed to have no knowledge of what had transpired at the Duomo, and they certainly didn't recognize me. The Dominican who rescued me took me to an older brother whose Latin was better, and I explained to him who I was.

"They gave me some clothes and some food. They gave me a place to sleep. It was clear they had no idea what to do with me, and I think several of them wanted to send me back to the hospital. But the old Dominican was adamant that I stay with them. Whatever they thought I was or what I was suffering, they knew I wasn't a vampyre. There were relics all over the house."

"Relics never bothered you anyway."

"Not much, that's true."

"Why do you think that is?"

"I think the relics that belonged to my teacher never bothered me because he never rejected me." Emotion colored William's voice. "He prayed for me, hoping I would find my way back to God. He never lost that hope."

"You believe, then? You believe in God again?"

"Yes, but I can say that I never stopped believing in him completely. You were the one who told me you thought my teacher would have compassion for me for reaching out to the Roman when I was in despair. Even as I took what he offered me, I regretted it. It wasn't what I wanted; I just wanted my teacher. I begged him to help me, and I know now that he did."

Raven shifted in her seat so she could see William more clearly. "The voice we heard during the exorcism, it said *despair*. What was that?"

"I'm not sure," William hedged. "From the moment I transformed into a vampyre, I felt the darkness of despair surround me. It was like drinking what I'd thought was the water of life only to discover it was poisoned."

"So vampirism was your punishment for giving in to despair?"

"No." William shook his head emphatically. "The Roman offered me power, and wealth, and sonship. Because I had given up hope of having a good life without my teacher, I willingly took what the Roman offered. But I regretted the choice immediately. My teacher said the transformation was incomplete. Perhaps that's why I could walk on holy ground and handle relics. I didn't give in to despair entirely, and because of that and the prayers of my teacher, I never acquired the full nature of a vampyre."

Raven pondered what he'd said. "I guess it wasn't a coincidence you were found by a Dominican."

William smiled. "I don't think so. The brothers could have sent me back to the hospital. I'm sure the Curia was looking for my body. But the brothers kept me while I regained my strength. Then, several weeks later, they took me to Fossanova.

"I had no memory beyond 1274. One of the Dominicans thought it might help to bring me to the monastery where my teacher died. A few of the brothers traveled with me.

"When we arrived, it was as if I'd never left. I was so convinced my teacher's body was there. I was so convinced my brothers were still there. Of course, they weren't.

"I spent a lot of time in the monastery and praying in the chapel, trying to figure out what had happened. I'd always had a good memory. I'd always been strong. I felt so weak, so powerless.

"One night I climbed to the top of a nearby hill." William cleared his throat. "It was the same hill where the Roman found me.

"I was there for some time, trying to figure out what to do. That's when everything flashed before me. I fell to my knees, overwhelmed by my memories. I remembered the Roman and my transformation. I remembered traveling to Florence and deposing the old prince. I remembered you."

He brushed Raven's knuckles with his thumb. "As soon as I remembered you, I wanted to leave. I'd made arrangements before Machiavelli's coup for you to have safe passage out of the city. I chose Prague because I thought it would be the safest place, away from vampyres and Curia alike. But even though I paid Sarah's network well, I was worried they'd failed. What if the Curia had you? What if they'd already erased your memories? I had to find you.

"I had nothing—no passport, no money. I went to the brothers and explained that my memory had returned. I was a businessman, I was married, and I urgently needed to get to Geneva so I could locate you."

"You lied?" Raven poked him in the side.

"You and I pledged ourselves to one another—first on the Loggia some months ago and again in the Duomo." He thumbed the ring she wore on her left hand. "We are married."

"Agreed." She lifted his hand and kissed the skin above his gold band. "What did the Dominicans say?"

"I think some of them continued to believe I was disturbed. Or they thought I was deceiving them. But the others believed me, and they secured a train ticket to Geneva and gave me money to travel. I didn't have a passport, but the Swiss rarely check passports at the border with Italy. I took the night train and made my way here." William exhaled loudly. "You know the rest."

Raven leaned her head against his shoulder. "How do you feel now?"

"Different." William passed a hand over his eyes. "I'm still adjusting to this body. It's strange to feel my heart beat regularly. It's strange to have to breathe. I have memories of my human life, long ago, as well as memories of when I was a vampyre. Sometimes I get mixed up."

"You don't feel the urge to drink blood? Or climb the sides of buildings?"

William pressed his lips to her temple. "No. The first human food I craved was roast venison. I still haven't had it yet. The Dominicans seem to subsist on fish and chicken."

Raven pondered his words as the warmth of his body radiated to hers.

"I don't know what to say."

"You don't believe me?" William's face was stricken.

"I believe you, but it's hard for me to balance what I know about the world with what you've just described. I don't believe in God or an afterlife. But I've seen things, strange things I can't explain. I don't understand the whirlwind we saw in the Duomo. I don't understand how I could watch you die as a vampyre and now you're sitting next to me, alive and human.

"I'm going to hold on to this." She clutched his arm with both hands. "You are here with me. You are human, and you are alive. For the moment, at least, we are safe. I'm not going to bend myself out of shape trying to figure out how we got here. I would like to know why—why you and why me."

She lifted a shoulder. "But human beings don't know everything. Perhaps that's best."

Chapter Sixty-Five

Three years later
Hope Island, near Bora Bora

Raven sat on the covered terrace of their villa, painting a vista of the island. The breeze blew her long, black hair around her face, forcing her to tie it back.

From her current vantage point, she could see part of the white sandy beach. A figure appeared, jogging barefoot across the pristine sand.

The figure seemed to search for her as he jogged. He waved.

She waved back.

Her husband continued his jog and disappeared from view.

She turned to look inside the house, through the enormous space where the side walls had been retracted. Beautiful paintings hung in the living room and beyond, in their bedroom.

The architecture and design of French Polynesia was at odds with the style of the Italian Renaissance, but she didn't care. This was their home. Their refuge. Their sanctuary.

The few original works of their collection they'd had shipped to the island were protected in a closed room that had carefully controlled light, temperature, and humidity. Both Raven and William enjoyed visiting the private galley that included paintings by Michelangelo and Botticelli, among others.

Beyond the villa, on a hill at the other end of the island, there stood a chapel where her husband spent time in meditation and prayer. Where he sometimes spoke to his teacher. Where she joined him on occasion as she navigated her own uneasy spiritual journey.

Raven spent her days painting and sketching, much of her work inspired by the island or their time in Italy. William explored the limits of his human body, learning to snorkel and surf. But their evenings were always spent together. They'd tell one another stories next to the fire, or make love on the beach, or simply enjoy one another's company.

Most of their art collection was still housed in Geneva, awaiting final decisions of where the various pieces should go. Raven and William had sold several works privately in support of their fund for abused children. The fact that they could continue their support from their island sanctuary gave their lives added meaning.

Perhaps a day would come when they could travel to America and she could see her sister again. For now, they lived a simple life together while their enemies appeared to be chasing other foes.

Raven had no idea why William had been spared. She had no idea why they'd been given a second life together. But she lived every day grateful and full of hope.

FIN

Epilogue

December 2013
Cambridge, Massachusetts

"Darling, can you get the door?" Julia called to her husband. "I have my hands full."

Clare was covered in milk. Somehow, in her exhausted state, Julia hadn't closed the baby bottle securely and milk had poured all over Clare's face and body as it splashed to the floor.

Clare currently sat in the kitchen sink while Julia attempted to separate her from her wet, milky sleeper.

"Did you order something?" Gabriel stuck his head into the kitchen on his way to the front door.

"No. It could be Christmas presents."

"From whom?"

The doorbell rang again.

"I don't know, Gabriel." Julia grew impatient. "Could you just answer the door?"

She heard her husband's solid footsteps crossing the hardwood. She heard the opening of the door, the faint murmur of voices, and the door closing.

Gabriel entered the kitchen carrying a very large box.

Julia eyed it curiously. "Who is it from?"

"Some shipping company I've never heard of."

"I meant who's the sender?"

"The name was left off the label."

Gabriel retrieved a knife and began opening the box.

He pawed through a great pile of Styrofoam packing material in order to uncover another box.

He cursed.

"Language," Julia whispered, angling her head toward Clare.

"Dada." Clare giggled and bounced on her backside, cheerfully half-naked and still sitting in the large kitchen sink.

Gabriel lifted the second, smaller box and placed it on the kitchen table.

He opened it and sifted through the contents.

Then he took a very large step back.

"What is it?" Julia was alarmed by his sudden movement.

Their eyes met.

Gabriel reached into the box and pulled out a protective sleeve. Then, very carefully, he opened the protective sleeve and drew out an etching.

Julia dropped the cloth she'd been holding. "Holy crap."

Clare mumbled something that sounded suspiciously like the words her mother had just uttered.

"There are a lot of them." Gabriel appeared bewildered. He pulled out more of the sleeves and began arranging them carefully on the table.

"Are they ours?" Julia's eyes grew wide.

Gabriel began checking the sleeves. He found the illustration of Dante and Beatrice in the sphere of Mercury and flipped it over.

There, on the back of the illustration, was a faint pencil mark. He showed it to Julia. "This one, at least, is ours. I remember the mark."

Julia covered her mouth. "They must have found them. Interpol must have found them."

Gabriel placed the illustration back in its protective sleeve. "I don't think so. Interpol would have contacted us. We would have known they were coming."

"Then who?"

He checked the sender's address label on the largest box. It showed an origin of Geneva, Switzerland, but no name.

He scratched at his chin.

Julia's eyes met her husband's. "Could it be…"

Gabriel placed his arm around her shoulder, drawing her into his side. "I don't know. I think it doesn't matter who they're from. Dante and Beatrice are finally home."

List of Terms and Proper Names

(NB: This List Contains Spoilers)

Alicia — William's fiancée from the thirteenth century.

Ambrogio — William York's servant.

Aoibhe — *Pronounced "A-vuh."* An Irish member of the Consilium.

Ispettore Batelli — Police inspector in Florence.

Borek — Florentine vampyre and commander in the Florentine army.

Cato — Lieutenant of the Roman.

The Consilium — The ruling council of the principality of Florence. The Prince is an ex officio member.

The Curia — Enemy of the supernatural beings.

Gabriel Emerson — The professor is a Dante specialist who teaches at Boston University. He is the owner of a famed set of Botticelli illustrations of Dante's *Divine Comedy*, which he lent to the Uffizi Gallery in 2011. His story is told in the Gabriel's Inferno trilogy: *Gabriel's Inferno*, *Gabriel's Rapture*, and *Gabriel's Redemption*.

Julia Emerson — Doctoral student at Harvard University. She is married to Gabriel and the co-owner of the Botticelli illustrations.

Feeders — Derogatory term for human beings who offer themselves up as a food source to supernatural beings.

Ferals — Supernatural beings who live and hunt alone. They display brutal, animalistic behavior.

Gaius — Vampyre Captain of the Roman army.

Gregor — Personal assistant to the Prince and head of security for the principality of Florence.

Human intelligence network — Human beings who are contracted to provide information to the supernatural beings. They also provide security and perform specific tasks.

Hunters — Humans who hunt and kill supernatural beings for commercial purposes.

Ibarra — A Basque former member of the Consilium.

Father Kavanaugh — Former director of Covenant House in Orlando, Florida, and friend of Raven Wood.

Lorenzo — A member of the Medici family and second in command in the principality of Florence. Also a member of the Consilium.

Lucia — Ambrogio's wife and servant to William York.

Dan Macready — Cara's boyfriend.

Niccolò Machiavelli — Famous Florentine and member of the Consilium. Head of intelligence for the principality of Florence.

Henri Marchand — Director of the Trivium Bank in Geneva.

Maximilian — A Prussian member of the Consilium.

The Medici — Famous ruling family of Florence during the Renaissance.

Gina Molinari — Friend of Raven Wood, employed in the archives of the Uffizi Gallery.

Old ones — A special class of supernatural beings who, by virtue of having attained seven hundred years in their supernatural state, enjoy tremendous power and special abilities.

The Prince — Ruler of the principality of Florence, the underworld society of supernatural beings.

Recruits — New supernatural beings, formerly human.

The Roman — Ruler of the principality of Rome and also the head of the kingdom of Italy, which includes all the Italian principalities.

Agent Savola — Interpol agent assigned to Florence.

Simonetta — The Princess of Umbria.

Stefan — A supernatural physician of French Canadian origin.

Tarquin — The current ruler of Venice, under the authority of the Prince of Florence.

Professor Urbano — Director of the restoration project working on the *Birth of Venus*. Raven Wood's supervisor.

General Vale — Commanding officer of the Curia army.

The Venetians — Supernatural beings living in the principality of Venice.

Dottor Vitali — Director of the Uffizi Gallery. He appears in the Gabriel's Inferno trilogy.

Patrick Wong — Canadian citizen and friend of Raven Wood. Works in the archives at the Uffizi Gallery.

Carolyn (Cara) Wood — Raven's younger sister. Carolyn is a real estate agent in Miami, Florida.

Raven Wood — American citizen and postdoctoral restoration worker at the Uffizi Gallery.

William York — A wealthy Florentine and patron of the Uffizi Gallery. He appears briefly in *Gabriel's Redemption*.

Younglings — Supernatural beings who have yet to attain one hundred years in their supernatural state.

Acknowledgments

I owe a debt to the cities of Florence, Rome, and Prague, their citizens, and to the incomparable Uffizi and Accademia Galleries, as well as St. Vitus Cathedral. Thank you for your hospitality and inspiration.

I am grateful to Kris, who read an early draft and offered valuable constructive criticism. I am also thankful to Cassie, Jennifer, and Nina for their feedback and support.

I've been very pleased to work with Ever After and Cassie Hanjian, my agent. I'd like to thank Kim Schefler for her guidance and counsel.

My publicist, Nina Bocci, works tirelessly to promote my writing and to help me with social media, which enables me to keep in touch with readers. I'm honored to be part of her team.

Heather Carrier of Heather Carrier Designs designed the book's cover. She did a beautiful job. I would also like to thank Jessica Royer Ocken for copy editing and Coreen Montagna for formatting the novel.

I am grateful to Erika, Deborah Harkness, and Lauren for their kind words about *The Raven*. Thank you. I also want to thank the many book bloggers who have taken the time to read and review my work.

I want to thank the Muses, Argyle Empire, the readers from around the world who operate the SRFans social media accounts, the Canal SRFansESP who create exceptional vlogs on YouTube, the Trilogia Gabriel for inaugurating a Spanish language book club on my books, and the readers who recorded the podcasts for The Gabriel Series and The Florentine Series. Thank you for your continued support.

While I was editing this book, I learned of the passing of John Michael Morgan, who recorded the audio versions of my books. My condolences go to his family and friends. He will be missed.

Finally, I would like to thank my readers and my family for continuing this journey with me. I'm proud to be your Virgil during this foray into the Underworld.

SR
Ascension 2016

About the Author

I am a Canadian author who is interested in Italian history and culture, as well as the city of Florence. I am also the New York Times bestselling author of The Gabriel Series.

I'm interested in the way literature can help us explore aspects of the human condition — particularly suffering, sex, love, faith, and redemption. My favourite stories are those in which a character takes a journey, either a physical journey to a new and exciting place, or a personal journey in which he or she learns something about himself/herself.

I'm also interested in how aesthetic elements such as art, architecture, and music can be used to tell a story or to illuminate the traits of a particular character. In my writing, I combine all of these elements with the themes of redemption, forgiveness, and the transformative power of goodness.

I try to use my platform as an author to raise awareness about the following charities: Now I Lay Me Down to Sleep Foundation, WorldVision, Alex's Lemonade Stand, and Covenant House.

Bonus Content

Oxford Gladiator

by Professor Gabriel O. Emerson
Associate Professor of Italian Studies
University of Toronto

I am not a man who makes decisions lightly. But when I want something, I pursue it. If a woman catches my eye, I won't rest until we've managed to press our bodies together, and she's panting my name. And I never back down from a challenge.

After I graduated Princeton, I went to Magdalen College, Oxford, where I studied Dante and Virgil.

My interest in these two poets led quite naturally to an interest in the customs of ancient Rome, especially the lives of the gladiators.

Gladiatorial contests straddled the space between public entertainment and religious sacrifice. On the one hand, Romans enjoyed the spectacle staged combat provided. On the other, the contests provided plenty of bloodshed and death to feed the appetites of the city gods. One could view the loser in such a match as providing a human sacrifice to the gods of Rome.

My interest in gladiators took a somewhat unexpected turn one evening when I was accosted by a group of loud, drunken Christ Church students. I was walking from the Bodleian Library to my room at Magdalen, carrying a book on gladiators, when I bumped

SYLVAIN REYNARD

into someone. He pushed me, cursing loudly. I called him a Neanderthal and shoved him back.

Catching sight of the book I was carrying, the Neanderthal, (who I will now call *Brutus*), challenged me to fight him like a gladiator. I was shocked that such a behemoth was literate, let alone able to string together a complete sentence.

I told him to name the time and place.

That's how I found myself on the meadow of Christ Church College just after dawn, holding a sword Brutus and his friends had conveniently "borrowed" from one of the suits of armor owned by the college. They'd also borrowed a couple of breastplates and two shields. I fastened the breastplate to my chest but spurned the shield. The broadsword weighed at least a kilo, and I would need both hands to wield it properly.

Brutus was a mountain of a man, tall and wide. He was easily a head taller than my own six feet, two inches, and outweighed me by about a hundred pounds. He also had an overabundance of facial and body hair, which gave him a bear-like appearance. He looked like someone who could have fought with the Germanic tribes against the Romans, centuries earlier.

As we prepared to do battle, a ragtag group of students gathered. I was the only sober one among them until a theology student was untimely ripped from his bed and told to act as referee. Poor chap.

"Right," he said, wiping the sleep from his eyes. "The warrior who draws first blood wins. Shake hands, gentlemen."

Brutus crushed my hand with his meaty paw. He winked before shoving me backward.

I swore an oath as I stumbled, struggling to regain my footing. With an incoherent cry, he rushed me, swinging his sword at my head. I dodged, then pivoted behind him and struck his kidney with the flat of my sword.

With a roar, he grabbed his back, flailing. I bobbed once again, plowing my foot into his knee.

He threw an elbow, which glanced off my jaw. I ran my tongue over my teeth to make sure they were all intact before spitting out blood.

Brutus grinned, raising his sword. The blade whistled through the air before the clash of metal against metal rang in my ears. The impact of our swords jarred my arm all the way to my shoulder. I could feel my entire body shudder, rattling my teeth.

I withdrew and swiped at his midsection, scraping across his breastplate. But I was wildly off balance. He swung at my side, striking the place where the breastplate ended, and I fell to my knees.

Brutus stood over me, slightly winded, before lifting his sword.

"*Et tu, Brute?*" I whispered before tackling his knees.

The giant fell like a great oak tree, cut down in his prime. I stumbled to my feet, clutching my sword.

As the last pinks and grays of dawn gave way to a pale blue sky, I pressed a knee to his chest and with the tip of my sword drew blood just beneath his left ear.

Breathing heavily and sweating profusely, I removed my breastplate, stabbing my sword into the grass. My opponent groaned and pressed a hand to his neck.

The crowd was silent. They stood aside as I passed through them, walking the slow steps of the victorious but battered warrior.

"Who was that?" someone asked, pointing at me.

I turned around. "Gabriel Emerson, president of the fencing club."

Outtake from
THE SHADOW
by Sylvain Reynard

July 2013
Florence, Italy

Professor Gabriel Emerson stood outside the Uffizi Gallery, staring. Darkness had fallen on the city of Florence and Gabriel, distressed and perplexed by the theft of his precious artwork from inside the famous museum, was searching for answers.

Inspector Batelli and agents from Interpol had descended on the Gallery like the wrath of God, swarming the grounds in uniforms and dark suits. But they found no signs of forced entry, no indication the security systems had been compromised, and more mysteriously, no fingerprints.

Several weeks after the theft, the investigators were gone. The Botticelli illustrations of Dante's *Divine Comedy* had disappeared without a trace, and Gabriel was left standing outside the building feeling angry that he and Julia had been robbed of their prized possessions—possessions that probably would never be returned.

The Uffizi was a multi-storied, U-shaped building. Gabriel stood in the center of the U, his blue eyes assessing. Yes, there were dark alleys near the Gallery, but lights on the sides of the building illuminated the area. There were few entrances, but many windows. Not all the windows could be opened, however.

And there was the terrace.

On top of the Loggia dei Lanzi was a small rooftop terrace that opened from the second floor of the Gallery. Patrons of the museum went to the terrace to admire views of the Piazza Signoria below or Brunelleschi's great dome that loomed in the distance.

Gabriel moved to the side of the Loggia in an effort to examine the terrace from the ground. One could certainly climb to the terrace, but would still be faced with locked doors and the security system if trying to enter the building after hours.

Gabriel walked to the bottom of the U and looked up at the Vasari Corridor, which led from the Uffizi across the top of the Ponte Vecchio and over to the Pitti Palace. The corridor was a point of entry into the museum, but it had a security system and was punctuated by a series of locked doors, each of which required a special key. The corridor would not have been a thief's first choice.

Gabriel gazed down at his shoes and the stones beneath them. There were tunnels and hidden passages beneath the city. The Uffizi was no exception. Most of the tunnels were impassable, as well as rat-infested. Still, if the thief was working with someone inside the Gallery...

A light breeze lifted from the direction of the Arno. Then, in an instant, it was gone.

Gabriel shifted his weight and began to examine his surroundings more closely. He felt the weight of a pair of eyes.

He heard music coming from the Piazza Signoria and elected to walk toward it.

Someone bumped into him. Hard.

The Professor went sprawling backward, the air knocked out of him.

Stunned, he looked up and saw a dark figure standing over him. The figure had a familiar face.

"A warning." The man addressed him in Italian, with a soft and steely voice. "This is my city."

It took a moment for the Professor to regain his breath, but when he did he scrambled to his feet. "Is your name Florence?"

The man scowled. "I've killed for lesser insults."

The Professor positioned himself like a boxer, fists raised. "You've never faced me before."

The man laughed. "Such *hubris*. I know exactly who I am facing. You are alive only because of her."

The man's eyes darted to the Professor's wedding ring. In the light from the Gallery, the platinum glinted.

The Professor's expression hardened. "Leave her out of it."

"She will be left alone, provided you abandon your search for the illustrations and leave Florence."

The Professor opened his mouth to protest, but the man interrupted him. "This is your final warning. The next time I see you, I'll kill you. Then I will hunt what is most precious to you."

The dark figure blurred past the Professor and disappeared down a narrow street to the left of the gallery.

Gabriel searched the courtyard for any witnesses.

He was alone.

"Julianne." Her name was a cry on his lips as he broke into a run, speeding toward the Gallery Hotel Art.

Outtake from
GABRIEL'S REDEMPTION
by Sylvain Reynard

"BODY PAINTING"

Selinsgrove, Pennsylvania

"I think you missed a spot." Gabriel's blue eyes twinkled as he gestured to a patch of wall near the doorframe.

He'd just entered the bedroom and stared at Julianne, who had splotches of white paint on her faded, old jeans and black T-shirt. Her dark hair was tucked under one of his University of Toronto baseball caps. She looked adorable.

"Where?" Julianne scanned the freshly painted wall, brush in hand.

"Here." Gabriel pointed to a narrow strip, approximately the size of a (pregnant) gnat.

"Very funny." She bent to dip the brush into a can of white paint.

"And you missed another spot here." He tapped the end of her nose with his finger as she straightened. "Did you get any paint on the wall? You're covered in it."

Julia glared. "I don't see you helping. What have you been doing? Contemplating all the ways you can make your graduate students cry?"

"I don't need to do that."

"Why not?"

"Because I already know all the ways to make a graduate student cry."

Julia rolled her eyes, much to Gabriel's amusement.

"I told you this morning I had an appointment to see the people who are working on the orchard." His eyes narrowed. "I also told you to let me hire someone to paint the walls. But as usual, you didn't listen and decided to do it yourself."

"It's a waste of money to hire a painter when I can do it."

"It's a waste of time for you to do it, when we can afford to hire a painter. I'd prefer you spend your time doing, ah...*other things*." He winked.

"You're impossible."

"And you're gorgeous, but paint-covered."

Julia extended the paintbrush toward him. "Now that you're here, you can help."

"No."

She lifted her eyebrows. "No?"

"No." He jammed his hands into the pockets of his jeans. "I'll make a phone call and hire someone. Then I'll carry you to the shower and take my time soaping every inch of your body. After that, we can see what other activities come to mind."

He grinned at her suggestively before heading to the door.

Impulsively, she flicked her paintbrush at him and an arc of white paint flew through the air, landing on his back.

(Had the Professor been dressed in black, he would have looked like a skunk.)

Gabriel turned around slowly, removing his hands from his pockets.

Scheisse, thought Julia.

"What was that?"

"Um, I didn't say anything." She hid the paintbrush behind her back, hazarding an innocent smile.

"Did you just cover me in paint?"

She shook her head. "No. Absolutely not. Why would I do that?"

He stalked toward her, and she backed up, still clutching the offending paintbrush.

He paused, twisting his neck so he could see his back. "These were my favorite jeans."

Her gaze flickered down to the jeans that were her favorite as well; not least because of the way the material clung to his very attractive backside. "It was an accident."

"And this was one of my favorite shirts."

"Sorry."

He lifted a hand and ran it across the back of his head. His fingers came away streaked with white paint.

"It's even in my hair."

She leaned her head to one side, examining him. "It gives me an idea of how you'll look when you turn gray."

"And the verdict?"

"You'll look good."

"How good?" He backed her up against a painted wall and grasped the hand that held the paintbrush, holding her in place.

"Really good. For an old man."

Their eyes met briefly before he captured her mouth.

"You're entirely too artistic for your own good," he murmured. "One day with a brush and you're Jackson Pollock."

"I just wanted to make Richard and Grace's old room ours."

Gabriel gave her a small smile before taking her lips again, this time pulling the paintbrush from her grasp. He pressed her firmly against the wall, and surprisingly, she did not resist.

"I think I'd like to join you." He hummed against her skin as his mouth moved down to her neck.

"In the shower?" Julia reached up to sift through his hair, resisting the urge to laugh at the paint-streaked strands.

"No." His fingers drifted down her front, passing over her breast, before tracing the sliver of exposed flesh just above the waistband of her jeans. "I'd like to join you in painting."

"Now that would be sexy."

Julia wrapped her arms around him, returning his kiss. A slick sound emanated from her T-shirt as it peeled away from the wet paint on the wall.

"I've backed into it, haven't I?" She looked over her shoulder, groaning in dismay at the sight of paint on her shirt.

"Yes, you have." Gabriel tried to hide his amusement. And failed.

She frowned. "You backed me into the wall on purpose."

"No. Absolutely not. Why would I do that?" He smirked.

She peered down at her jeans. "It's even on my backside."

"Let me see."

She presented her bottom to him, and he made an appreciative sound.

"It's incredible." He reached out and squeezed her backside. "I'd like to paint it."

Julia quickly grabbed the brush from his hand and flicked it at him again, causing paint to spatter down the front of him. Now his front matched his back.

The smirk slid off his face. "That was uncalled for."

"I'm sorry." She clasped a hand over her mouth, giggling uncontrollably at the speckled (and pissed-off) Professor.

"I'll bet you are."

His eyes glinted before he smiled sweetly, drawing her into his arms. He kissed her, pressing their bodies together from shoulder to thigh. Spots of paint transferred from his front to hers as they moved against one another.

She was so focused on the way his tongue teased hers, she didn't notice that he'd pulled her shirt up. With the barest hint of movement, he began running the paintbrush across the skin of her naked back. Up and down and back and forth.

She shivered. "What are you doing?"

"Nothing." He continued his tantalizing pattern, whispering the strands of the brush over the surface of her flesh.

"You're painting me, aren't you?"

"This is my only chance to paint a masterpiece."

"Gabriel," she murmured.

"I'm only speaking the truth. You're a masterpiece to me." He kissed her again, slipping his tongue inside her mouth.

The movement of the brush against her flesh matched the stroking of his tongue against hers. Julia gently explored his mouth, moving her arms up to wrap around his neck.

After a moment she sighed and brushed a kiss against his stubbled chin. "We should move this to the shower."

"Wait." He pulled off her baseball cap, tossing it aside. He ran his fingers through her hair as it spilled down to her shoulders.

Then in one movement, he tugged her shirt over her head.

"Beautiful." His eyes drifted lazily from her face to her chest.

She watched as he moved the tip of the brush up and down her ribs, and down to circle her navel, the strands gliding sensuously over and around.

He traced the tops of her breasts, above her black lace bra, as her eyes latched on his.

She grabbed his hand, stilling it. "Let's take a shower."

"The shower can wait," he rasped. "Prepare to get wet."

Then he pulled her to the floor, still clutching the paintbrush...